HOUSE OF A HUNDRED ROOMS

Stories
the
Ghost Tour
Guides
Do
Not Tell...

KEITH J. SCALES

ISBN-13: 978-1978086883
ISBN-10: 1978086881

HOUSE OF
A HUNDRED ROOMS

is respectfully dedicated
to the 1886 Crescent Hotel
and all who pass through
her doors. In this building
reside many stories,
some lost to time,
some in living memory
and some, yours for example,
still going on.

Let us go forth, the
tellers of tales, and seize
whatever prey the heart
longs for and have no fear;
everything exists, everything
is true, and the earth is only
a little dust under our feet.

W. B. Yeats
The Celtic Twilight

HOUSE OF A HUNDRED ROOMS
Tales the Ghost Tour Guides Do Not Tell

PRELUDE:
Landing, Fourth Floor South

A little girl was left to play on a top floor landing and instructed not to go near the railings. She did as she was told, every day, inventing worlds for herself and her small toys and dollies, stories in which she was not left alone, every day, while mama went away with mops and brooms. As time went by she grew bolder and began to explore her surroundings: the hall around the corner, the window overlooking where people walked, the big hole behind the railings she would peep down into sometimes. One day mama came and found her leaning over the ledge and shouted at her and shook her to make her cry. 'You listening to me? You fall down there you won't come back up!'

So the little girl did as she was told, every day, playing with her dollies and Teddy and staying away from the railings. But one day Teddy made her really mad and she took him over to the railings and put her head and arm through and held Teddy over the abyss. 'Teddy say sorry!' She shook him to make him pay attention. The sound of her mother's scream filling the long hall made her jump so hard she let go with her spare arm and suddenly she and Teddy were flying down into the empty place together, laughing. Falling was fun!

The little girl only knows one place, the top of the stairs. She had a bed in mama's room, but she doesn't know how to get there. So she stays at the top of the stairs, playing her games of being someone else, somewhere else, and looking forward to the ghost tours at night. She likes people, especially little girls, though most of them act as if she's not there, even when she tries to talk to them through that thing that blinks. Sometimes she gets so mad at someone, something they say about her mama, or just the fact she likes them and they are ignoring her, that she summons all her self together and gives that person as hard a poke, right in the belly. She has been known to go into rooms at night, but only those in sight of the top of the stairs at the fourth floor landing south. Sometimes she follows along behind the crowd down the hall a little way, toward Miss Theodora's room, but soon runs back to her place at the top of the stairs again, where she waits with her dollies and Teddy for the next ghost tour.

PART ONE: WHO'S THERE?

If anything in these legends
should shock the faith of the
over-scrupulous reader,
he must remember....
that he treads the halls
of an enchanted palace,
and that all is haunted ground...

Washington Irving
Tales of the Alhambra

Chapter One:

House of Ghosts

There are more guests at table than the hosts
Invited; the illuminated hall
Is thronged with quiet, inoffensive ghosts,
As silent as the pictures on the wall.

Longfellow
Haunted Houses

CHAPTER ONE
House of Ghosts

The odd little town of Eureka Springs materialized overnight in the Ozark hills a century and a half ago, when a legendary Indian healing fountain was rediscovered in a hidden valley. A boy's eye disease was relieved, the ulcers on a judge's leg disappeared. The news spread like wildfire and within weeks ten families were gathered in tents and wagons around the magic fountain; within months the impromptu encampment was famous across the nation and growing rapidly. Sick and ailing people were finding their way to the healing place in the wilderness at the rate of one to two hundred a day and according to surviving testimonials, many were healed. Five years later Eureka Springs was the fourth largest city in Arkansas with an international reputation as a fashionable health resort.

Still hard to find from any direction, Eureka Springs today is a random tangle of sturdy stone walls, hanging gardens and almost vertical streets defying negotiation or explanation, where cottages and mansions, shops and hostelries, no two alike, perch precariously on the edges of steep ravines, out of place, out of time; the Victorian mansion, the Frank Lloyd Wright and the log cabin cling to the cliffs, side by side. Sheltering a population a tenth the size it once was, Eureka Springs is yet so contained that anywhere you are, in the bewildering maze of overgrown thoroughfares, you are on the street where you live. Beyond the rooftops the barely penetrable forest stretches in all directions as far as the eye can see.

The air is still sweet in Eureka Springs and, possibly because the streets are so steep, those who have chosen to live there look and act younger than they are. And at the heart of the town the legendary Basin Spring still flows.

Above the town, the highest hill in the region is surmounted by an imposing stone structure from a period of history difficult to identify: an aged stronghold with walls as stout as a castle; a view to the horizon in all directions; and one road in and out winding down to the village. Why is it here, and what was its first purpose? Is it a fortified villa, a well-appointed fortress, a manor house designed to intimidate? Someone's home? With its great dry-stacked stone block walls, square turrets and countless windows, is it a palace, a resort, a place of learning, some kind of institution? Definitely an anachronism, a mystery and a complete surprise to travelers not expecting to find a gothic mansion in the barely accessible Ozark hills, the mysterious edifice dates from within five years of the eruption of the town and, like the Basin Spring itself, is the stuff of legend.

In the twilight her towers are gilded by the sun reflecting off the long narrow windows as it sinks. The air is still and moist. In the faint green light the shadows of the tall trees all about creep up the great stone walls like fingers of darkness. Thunder rumbles somewhere not far away. Night is close. With dark flying clouds above, blank windows gazing ominously down, darting bats and a black cat prowling, it is not difficult to believe the stately 1886 Crescent Hotel is what it has been called: the most haunted hotel in America.

The Grand Old Lady of the Ozarks has seen the ends of eras and the beginnings of others; from the first construction, ton upon ton of great square-chipped limestone blocks hauled high by mule-teams and block-and-tackle winches and levered into place by hand; to the age of the ubiquitous, palm-held, hard-plastic gadgets that enable us to observe, from an armchair in the lobby, what is happening at this moment on the other side of the world or thirteen minutes ago on Mars.

For thirteen decades of the world's history thousands of stories, linked to thousands of other stories, have been brought to the Crescent Hotel and played out in her hallways and rooms by hundreds upon hundreds of guests each and every day, including today. Every story gains strength from being told; and every story, when it ends, leaves something of itself behind. Some say, the greater the passion the more prevalent the residue: the dead woman rises on the day of her murder; the lovers who were unable to complete their union seek each other forever in these endless halls, calling each other's name, in room 416, where a woman swallowed handsful of pills and then hurled the empty bottle because she regretted what she had done, the mirror on the vanity keeps breaking.

A century and a quarter of history suffuse these walls and

rooms and halls and, it may be, various inhabitants of the past are continuously present, sometimes in plain sight yet rarely observed. The old man who comes in every morning and sits in the armchair by the fireplace for a few minutes, waiting for the bus that stops at the hotel doors – has anyone ever spoken to him? Or seen him get on the bus? When laughter is heard on the floor above, who goes up to check if anyone is really there? The men you see walking dogs around the grounds and parking lot, who knows where they come from or go to?

In the Crescent Hotel are many presences, lingering near the living because they no longer have lives of their own to lead (although they still have their secrets), watching and listening; but the presences are only perceptible to those who pay very close attention, and most of the living are too preoccupied to be aware of them. The face at the window, the slowly closing door, the music in the pipes, the gust of air in the closed room go mostly unnoticed in the excitement of a weekend getaway at the Crescent Hotel in Eureka Springs.

However, visitors to the hotel do have an opportunity to learn some of her secrets.

Any given evening, on each floor of the Crescent Hotel groups will be gathered around ghost tour guides, listening to tales of mysterious deaths and apparitions of the dead, handed down over the decades, told where they took place: in the long hallways or on the observation deck, in the lobby, at the vertiginous summit of a stairwell, outside the looming annex, inside the notorious Morgue.

The Girl in the Mist, the Lady in White, the little boy with the ball, the little girl who fell through the railings, the unnamed college girl who fell from the balcony, the young Irish stonemason who fell from the unfinished building – an omen, or perhaps the reason the hotel is home to so many of the disembodied in descent? The dapper little man waiting for someone unknown at the window table in the Crystal Dining room, the older lady fumbling in her purse, the tall man who vanishes at the second turn of the first stair... Who were those people whose stories, fragmentary but persistent, the tour guides still tell? And all the others, recurrent or occasional, that have been reported over the years, who were they when alive? And why are they still here, dead?

The reasons for the return of those who passed over we may surmise but can never fully understand, any more than we can contain the immensity of even one galaxy in our minds. And yet the well-told ghost tale will arrest the attention of all walks of listener; strangers learning together of eerie and inexplicable events can for once feel comfortable sharing an experience; all defenses are down in the contemplation of the last and greatest fear that haunts us all: leaving the land of the living.

Of the ghosts who have always been said to haunt the hotel, we have only verbal reports of impossible appearances, and only guesswork as to who they were in life, what they were like, what it felt like to be them, then; and how it is for them, now.

We can only imagine.

Chapter Two:

The First to Fall

In Ireland this world
and the world we go to
after death are not far apart...

W. B. Yeats

CHAPTER TWO
The First to Fall

Micheal Ó Seachnasaig is, literally, on top of his world. Newly brought out of the old country where the effects of the potato famine are still felt - - now less in the stomach than the gut, as hatred of the invader poisons all wells - - Michael remembers: *Whose side are you on, feller, what religion do you profess, are you for the revolution or against it, make up your mind or we'll decide for you, feller... O'Shawnessy? Catholic, is it? Watch your step, feller, these are dangerous times...* And Michael thinks, I'm not there, I'm here - in a new state in the new world, high up on the rising wall of the building they say is going to be the finest hotel this side of the Mississippi River, and I'm helping my Da to build it. I don't care if I never go back to Sligo.

Most of the workers, when they're finished up top get down from there as soon as they can, but not Michael. As sure footed as any goat, as all the stonies agree, he walks around on the heights just as easy as along a country lane; he likes it up there in the clouds.

On the first really hot day of summer, Michael watches for the signal from the loader to remove the wedge from the block-and-tackle; freeing the rope so that when the mules are commanded to move away the next block can start rising up from the ground, inch by inch, turning slowly, shedding dust. If the mules start off with a jerk the block will be set swinging dangerously, and that's a time when every man on the worksite must watch out for himself, even a slight knock from a one ton block can break a shoulder or cave in a skull. Many are the stories told around the bankers or over the bottle, of good men sent to their rest by looking the wrong way when the mules were on the move.

He stands on the wall not much wider than his arse, watching the huge limestone block inching upwards. When it is slightly higher than the top of the wall he gives the signal, one clear sweep of the right arm, to halt the mules, and as the rotating block slows, turns the crank to move the swing arm over to the wall. Then comes the dangerous part. Using a long iron lever he adjusts the angle of the stone. When he is sure it is straight and true to the wall he gives the final signal to drop the stone the last few inches into place. He climbs up onto the newly-placed block, loosens the straps and gives the thumbs up. The mule skinner backs his animals into place with his mysterious clicks of the tongue, and when the harness reaches the ground Liam and the others start to strap in the next stone. As Michael hammers the wedge back into place on the rope-drum sweat pours down his neck and he feels his shirt soaking under his arms. The bright sun reflects upward off the limestone, hotter every minute.

*

Michael and his little brother Tigh were the last of the family to arrive. His Da and Liam had been in the New World for going on four years, and Michael had spent those same years dreaming about being with them all together, all except Ma, who got bad sick and went gratefully to her grave. Michael remembers: her old, tired face; the cozy feeling of blankets that she warmed before the fire; the tilt of her head with its stringy gray hair as she turned to the firelight, squinting at the letters from America that came once a month, that she read once a week.

Michael and Tigh were made welcome from the day they climbed down, stiff and bruised, from the stagecoach after a nine-hour ride from Pierce City. The fellows on the site all had so much respect for Da they took it on themselves to teach his second son all they knew, and to treat the youngest like a mascot. Tigh is barely up to Michael's shoulder and it's understood that all the men look out for the little boy on the job site, keep him away from the back end of the mules that are mostly docile but can launch a hefty kick when they're irritable in the late afternoons; always make sure he stays away from the area where the slabs are dumped and doesn't stand too close to the bankers where they're carved and the flying chips can get in an eye; and never let him anywhere near the boiling pitch pot.

The stonies had all worked with Da for a long time in St. Louis, a city Michael is in no hurry to see. He likes it right where he is, on a mountain top with green forest all the way to the horizon in all directions.   When the day's work is done and the sun almost down they will walk in a group on the dark trail through the woods leading to the train station, for the exciting ride home in the big, puffing iron monster with great steel wheels, chugging, whistling along by Leatherwood Creek and the huts where all the Irish live, right beside the just-begun quarry where they have their pick of pure pink limestone. When the train whistles to a stop, chug, chug, hisssss, they stand and stretch, leaving white dusty patterns on the bench-slats.

Ale and more meat than Michael has ever seen in one place for dinner, eat as much as you want, there's plenty more game in the forest. After dinner the fellows would have their second wind and be wanting to wrestle or put stones from the shoulder in strictly supervised competition. Michael has been wrestling with Liam as long as he can remember and never got the better of him once, even though he knew Liam was not really trying. But Michael can feel his stringy muscles getting tighter every day and every day he feels he can lift more in a sack or a hod and one day he knows he will get Liam down and hold him there.

To end up the night they will play a few tunes on the fiddle around the fire, reminisce about the old country, wish all who are still there well and praise Himself for setting them all here on the hill above the famous Eureka Springs, on their feet, in work, and plenty more where that came from. The restless sleep of men without women; then a hunk of bread and a glass for breakfast, back on the wonderful train, back up the trail, maybe singing a song they had enjoyed the night before, to the worksite in the middle of nowhere.

*

Michael surveys the scene laid out so far below that he could be a small boy examining a model. Over there, the bankers where the rough stones are trued up; back by the trees, the slash pile; the fenced area where the mules are held at night; Da's shack, where he'll be drawing up next week's work plan and where the men line up for beer at eleven – stonemasonry is thirsty work! – and a shot of whisky when the sun goes down. Good times. Good place to be.   All I need now, Michael thinks, is a girl.

Long red hair, freckles, big friendly smile and a jaunty walk, she likes to be chased, and she likes to be caught.   Some day. She's out there, somewhere and maybe she's here, in Eureka Springs, the magic

17

town that appeared one day in the Ozark mountains. She's Irish, Michael knows that, but not opinionated, please God, and to put it plain as long as she likes to be caught her hair shall be of what color it please herself.

From his height he is the first to spot the big boss, cantering uphill, and he gives out a sharp whistle, pointing to the road up from town. The Brigadier-General clip-clops through the worksite on his great stallion, a sight to see. Straight as a stick, he handles the reins, climbs down from the saddle and takes the bridle all with the same hand, the one he didn't shoot off with his own gun, though no one mentions the fact in his hearing. From far above, Michael watches the general as he marches about the site with Da, pointing and putting questions. Da replies, pulling on his ear lobe, a gesture Michael recognizes, alright.

Michael knows that Da and the general don't always get along. Not a lot of people do get along with Clayton, except the really bigwigs. Still, he's not quite the hoity-toity as you meet in England, or even in Ireland. He's high-handed right enough but they say he's that way with everybody. He talks to the stonies the same as he would talk to judge or a priest, and so he should, he has the right men for the job.

Michael's Da knows more about stone than any man living; as much, anyway. His drawings are always spot on, he sets up a worksite where everything is easy to get at and his buildings stay up, stay put, and stay dry. 'You have to let a building breathe,' he says, 'especially at the corners.' He likes the job he's on now alright. Apart from the snakes and scorpions. If all goes well, everyone stands to make out on this one, saving thunderstorms, accidents and the yellow fever. And the governors have the wherewithal, nothing fly going on here, these fellers run the railroads, they're not short of the ready.

The general's a bit of an engineer himself, which is no bad thing, he knows about drains and access roads, and that was a good bit of work, piping the water up here from the spring halfway down the mountain, can't dress stone without water; but Michael has to laugh up his sleeve when he sees Clayton telling Da how to go about putting up the walls. Da nods and winks, grinning under his great hedgerow of a moustache, rolling up his drawings, yelling at the fellers about what he wants to see finished before the day is done, and offering to shake the Brigadier General's hand that he hasn't got. He'll take a drink in the evening and that's when his true feelings will come out. But he'll be first on site the next morning, him and Michael and Liam and Tigh, and the job will be done his way.

Still, watching the general swing himself singlehanded onto the horse and make it rear and gallop away down the hill, upright as a stick, there's something you have to admire.

As the morning wears on the air falls still. The sun is seemingly concentrated onto the bare hilltop where the Crescent Hotel rises to meet its uninterrupted burning rays. Michael reaches for his water jug and is surprised to find it almost empty. He has been taking sips more often. He takes off his hat to wipe the sweat from his face and fills his eyes with limestone dust, which his companions on the job warned him to avoid. 'Keep your eyes as long as you can son, you'll be lost without them, as the blind man said, it's one of the curses of a stonie's life.'

He uses some precious water to bathe his eyes and clean out his eye-sockets, sitting with his back against the winch and his legs along the wall. He wishes he had more water. He could get some at the beer break but they had six stones to place yet. It must be almost time for the next block, but no one's given the whistle. They don't have sunshine like this in Ireland.

He tugs his hat down as far as it will go, as he turns on the sole of one foot and suddenly freezes, staring down the wall he is balanced on. He stares, barely breathing, trying to come to terms with an apparent movement of the wall, and with a new image in his mind; of footing missed. Quite a drop, whatever side you went over. Straight down on the outside, onto bedrock; inside, evenly spaced thick white oak beams to break you in mid-fall. He stares down the face of the wavering wall until it stops moving.

He sits against the winch, holding onto a timber with one hand. He hears the forest sounds, the songs of a hundred birds, frogs in a pond somewhere. But no voices, no hammering, no mules. Just a strange, empty quiet, in the relentless heat. Where is everybody? Hiding, like him, from the sun? He climbs to his feet, unusually cautious, in case the unfamiliar vertigo should return. When he steps out of the shade of the winch the sun strikes his face like a slap.

The worksite is empty. Michael doesn't see any of the stonies, or the day laborers. Has something happened? Where did all the fellows go? Probably keeping out of the sun, as he would like to be doing. But where? The sun was straight overhead, no shade wider than a chisel anywhere on the site. Would they be over there in the forest? As he peers under his hand he sees a movement in the trees and a figure steps out of the shadows into the light. It is a girl.

19

Shading her eyes, she crosses the empty space between the forest and the building, looking up. She'll get herself shouted at, any minute now: *Don't come any closer miss, 'tis dangerous, so it is...* But no one shouts.

She has on a long dress that seems to ripple despite the stillness of the air. Her arms are bare and a mane of long hair flows all about her face. She stops below where he is standing, looking up. At him? Does she know him? He doesn't know any girls here at all, nor fellows either except his own and the Brigadier's men. What should he say? He wouldn't want to appear insolent. She stands, staring up at him, running her fingers down the tresses in front of her face. He lets go the winch block, to raise his hat.

'Good morning!' he calls, wishing he had a wittier thought in his mind, a more amusing thing to say.

'Evening you mean,' she calls back, with a toss of her hair.

'Right you are,' he says. 'Afternoon, anyway.' For an instant the thought crosses his mind – has he lost track of time, and have all the fellers had their shot of whiskey and gone home for the day? Liam, Tigh and Da, all forgotten him?

'Aren't you afraid to be up so high?' she shouts. Is she Irish? She sounds Irish.

'Not at all,' he shouts back, and lets go the winch rope with his other hand. 'Safe as houses, sure!' And he dances a little jig step on the edge of the parapet with his fists on his hips, to show her that he is Michael the mountain goat and height does not bother him at all.

'Stop!' she says. 'For the love of God!'

'Sure,' he calls down, 'I'm perfectly at home, so I am, it's the high places I prefer.' And, already in love, he throws his arms wide and stands on one leg, laughing.

'Be careful!' she cries, hiding her face behind her hair. 'You'll fall!'

Chapter Three:
Under the Stairs

Yesterday upon the stair
I met a man who wasn't there...

William Hughes Mearns
Antigonish

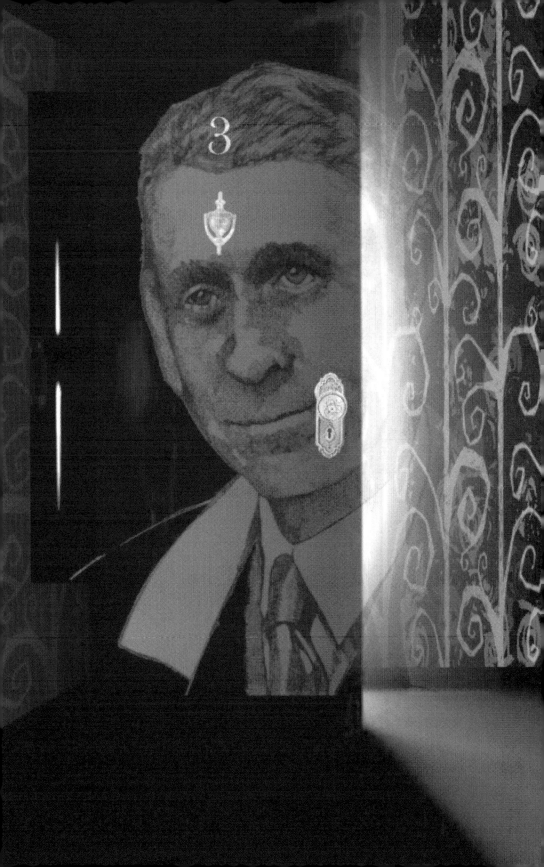

CHAPTER THREE
Under The Stairs

The Crescent Hotel today looks much as it did in 1886, though the interiors have been re-imagined and the grounds redesigned many times. We can see, from the old photographs lining the walls, the lobby when it was a series of parlors, at another time decorated as gaudily as any circus wagon; the front door when it was the back; the tennis lawns and basketball courts, now gardens for wedding ceremonies and eccentrically-themed parties. And yet much in those old photographs remains unchanged: the giant limestone block walls, the convenient balconies connecting otherwise discreet rooms, the sinister annex... All is recorded on the hallway walls, with varying degrees of distinctness, for we who come after.

A place is more than a thing, it's every thing that happens in that place, and a building is more than its walls. The Crescent Hotel is a crucible where Life flourishes in generations of lives, beyond the individual span, defying Time's Arrow; in some sense, the brigadier, the nurse, the shyster, the girls of the conservatory, the painters and the pastry cooks are all still here, almost but not quite substantial.

The faces of individuals who lived for many years under this roof – Governor Powell Clayton; Senator Claude Fuller; the girls of Crescent College and Conservatory for Women and their teachers; Richard Kerens, builder of railroads and chapels; the director and staff of the so-called Cancer Curable Baker Hospital - look out at us from books and photographs and paintings, as do Mary Baker Eddy, William Jennings Bryan, James G. Blaine, Willie Nelson and a thousand others, some remembered, most forgotten. We are familiar with some of their expressions, and with a few of their thoughts. But a person is more than a portrait.

The hallway walls of the Crescent Hotel are olive green, textured like orange peel or reptile skin, creating shapes into which one would be ill-advised to stare too long. All sounds seem to come from somewhere else. If you listen carefully you can hear throughout the building a low murmur, many voices in many rooms and moods, filling the emptiness; and who is to say it is only the living who are speaking?

Presences permeate the rooms, the hallways that tilt unpredictably, the Crystal Dining room, too vast to assimilate at a glance, the whimsical ornamental gardens and of course the morgue; the living of today walk among the dead of the ages, everywhere.

Stand outside today, look up and you can still see the peculiar purple chimneystacks, legacy of the despicable genius, Norman Baker. Little Breckie bounced his ball under that great oak tree outside the laundry room. Close your eyes and you can see the soldiers and 'telephone operators' stepping down from the bus from Monett, hear their laughter, see the awe on their faces as they look up at the great stone castle in the forest, where they will let down their hair for the next few days. How many times did the president of the Conservatory, Richard Thompson, and his wife Mary Carson Breckenridge pass through the great glass-paned entrance doors, together or separately? And how many have held those doors open for others?

No one knows these halls better than the staff of the hotel, and none are more familiar with the dark corners and repeated inexplicable occurrences than the ghost tour guides, who walk these corridors every evening till after midnight. Ghost tour guides are like the houses in Eureka Springs: no two alike. They all have their own favorite incidents and characters and times of the past, they have their costumes and their aliases, their masks and their secret beliefs.

The tales to be heard on the tours have been told for generations and change only a little with each storyteller. And the company of guides changes, too, some seasons composed mostly of the ambitious young, stepping on the stones of the Crescent Hotel on the way to other destinations; in other years the guides are older, with tales of their own to tell. The tour guides are the bearers of legend, the keepers of history, the presenters of the past to the present; their fingers point to the moon across the bright face of which pass shadows and barely decipherable shapes that may or may not exist in this reality but certainly do somewhere, the shades of night flying above the 1886 Crescent Hotel, on a mountaintop in a thick forest, hard to find like the Grail Castle of old. At a certain point somewhere in space and time, one of the company of guides was a rotund little fellow named Davies.

The stairs at each end of the long halls turn in rising squares, you would see a person following you up or down, though the lighting is everywhere dim and flickering. As you descend you sense you are being watched, from above: you look up, the watcher is glimpsed and gone, your primeval instincts are awakened, will you be the hunter or the prey? Stay alert, says your adrenalin.

On the night he became a story on the ghost tour Davies was five minutes early for work, but as he edged his battered vehicle into a parking space the engine died, the brakes gave out and the car crunched into a rock wall. He heard the tinkling of various falling parts. When he had calmed down a little, after blaming various deities for the mishap, he breathed a raggedy sigh with his head drooped. 'Business as usual...' he said, and then, 'Could have been worse. Could have happened on the highway.'

He turned the ignition off and on again, several times, with zero response. Great. Poor Davies. He hadn't even wanted to work tonight but could not afford not to, and now he had no way of leaving even if he were offered the night off with pay. Some hopes. First: figure out how to get home tonight. Then what to do about the car. Then how to pay for it. *And will I have to pay for the damage to the wall?* Poor, poor Davies.

He lumbered up the wide burgundy-carpeted steps to the crystal glass doors, held open for all who arrived by a perpetually genial doorman who had been working there longer than any other member of the staff, no one knew how long. The lobby, a sea of rich carpeting where plush couches floated, was loud and crowded. Under the fuss and kerfuffles of check-ins, inquiries, complaints, wandering conversations with telephones, the bustling dining room, the glass-walled conservatory where a spirited wedding celebration was already getting out of hand, gentle, soothing period music played softly on, unnoticed and mostly unheard. From a niche in the central marble fireplace a mysterious hand-carved stone misericord, a combination of bat and owl, stared out at the milling guests. Light reflected inward from a multitude of darkened window-panes, to gleam in polished wood doors and balustrades. The concierge desk - a curious hexagonal affair inherited from a brilliant quack whose practices once brought prosperity to the town and its citizens but proved too shameful even for Eureka Springs – guarded the passage to the capacious Crystal Dining Room. Behind a reception counter with etched glass panels stood rows of pigeonholes and an unapologetic safe with about the capacity of a small person.

'Hey! Davis! Got a message for ya.' Antonio, a front desk clerk with distinctly Sicilian ancestors and an obviously voluminous capacity for pasta, called out through his window. 'Billy Bull's looking for ya –' The phone rang. 'Follow-your-bliss-at-the-1886-Crescent-Hotel-and-Moonshine-Spa-this-is-Antonio-what-service-may-I-be-allowed-to-perform-for-you-today-with-the-promptness-and-courtesy-you-deserve?'

Davies noticed, standing behind Antonio and largely hidden by Latin bulk, someone he had not seen before, a new employee apparently. She stood in a corner, stroking her long hair over her face, separating the strands and peeping out from in between, at Davies.

He gave a pleasant, noncommittal nod, not to frighten her on her first day, and looked away, waiting for Antonio to finish booking a room. When he looked back the girl was gone, presumably into the back office.

Antonio wound up his transaction. 'You're very welcome and we certainly look forward to having you stay with us at the 1886 Crescent Hotel and Moonshine Spa and really making a fuss of you, you all have great day now, Billy Bull's looking for you and he ain't too happy, he's about to fire your ass.'

'*Fire*? Me? Why?'

'What do I know? Timekeeping, weren't you supposed to be here by now?'

Davies checked the time on the great Roman numeraled clock behind the front desk and added the five minutes that it was always slow.

'I'm not late, what's the problem, why would -?'

' ey! Not my business –' Antonio threw up his arms as though about to launch into an explosive drum solo. 'Don't shoot the mailman!'

'I'm not late,' Davies said, anyway. 'My car ' 'The phone rang.

'Follow-your-bliss-at-the-1886-Crescent-Hotel-and-Moonshine-Spa-this-is-Antonio...'

Threading his way through gliding waiters, dashing bellboys, chattering concierge and desk clerk dressed in black, families with ice-cream cones and cupcakes; and wedding guests uncomfortable in tuxedoes and cocktail dresses having their pictures taken, Davies went over the weekly schedule in his mind. Yes, he was sure, he was not late. Not early, but not late. In a way, he hoped Billy Bull would yell at him so he could graciously point out the mistake. *Davies - one, Billy Bull - nil.*

He waited at the elevator that, despite the promise of its bullet-smooth, glossy brass door, moved with the speed of lead.

Fired? Billy Bull had been at the Crescent Hotel for less than six months, Davies for seven years. *Fire me?* The worst of it was, Davies had little doubt that Billy Bull would do it, would enjoy doing it. He checked the exact time on his smart phone: less than a minute to go before he was due at the Faculty Lounge. Thirty seconds, fifteen, ten... slowest elevator in the world... And he realized he had not pushed the call button. Which he then did, with considerable gusto, now officially a few seconds late plus however long it would take for the elevator to arrive. *Great.*

At last the brass door slid jerkily open. A man in a white suit stepped out and Davies stepped in, followed by three others. He kept his eyes fixed on the elevator floor, reluctant to communicate until he was in costume.

The thought of losing his job was even more depressing than coming to work. But it's important to be cheerful when you're leading groups of strangers through old, dark halls, telling stories of death and murder, haunted hotel rooms, poltergeists, apparitions and ghosts condemned to eternal repetition. You tell your stories, incidentally providing anecdotal evidence for the indestructibility of consciousness and the possibility of life after death, to everyone from ninety-year-olds tottering on the brink of the unknown to three-year-olds who steal the focus; you try to keep it light but keep it honest and still get good tips - for the three thousandth time. That's what it means to be a ghost tour guide.

The elevator juddered to a stop, the door opened indecisively and Davies stepped out, checking the time on his phone. He was now two and a half minutes late. But he was on the premises. Billy Bull had no cause for complaint or reason for reprimand, Davies was when and where he was paid to be. The elevator door closed behind him. *Wait!* He was on the wrong floor. Third floor.... He pushed the call button a split second after he heard the whine of protest from the rising elevator. Now it would be more like five minutes late. Great! He raced for the stairs.

Rounding the corner of the third floor north, Davies stopped dead. Something was different. He could not have told how many doors were lined up like cardboard soldiers along the halls, in all those years he had not taken enough notice to be able to recite the numbers they displayed, but he had rounded the corner of the third floor north thousands of times and something was different.

*

Not all the phenomena we call Paranormal are glimpses of the abiding dead. Phenomena of many kinds haunt the 1886 Crescent Hotel: some had their origin in people and events now past; some are forms of existence that humans may recognize, someday; and there must be other orders forever beyond the perceptions or comprehension of the human mind.

Some of the more subtle, more formless spirits linger in hidden parts of the building where the life forces were once seething and vital; in abandoned bat sanctuaries and the nests of long departed wasps and ants; in the meticulous workmanship of spiders that span empty space to lay their traps, at first almost invisible but over uninterrupted time as thick as blankets; in the unreachable corners of bathrooms; in the paste beneath the wallpaper; within the hollow inner walls of kitchens and wine-cellars.

Occasionally some of those existences drift away from the dark corners for an hour or eternity - they know no distinction - into the halls and rooms of the hotel; and on their peregrinations they carry from their habitat odors, fine dust, quanta of electromagnetic or other, so far unrecognized, forms of energy. Given eternity, some presences far older then the hotel have learned to employ their accrued detritus, like the debris ball behind a tornado, to manipulate the world of matter inhabited by you and me.

If left in peace, they lazily draw together all their drifting parts to revolve, revolve in all directions of spin, until they are formed into a perfect ball, a diaphanous something where before were only shafts of light, that hovers sometimes but mostly zooms, and does not remain an orb for long but returns to the nebulous, shapeless, smoke-like phantom that it was before; or morphs into other forms, yet stranger.

They are most often perceived by animals and small children; cats are especially alert to their passing by. Consciousness may be too precise a word to use for these alternate reality forms, yet they do appear to be aware of us, here on the mundane plane, and to operate sometimes with unmistakable intent. Sometimes they get irritated for reasons none of us can understand and then look out, the wraith is awake and wrathful; but mostly they like to play tricks, make mischief, just to entertain themselves.

*

Under the stairs was a door Davies had never seen open. If asked, he would have said he thought it was probably a storage closet, probably for cleaning supplies. The tour groups gathered near that door every night, to be told stories from the 'forties. But tonight the door stood wide open, revealing a bed, a bedside table and a small chair. He was about to resume his breathless dash to work when, 'Davies,' said a low voice. From inside the room. 'Could you come in for a moment?' And now he saw the chair was occupied, by a slender man with gray hair in a gray suit whom Davies had inexplicably not noticed.

Davies heard himself mumble, 'In? Me?'

'You have a tour to give?'

'In a little bit...'

'I won't keep you. Just want to let you know I'm moving on.'

How the old man knew his name and that he was a tour guide, and why he should want Davies to know his movements were questions that would doubtless be answered fairly shortly. *In all situations and at all times, the satisfaction of the guest is the primary concern of the staff, including ghost tour guides.* 1886 Crescent Hotel Employee Manual, Section iii: Staff/Guest Relations. *When interacting with the guests, staff should always behave like Ambassadors for the hotel, especially the ghost tour guides.* Screwed if you do or don't.

'You're checking out, sir?'

'Finally. It's been long enough.'

He looks awful, Davies thought, thin, gray...

'So – you stayed for a few days?'

Gray man chuckled. 'A few years...'

'You've been coming here for a few years, quite a few?'

'I haven't left for quite a few years. This room is my home. Or - it was.'

Oh-oh, Davies thought, he's going to tell me he's dying...

'And you want to know something? When I finally take my

31

leave, say goodbye to this old hotel and walk out the front door, there will be no more friends out there waiting for me than there were the day I arrived, one sultry July afternoon, the sweat pouring off my back and my suitcase which, not being in a position to hire a cab I had hauled up from the train station, about to dislocate my shoulder. I stood outside, looking up at the famous Crescent Hotel and thought, Looks expensive. But if all goes well with Tony Harmony, when it comes time to settle up with the hotel I'll be able to afford it, many times over and leave a good tip, too. And I was really hoping it would go well. Tony was unpredictable, unforgiving and unbalanced. If he didn't buy my figures, chances are I would buy the farm.

'But one thing I knew: if Tony Harmony had brought me to Eureka Springs to take me out, he would have brought his whack man with him. The Ferret, they called him in Chicago. Tony liked to keep his hands clean, he was always wiping them with a scented silk handkerchief. He never went anywhere without a goon on each side of him, but if the Ferret was along too, someone would not be closing down the clubs that night. Nobody knew where the Ferret spent his time when he wasn't on a job for Tony. It was rumored he stayed by the phone in a one-room apartment in Cicero, reading the phone book.

'I'd never been in Eureka Springs but I'd heard the stories. Big games every night, the local landowners on one side of the table, the Chicago contingent on the other. The city boys always had cash, suitcase loads; the locals put up their houses, their farms, businesses, hotels. And they were no slouches when it came to the game; they knew a Full House from a Royal Flush. And they carried their equalizers out in the open, just like in the cowboy movies.'

'Yes, I heard those stories, we tell some of them on the tours, oh my gosh, I'm late for my tour, nice to have – '

'Lemme explain something to you.' The Gray Man chuckled, his pockmarked cheeks deeply creasing. 'See, we were all supposed to check into the Basin Park Hotel, where the city boys liked to stay when they needed to duck out of sight for a while, or something was going down that needed to be discussed at length in private, and where there was some good gambling going on, big chips. Tony told me he wanted to see me in his room. For accounting. The Basin Park is where he keeps the big bills, is what he told me. And big bills is what he owed me. On paper, anyway.

'I figured that if he had been tipped off about my habit of lowering the totals on the nightly take, he would have called me into his office in Chicago. Nah. If Tony brought me all the way here - sent me the train ticket, right? - it must be because he's expanding the operation and he wants to include me in. Or not. It all depended on whether Tony Harmony had brought the Ferret to Eureka Springs with him.

'Which is why I booked into the Crescent Hotel instead of the Basin Park - to give myself a chance to scope out the situation before laying my head to rest in a hotel bed I might never get out of. I would make the meet next day, and with luck I was up for promotion, but I would spend tonight where no one knew how to find me. Just in case.

'I check in with one of my private IDs: Jack Rabbit; haul the suitcase up to this room, and lay down on the bed for a rest. It's ninety-five degrees outside and the ceiling fan is not much help. Stay calm, I tell myself. Just remember: Tony Harmony is smart; but you're smarter. He's lucky to have you in his outfit. And even if I was making a little more off his scams than he knew about, he could afford it; and I was not the only one finessing the numbers. Maybe what I know about who is doing what could buy a little leverage if it comes down to it. Which it won't. I drifted off to sleep.

'When I woke up it was cooler and I was feeling better about everything and looking forward to raising the stakes, moving up the ladder with Tony Harmony, sweet! I was ready to check out the town, find some dinner and something to drink with a kick to it. But first I needed to locate the Basin Park Hotel and scope out the joint for signs of the Ferret. I freshened up and put on the outfit I liked to wear when I didn't want to stand out in a crowd: conservative three-piece, white shirt and dark tie, panama, shades. I put my lucky ace up my sleeve and step out whistling into the hall at exactly the same moment the door opposite opens and Tony Harmony with two big goons right behind him appears, wiping his hands with his silk handkerchief.

"Well, would you look who's here!" Tony is clearly as surprised as I am. "You're supposed to be at the Basin Park," he says.

'I laugh my super friendly, all good buddies together kind of laugh, shrug included. "So are you!" I say.

"Yeah. But I ain't," he says, and steps to one side to allow the Ferret out of the room. "This is him," he says, jerking a thumb in my direction.

"Him? Okay," the Ferret says. He slips his hand under his lapel and in one smooth motion slides his snub-nose out of his shoulder holster and shoots me square in the forehead. Amazing, really. Right outside the door, there. I fell back in the room, they closed the door on me and hung up the Do Not Disturb. I wasn't found till a couple of days later, when housekeeping came to see why I hadn't checked out.'

Oh-oh. His mind has gone. He's on the threshold, he's about to go over, and he's losing it. Confusing some gangster movie with reality. And now I'm seven minutes late. 'But I was attending to the needs of the guest in the room with no number…'

'You don't recognize me.' He brought his face close to Davies'. 'I pass by you about once a week, while you're telling your stories.'
And Davies thought then he had seen the small gray man, somewhere. Elevator? Gardens? Lobby?
'I enjoy the way you put things. Big difference in the way it happened and the way you folks tell it, of course, but it's good to know we're not completely forgotten, the past is not gone completely. Although I've heard some whoppers over the years – that Glenn fella, what an imagination! And the Brigadier General – you guys have no clue who you are talking about. There was a man. Do you know that in one night – one night, one long game - he lost twenty-five thousand bucks? He was a poet, too. Still, you're not as bad as most of them. What I like about you is, when you don't know, which is most of the time, you say so, you don't make stuff up.'
'Ah – we try to get it right. We only have books to go by, old reports…'
'That's right. You only have books… Time was, not all that long ago really, when a gun and a knife was what you needed, in the wilderness, right around here. Not long after that it was a tommy gun. Today? Smart phones do just about everything, except kill. Directly, anyway. Times change, men change, but this old lady stays the same.' He looked up at the ceiling, gestured to the walls.
'So – you're moving someplace out of town?'
'Moving on. Something stops, something else begins, a door closes, other doors open…'
Wow, Davies thought. 'That's…yeah,' he said.
'What time is your tour?'
'Ah – right now…' Davies started to flap.
The gray man nodded and raised his right hand. 'Don't pee your pants.' He grinned broadly. 'Go to work. We'll meet again.'
Nodding and smiling, Davies backed out of the room then

bolted to the elevator, over eight minutes late. He had an excuse: he ran into a loony guest and couldn't get away without being rude.   But would Billy Bull listen? *He never has...*

Chapter Four:
Kissing Ghost

The force that through
    the green fuse drives the flower
Drives my green age...

Dylan Thomas

CHAPTER FOUR
Kissing Ghost

For the first third of the twentieth century, the halls and stairwells of the great stone house on the promontory were loud with the laughter and chatter of young women. Each term eighty or more students filled these rooms, all from families, European or Native American, with one common advantage: their parents could afford to send them to Crescent College and Conservatory.

Mostly confined to the castle on the hill, riding in the surrounding park or boating on a private lake, the girls were occasionally let loose on the town below - to the delight of the shopkeepers and local young men, who doubtless used every means at a farmer's son's disposal to impress the fine young ladies from the College.

Some fellows would get invited up for special visitors' day events. Some fellows would sneak up at night. But you wouldn't want to get caught. If President Richard Thompson found any young fellow messing with any of his girls he would have him put down.

November 14, 1917

In Room 318 four girls in white cotton nightdresses, faces bathed in candlelight, sit in a half circle on the floor listening as a fifth, perched on a single bed and hiding behind her hair, reads aloud from her journal.

'Today I salute our brave young men, fighting for freedom across the seas, gallant soldiers defending the lands so many of our families came from...' Dee pauses to turn her journal toward the light.

'Dangling preposition,' Agnes points out.

'...so long ago.' Dee concludes and puts out her tongue at Agnes, who turns bright red. 'And I give thanks that this conflict will be the war to end all wars, and soon our valiant warriors will return again to the plough and the factories they love so well, and our family lives will be restored to normal. When I think how much the children of today, our little Breckie included, will owe to the sacrifices that our brave young men have made, my heart swells with pride...'

'And women, we make sacrifices too!' Vera declares, and strikes her heart, head thrown dramatically back.

'You should say our *generation,*' Agnes insists.

'Shall I just stop?' Dee lowers her diary into her lap.

'No!' Laetitia reaches out her plump white arms. 'We're listening!'

Dee begins to read again, the book in her lap, her face completely hidden. '...my heart swells with pride that we – our *generation* – have - *has* made the world a safe place for Breckie to grow to manhood and realize his full potential, along with all children, everywhere.' She peeps out from behind the tress that hangs down over her face, like a small nocturnal animal emerging from its hideaway at moonrise.

'Dee, that's *beautiful*...' Vera sits on the single bed, thin face laid on Dee's bare shoulder, one hand creeping about her waist. Dee feels eyelashes wet on her skin. Agnes, gripping the hinge of her eyeglasses, shifts till she is sitting at Dee's feet. Laetitia sits beaming at Dee, one hand on her ample heart, her bright, half-crying eyes pouring love. Dee runs one hand repeatedly down a long tress, becoming more frozen, waiting for the outpouring of affection to be over. Louise leans against the armoire, watching everyone.

Laetitia says, 'Full moon tonight. Good for ghost stories.'

'Laetitia –' Agnes releases her glasses to point in the general direction of Europe, 'we're talking about the *war*...'

' We always used to on full moon nights...'

'Not since that night with the Ouija board...'

'Don't. Don't remind me.'

'Everybody shut up,' Louise commands. 'Dee - go on.'

'I have one more page.' Seeing all faces turned her way she reads. 'Mrs. T. very brusque in Health and Hygiene this morning. Scolded self for inattention. Self was paying attention, just not to her. Self was dreaming a poem, of distant hills, lilies and rills, not thinking about bandages and disinfectant...'

'What's a *rill*?' Laetitia's plump cheeks gather in distaste.

'Small stream or brook,' Agnes supplies instantly. She sits with her back very straight, as still as a chair.

'Rill....' Vera repeats, dreamily. 'I love that word...'

'Less than half an hour later, in gymnastics, self caught Mr. T. staring at self in a way that Conservatory principals should not stare at students.'

'I know *that* look...' Vera says. She reaches out her bare foot to touch Dee's, which jerks away like a small animal fearing attack.

'Interesting how Dickie Dick always finds a reason to drop in on gym...' Louise drawls.

'He's not interested in Mrs. T, that's obvious – '

'She's only interested in Breckie, writing down every word he says and counting his vegetables...'

'Giving in to his every whim...'

'It's the modern way...'

'It works! I never knew a four-year-old to laugh so much!'

'She spoils him.'

'Spoiling is better than speak-when-you're-spoken-to, do what you're told, bed without supper or a whipping, the way my brothers were raised...'

'We'll see how he grows up, won't we?' Louise is doing side bends, fingers linked behind her sturdy neck.

'Will we?' Vera stares into the candle-flame. 'Do you think we'll come back here, once we graduate? Do you think we'll remember nights like this?'

'I will,' Laetitia says,' her eyes brimming, 'I'll never forget any of you. Never, never, never.'

'Dee – 'Agnes says, 'you are so talented. You ought to be a writer. Like Mary Shelley –'

'- George Sand – '

'- George Eliot – '

'- Kate Chopin...'

'Vera!'

'I am a writer,' Dee says.

Agnes points a finger at the ceiling and declares, 'But you must use your own name, your woman's name. The time for ambiguity has passed!'

'I've always been a writer,' Dee says to all of them, 'It's who I am.'

'I love your mind...' Vera whispers in Dee's ear.

'When I'm writing I don't think, I just let it flow from my pen, I never know what I'm going to say or what's going to happen next...'

And suddenly they hear, through the open French window that

lets onto the balcony, a long, low, melodic, three-note whistle, sustained by a powerful breath, wafting up from the shadows on the warm breeze that chose that moment to stir the curtains, and fading beautifully away leaving an invitation on the air.

They look at each other, breathless, big-eyed.

'Who's that?'

'Don't know... Who is it?'

The enticing tune comes again, and this time it is louder.

Vera whispers, 'I'm not expecting anybody...'

They all jump suddenly when the door opens, letting in the yellow light from the hall, but it's only Fanny from next door.

'Who's out there?'

'He'll wake everybody up!"He'll wake up Dickie Thompson...'

'He woke me up!'

'Mmm – me too,' Vera weaves little spells with her fingers. 'I wonder what he's like...'

They are all wondering the same thing, privately, when the whistle comes again: peremptory, candid, demanding, reduced now to two notes and as loud as may be heard on a building site, precipitating a rush to the balcony by seven pretty young maidens, all laughing and falling into each other. They lean over the balcony, hissing 'SSSHHH!!!' loud enough to rival the locomotive at the bottom of the hill.

A figure below, a young man in a rumpled suit who should not be there at that time of night, tips his broad-brimmed hat with one hand and gives a cheery wave with the other, the full moon glinting in his eyes.

The girls throw down questions, like roses.

'What do you want?'

'Are you looking for someone?'

'Who are you?'

'What do you want?'

The young man replies not at all, but throws back his head in a silent laugh, shrugs his broad shoulders, points to himself and then, with gesture clear and unmistakable, indicates the balcony on which the girls are gathered

'You're not supposed to be here!'

'It's after hours, we're not even supposed to be awake...'

'What do you want?'

Again, the mute suggestion that he should be on the balcony, too, among them.

Vera laughs, looking at the others with mischief in her eyes.
'Shall we?'

'Who is he? How do we know he's not a murderer?'

'Or boring...'

'If he is we'll send him away.'

'We have to find out what he wants,' Laetitia says. Vera and Fanny catch each other's eyes and splutter.

'Perhaps he has an urgent message for someone?'

'That's probably it, Agnes...'

'What do you think, Dee?'

Dee ponders, but the young man puts his fingers in the corners of his mouth and takes a huge breath. Hastily: 'Nothing ventured...'

'Wait right there!' Vera tells the young man.

'Don't move,' Louise clarifies.

The girls drag a large wooden laundry basket from its usual position in a corner of the balcony to where a rope hangs from a pulley, a device employed by the chambermaid and the laundresses to lower the linens to the gardens below. Louise runs the rope through the pulley till the hook appears while the others, nudging each other breathlessly, watch the young fellow below, sauntering in a widening circle with his hands in his pockets, kicking a stone.

'Ready?' Louise indicates where each girl should grasp the laundry basket. On her, 'Lift!' they hoist it between them onto the rail, balance it while Louise attaches the hook to the handle, haul on the rope to raise the basket off the rail and lean over to push it clear of the wall as Louise lets out the rope. The basket descends, spinning slowly, almost regal.

'Come on!' Fanny calls down in a loud whisper, waving. 'Get in the basket!'

The rope is tugged. The girls gasp and almost shriek, cover their mouths.

'Let's go!' Louise grabs the rope. Willing hands lay on, and moments later a hat appears above the railing, wide brimmed, almost conical, and beneath, a dusty tanned face creased with laughter lines, teeth that flash in the moonlight. With a goat-like leap he lands on the veranda, gives a slow cordial bow like a diplomat at a royal wedding but not nearly as controlled, raises his head and laughs and the girls all giggle with him.

'Come inside,' Fanny says, 'Someone will see you!'

The young man shrugs, tosses his devil-may-care head and

allows the ladies to shepherd him into their boudoir.

They make him comfortable and take his hat, releasing a tumble of long brown hair. They bring him lemon water and cookies and introduce themselves and show him where they sleep, telling him secrets about each other - *She snores...she gets up ten times a night!* – and whose bed is always a mess and who is as neat as a new pin.

'My family is just about the most important ever represented at this conservatory. We're oil.'

'We didn't have to go digging in the dirt for oil—'

'My family is the oldest, we came on the *Bona Nova*. My ever-so-many great greats-grandfather was a master stonemason...'

'All the men in my family are Masons to this day – sssh!'

'I myself toured old Europe but last year. We were in Venice, Hamburg, Paris and London.'

'I've been to Mexico and Canada both. We live in New York, on the island of Manhattan.'

'You should see her house! Big enough to get lost in...'

'It takes two whole days to ride across our ranch...'

'You'd get lost anywhere! She got lost in Crescent Park but yesterday...'

'It's true! I have no sense of direction, *absolument rien!*'

'She's top in French. Dickie Dick's favorite...'

'I'm told they do a lot of kissing in France,' Fanny says, and everyone stops talking.

'Oh, no,' Agnes says.

The young man looks around at his companions, grinning so that the creases around his mouth grow deeper, his cheekbones even more pronounced; the twinkle in his eye is a promise and a dare as it settles on Dee.

'Do *you* like kissing?' Fanny says, offhandedly.

'*I* do,' Laetita says. He chuckles, shrugs, twinkles.

'Boys like kissing, don't they?' Louise challenges.

'*He* likes it, you can tell.'

'What would you know about it, *Fanny?*'

'I don't need to talk to you about it, *Vera.* You live your life, I'll lead my own, thank you!'

The young man and Dee have been staring at each other for some time, both seemingly about to break into laughter. Abruptly, he takes her by the shoulders and holds her still while he plants a kiss on her lips that is brief, but enough to reduce her to an apparent state of catatonia. Agnes slips out the door.

Much murmuring and excited laughter as the young man, with an impertinent grin, looks about for his next volunteer. He does not wait long.

Sometimes he has one in each arm, favoring them each in turn with his lips.

The girls watch each other's amorous indulgences, alert to the slightest of improprieties, urging each other to just calm down when the activity becomes too breathless. They catch each other slyly observing the young man for indications of excitement, and stifle screams of shared embarrassment at their own inexcusable curiosity. The young man laughs with them, his eyes glittering. Louise, in the corner by the armoire, watches in silence. At last, when all but she have taken a turn at being kissed by the young man, she strides across the room, seizes the young man's face and flattens her lips against his. Both keep their eyes open.

'Look at Louise!'

'Louise! Don't eat the poor thing!'

Louise releases the young man and wipes her lips on the sleeve of her nightgown. 'Hmm,' she says, and returns to her place by the armoire.

When all the girls have had one kiss each Laetitia suddenly exclaims in a loud whisper, *'Zut alors!* look at the time! The watch will be passing any minute, we have to get back to our rooms, now!'

'We have drill in the morning,' Louise reminds everyone.

Bustling begins. Much urgent scuffling follows as the girls pull the young man by his arms, through the French window, across the balcony to the railing where the basket swings, and hand him his hat. The young man adjusts his vest, surveys his admirers, and with a cock of his head, jams on his hat and leaps back into his vessel.

The hands that hauled him up are about to lower him down when suddenly Dee, leaning so far over the rail her feet are hardly touching the balcony deck, throws her arms around the young man's neck and whispers something into his ear, then puts her ear to his lips. He seems to whisper something back. Dee stares into his eyes a long moment then kisses the young man softly on the lips - an extra, unsanctioned, stolen kiss – whereupon those who have been patiently holding onto the rope, expostulate fiercely.

Louise unlocks the pulley and the young women let go the rope hand over hand, glancing at each other with the scarcely contained glee of those who have broken rules and got away with it, complicit in the enjoyment and excitement of their respective encounters, each holding their own memories of the few moments experienced in the strange young man's embrace.

They take a last look over the rail to wave goodbye to their vicarious lover, to the latest increment in their growing understanding of the life that is quickly unfolding for them, real, unreal, inevitable and filled with surprise, in a world that will be changing faster than any alive that day could imagine, yet still driven by ancient forces.

'Where did he go?'

'Is that him? Over there? No – that's a bush...'

'How can he have disappeared so quickly?'

'We never found out his name!'

'We never asked!'

Dee, her eyes wet, whispers behind her hair: *'Michael...'*

Chapter Five:
In the Faculty Lounge

I shall not commit
the fashionable stupidity
of regarding everything
I cannot explain as a fraud...

Carl Jung

CHAPTER FIVE
In the Faculty Lounge

Your Tour Guide is a member of an ancient and noble profession. Some prized territories in old Europe are shown off to tourists by dynasties going back generations; you don't just fill out an application for a temp job at the Palace of the Medicis. Ask anyone who has ever taken a tour anywhere and all will agree, whether it was of the catacombs of Palermo, the upper reaches of the Amazon or backstage, the experience was rewarding or otherwise depending on the guide.

A guided tour is a medium of communication – information delivered by one person to a couple of dozen newly-met individuals of all ages and attitudes, on the move. Practiced yet personal, informal yet concise, a tour is an improvisation, an art form, a performance that must not appear contrived delivered feet away from a shifting crowd, strangers to each other, some bored and tired, some hyper-excited and all ports between. But by the end of the tour, a skilled and friendly tour guide will have unified the group – a task that begins in the first moments - and perhaps some of those who meet on a tour will maintain lifetime associations. One of the ways to measure a tour's success is by how long it stays in the memories of the guests.

To qualify for the responsibility of giving each of the multifarious guests their moneys' worth requires extensive study, with retention; an accurate internal clock; social finesse - tact, a sense of humor - and perhaps a black belt. Genuine personal excitement over the material and reliable historical context, with details, make a good tour guide great.

The ghost tour guide has, obviously, an added area of reality to juggle, the very fount of extremes of opinion in the misty territory where ghosts either do or do not exist: the stories that ghost tour guides tell start in this world and end in the next. And, if there is truth to the stories, they are told within earshot of the characters in them, who presumably have feelings. The ghost tour guides walk a tightrope

51

in uncertain light, balancing the faith and the cynicism of a living audience with ordinary respect for the departed individuals, never met, whose stories they tell; ghost tour guides must offer the Invisible Ones the same courtesy they give their guests.

*

'You're late!' Billy Bull snarled, so loud that several pairs of guests jumped and scurried away.

'No, I'm not...' Davies flapped penguin-like, an impression reinforced by his pear-shaped physique.

'Late!' Billy Bull's verdict reverberated down the elevator shaft to disperse in the lobby far below.

With his waved hair, straw boater, big spotted bow tie, shiny satin vest and patent leather shoes, Billy Bull was the quintessential undersized song-and-dance man, the entertainer with no skills except to make people laugh and dazzle them with footwork, fallen in his later years, unfortunately for the entire Crescent Hotel ghost tour department, into a position of management. In the six months since he had replaced the legendary, god-like manager, Keith, Billy Bull had effected major changes in the ghost tour operation, principal of which was driving away most of the loyal guides. Davies would have gone too, except he could not afford to miss even a day of work or he would be out of his apartment.

Billy Bull carried always a pair of scissors which he waved dangerously as he clack-clacked at the air in emphasis of his continual but usually indefensible assertions. He marched along the hall, clacking and jangling his keys in time to his endless reprimand. Davies drooped alongside, having long stopped listening.

'When I say five I mean five on The Dot, when I say four thirty I mean four thirty on The Dot, not five minutes before or five minutes after, well five minutes before is okay, fat chance of that happening, I need people working for me who can get here on The Dot, you hearing me, Davis?'

'I was here on time – '

'No, you were not!'

'I ran into this crazy guy, one of the guests, in a room I didn't even know was there, he seemed to think he was a gangster, I couldn't get away from him -'

'LATE!' Billy Bull unlocked the glass-paned doors of the Faculty

Lounge, propelled Davies into the room with two fingers in the back, took a last quick glance up and down the hall, closed the door and, one hand on Davies' shoulder as though guarding a hostage, got started. 'It keeps happening,' he said, worrying the punctuality bone.

'I'll try to do better – '

'Don't try, just do it! Listen, Davis -'

Davies had failed to plug a hole in a dyke, and inundation by recrimination and supposedly friendly advice was imminent and unavoidable. The question was, would this night's tirade conclude in dismissal and potential homelessness?

'Aren't you happy here? That's usually what lateness is a sign of, it's an indication that your job is less important to you than other things in your life, I was just reading that in a magazine - someone who exhibits those characteristics is probably ready to move on, and lemme tellya if your enthusiasm is out the window the guests are not going to have a very good tour and they won't come back, they won't tell their friends, they're writing reviews, next thing you know we're all out of a job, me included! You ever think about that? You ever think about other people?'

Davies would have been glad of the opportunity. But as insufferable as Billy Bull's invasion of his privacy, time and dignity was, even more infuriating was his own lack of whatever it would have taken, he genuinely did not know, to tell Billy Bull to bug off. And lose his job. And his apartment. He could have rolled his eyes and sighed expressively, but Billy Bull's face, inches from his own, was trying so desperately to deliver a message actually about Billy Bull, and Davies was working hard on Noncommittal.

'Forty-five years on the boards, musicals, comedies, whodunits, dinner theatre, I've done it all, I'm a performer, it's who I am, and I'm good! I'm very, very good! But you know what makes a performer great? Discipline! Hard work! Devotion to the craft! Talent will only get you so far. And if you don't have talent you have to work twice as hard but you don't mind that if your heart is in it, you have to love what you do, do you love what you do? Can you honestly say to me, I love what I do, because if you can't... You better mind your Ps and Qs, and that's all I'm saying. ' Billy Bull writhed inside his seersucker suit as though he were sharing it with something small that wriggled. 'This room's a mess. Where the hell is the Dream Queen? Help me straighten these chairs out, it's almost time for her tour, they're starting to arrive outside. That woman is a total wingding, she's got a head like a bucket with a hole in it, vegetarian! Hippy dipshit! She's another one better mind her Ps and Qs, why do I have to keep reminding everybody? The question is, What, are we *here* for?' The gestures with which Billy Bull accompanied his question were suggestive of Man, Drowning, perhaps by Giacometti. 'What... are we here for?' And he began to rearrange the chairs that Davies had already straightened.

Davies was preparing an answer but before he could offer it, the broom closet-cum-changing room opened and DreamCloud Detroit emerged, like a fairy *en pointe*, in floating scarves like butterfly wings, hair in various shades of pastel most attractively tousled and, strapped to her third eye and flashing like a firefly, a tiny digital light.

'We're here to love each other,' she said, musically, 'and say nice things about each other, always.' Flimsy multi-colored layers of chiffon floated liquidly about her frail form. 'We make our own universe, it's up to us to love, and teach others how to love each other,' she said. 'The poor things, they need to know it's OK to care about each other, our parents, animals, the rain forest, Mother Earth...'

'Don't gimme that woo-woo crap,' Billy Bull said, 'I get enough of that in church on Sunday morning, I had my sermon for the week, but we're not at church we're at work, and what are we at work for, why are we here, it's very simple: we are here to make money! Bottom line! Right, Davis? Right? Money, money, money!'

Davies resented being recruited to support Billy Bull at any time but on this evening - despite his job insecurity and precarious grasp on shelter, with daring possibly attributable to the presence of DreamCloud Detroit who always seemed to be teetering on the verge of lucidity but Davies wanted her to like him nevertheless - before he could stop himself he found himself challenging his supervisor.

'It's not *just* about money, is it?' He folded his arms high on his chest, hands grasping his elbows. 'That may be the reason the hotel offered the ghost tours in the first place, but there's more going on here than buying and selling. We talk about serious stuff, we address the question that everybody on the planet asks, What happens when we die? And sometimes it's urgent.'

Billy Bull stood very close to Davies and stared up at him as though preparing to bite his chin. 'Bullshit,' he said.

Attempting to behave as a truly enlightened person might, Davies plunged on. 'People come on these tours for different reasons, they're not all here on a lark. Everybody's different...'

'That's so true!' DreamCloud Detroit said. 'That's what makes them all so beautiful...'

54

'No, they're not!' Billy Bull shouted and DreamCloud flinched. Davies felt protective of her, pretty little moth that she was, but he flinched too. Billy Bull, remembering that the people he was about to revile were sitting just beyond the Faculty Lounge door, lowered his voice. 'These are not people, these are guests on your tour. You know what that means? Twenty two fifty a pop, that's what a guest is, who cares what they think about when they're not here? Get 'em in the door, give 'em a quick tour, send 'em home, bye-bye, there's another tour behind us, don't forget the tip jar on your way out. The rest is...' He made an embarrassingly plausible masturbatory gesture in the air with his little pink fist. 'You are no more important in these people's lives than a busboy and you know what? It's easier to find a good tour guide than it is to find a good busser, so mind your Ps and Qs, don't give me any more of this sanctimonious crap! The numbers are down again this month, that's what we need to worry about! There must be something wrong with the tours, you listening to me?'

'The people on the tours are not just numbers –' Davies interjected.

'Oh, no,' DreamCloud Detroit fluttered, scattering patchouli.

'The people on the tours are kooks!' Billy Bull stamped his foot but remembered to keep his voice down. 'Tell them what they want to hear and keep it moving, that's four hundred bucks every half hour, five hundred if we cram them in, hey, we're not here to smell the daisies, we're here to make *money!*' He re-readjusted the angles of several chairs as though to prove the point.

'Yes, I see that now,' DreamCloud Detroit soothed, 'it's a business! Thank you for reminding us, we need that sometimes, it's so easy to get caught up in everything that's going on with them, I mean, Michael is getting out of hand, so jealous! I must go now to prepare myself to serve my guests but there is something I need to impart, to you especially, Mr. Davison – '

She paused, grasped an amulet about her neck and stood a moment with eyes closed, apparently communing with someone perceptible only to herself. Billy Bull looked up at Davies and described with a fingertip a gyre in the air emanating from his temple. Returning, DreamCloud Detroit took each of them by the wrist in surprisingly strong fingers. 'The Crescent is soooo active tonight, I mean it. Oh, my goddess...' And she slipped out the Faculty Lounge door, presumably to the Ladies Restroom for the standard pre-tour pre-emptive pee.

'I'm not saying we're not here to make a profit, but we're not selling pots and pans,' Davies paused in his second circuit of chair re-straightening, 'we're giving these people raw material for their personal inquiry into the possibility of life after death...'

'How can there be 'life' after death?' Billy Bull gesticulated his way around the entire room, his semaphore especially energetic when crossing the stage area, before returning to adjust the chairs that Davies had just placed, for the third time. 'You just contradicted yourself, right there. Death is Death, that's what it means - no more life. Kaput, kablooie, poof, lights out! And there's no money in retail hardware, let me tell ya, ever since they got container ships. Money is hard to find, and you gotta have money. Unless you're a ghost!'

He stopped to laugh at his joke, leaning on the back of a chair, a little breathless, tilting his boater forward to scratch the back of his head. Davies watched him as he stared into space for a long moment, almost as though he were watching someone else in turn. At length, 'I could be at home, watching the game, if I didn't care about making money. But this ghost thing won't last forever, y'know.' He started in on the chairs again and Davies gave up. 'Something else is going to get their attention, a war or something, and we'll all be out of work. Ghost tours will be nothing but a memory, they will have proved by science there's no such thing. I should know, I've tried everything. Including show business. I was a hoofer, did you know that? But you know what? Football will never die. That's where the real money is today - sports. There will always be people willing to pay big bucks to get into a game. Ghosts? Gimme a break!'

Davies was the last person in the room to be defending the authenticity of what he did for a living. And yet on *this* night, just before what could very well be, from his supervisor's attitude, his last shift telling ghost stories, he found himself defending the profundity of the act, the value of the profession, the importance of the discussion; and having strayed thus far from the timorous way and in the grip of a strange new feeling of exhilaration, Davies threw job security to the winds and dropped a question on Billy Bull's plate: 'What about the immortality of the soul? Don't you ever think about that?'

'You mind your P's and Qs!' Billy Bull had had enough metaphysical speculation for one day, thanks very much. He peered through the curtains on the glass doors like a felon every time the door bell rings, in the movies. 'They're starting to arrive. Nice crowd. Get in character, I need you to take tickets.'

'The schedule says you're taking tickets tonight – '

'That changed. Didn't you get my email? No? Whose fault is that? Chop, chop, the house is opening! '

'Shouldn't we wait for DreamCloud?'

'Davis! You don't hold the curtain except in the case of a death in the house, let's go, you're keeping the faithful waiting. Who do you think you are, the Pope! Aha! That was funny!'

Davies tied the strings of the black velvet floor-length cloak on his shoulders, hung the ancient Egyptian symbol for hierophant around his neck and set the black, four-cornered hat on his head. Billy Bull continued to clack his scissors and peer through the curtains every few seconds.

'Davis! Folks have been waiting five minutes already, let's not start them off in a bad mood, you never know who's going to give you a bad review these days, piss 'em off and they crucify you – ready?'

'Wait! I forgot to clock in!'

'Davis! The customer? The guests? You're on!'

Billy Bull flung open the door of the Faculty lounge and sailed out into the hall, announcing: 'Ladies and Gentlemen, welcome to the 1886 Crescent Hotel ghost tour! My strange friend here is ready to take your tickets. And may the ghosts be with you!'

Chapter Six: Candlelight

I know that I am often
with him when I sleep
and that the passing months
are not so much severing
as uniting us.

Mary Breckinridge Thompson

CHAPTER SIX
Candlelight

October 1919

In Room 303 four girls in white cotton nightdresses, faces bathed in candlelight, sit in a half circle on the floor, all talking at once.

'As far as I'm concerned,' Harriet raises her palms, 'they can keep their old emancipation, it's so boring, just one more thing to have to think about, I want to have a good time while I'm young, not go to a lot of meetings and shout ...'

'That's fine!' Agnes mirrors the gesture. 'As long as you *vote!* Women have been imprisoned, beaten for the right to vote, we can't just not use it!'

"But how will I know who to vote for?' Harriet begins to brush Vera's hair.

Louise, stretching her ham strings against the armoire, drawls, 'Ask your father how he votes and then do the opposite.'

'Vote for Harding - he's promised to fight for equal rights for women.'

'I don't trust Harding.' Vera has dark circles under eyes.

'Why not?'

She shrugs. 'Just a feeling.' 'Politicians promise whatever will get them elected. Then they forget their promises.'

'You can't vote with your *feelings!* We have to stay informed!'

'I always go by my feelings,' Vera says. 'My instincts. As an actress, one must.'

'Going by our instincts at this time would probably start the wars up again.'

'But there's always so much going on!' Harriet drops the hairbrush in Vera's lap and turns her back. 'Revolutions, strikes, anarchists, Bolsheviks, League of Nations, Spanish flu - I can't keep up with current affairs, and you don't know how much of it is true anyway, so I'm just going to not bother. I'll find a nice man to marry and let him take me around the world...'

She nudges Vera, who takes up the brush.

'Harriet –' Agnes pushes up her glasses, one fingertip on the bridge. 'The times have changed, the old ways are obsolete. We do not have to put our lives in men's hands any more. Women are finally going to be on the same level as men in all walks of life, for the first time in history! In our lifetimes!'

'But I don't want to be on the same level as men...' Harriet squirms as Vera finds a tangle in her hair. Vera drops the brush in Harriet's lap, lies back with a quiet gasp.

'You want to be underneath!' Louise works her spine.

The girls fall about, muffling their squeals, despite Agnes' best efforts to restore dignity to the room, and when Vera proclaims, 'On top! Why not?' they lie giggling helplessly and holding their stomachs, even Agnes.

Dee comes in, ever-present notebook in one hand, a carefully coiffured tress of blond hair hiding one eye. She is followed a moment later by Laetitia, wiping crumbs from her cheeks.

'Hilarity? The cause, pray tell.'

'Agnes is being a suffragette,' Harriet says.

'No, I'm not! Well, I might be. I just think that now women are beginning to be recognized as equal to men, the problem is, people are not going to change their ways.'

'But we're not all equal!' Laetitia looks at Dee. 'Are we?'

'Everyone in this room is capable of managing a corporation or starting a business – '

'Competitive sports!' Louise throws in.

'- and women must run for office –'

'Politics!'

'- it's the only way progress is going to occur! Show of hands – how many budding U.S. congresswomen do we have in the room?'

Dee physically shies away from the thought.

'Not I.   I'd rather live in Paris and 'ave lovairs and drink *absinthe.'*

Laetitia is wide-eyed and horrified. 'You would not!'

'I think about it. That's where all the real writers are going.'

'I can see your family agreeing to that!' When Agnes is

disappointed she brings common sense to bear.

'They don't have to.' Dee does not speak the blasphemy loudly. She does not have to.

'Paris?' Laetitia shudders.

'And how do you intend to support yourself?' Harriet hates the thought of Dee in Paris, as does everyone in the room, for different reasons.

'Whatever do you mean?'

'How do you propose to pay the rent?' Louise pantomimes throwing a basketball at Dee. 'Buy your *absinthe*?'

'Her *lovairs* will keep her in luxury...'

Vera, with an extravagant gesture that billows the sleeves of her nightdress. 'Dee is being a *flapper!*'

'And there we are again, depending on men! We have to fend for ourselves!'

'I will not be the plaything of men, I assure you, friends of my youth. Rather... men will be playthings of mine....'

'But how will you live?'

'I shall live off my writing, *naturellement.*'

'I can see you now, in your beret and cheroot –' Vera pantomimes.

'Lounging about in cafes...' Louise lounges against the armoire.

'All your admirers whispering in your ear...' Harriet is suggestive.

'Things in *French!*' Laetitia is reproachful.

'Slaving over my typewriter till the sun rises over the Seine...'

'While your latest lovair sleeps it off!'

Louise's bitter tone stifles conversation and the room is quiet. Eventually, Dee addresses everyone present, though her face is barely visible behind the single lock of golden hair dangling to her chin.

'Am I to marry a nice local boy and live on a ranch, nothing but cattle as far as the eye can see in all directions?'

'A great many people in Europe today would be happy to change places with you,' Agnes reminds the room.

'With any one of us,' Vera says, to the candle flame.

'Mrs. Thompson says it's a dreadful mess over there,' Harriet says. 'All the buildings fallen down and nothing works. Everybody running around trying to put everything back together again, like Humpty Dumpty. '

'All the king's horses...' Laetitia begins, but Agnes interrupts.

'We must never let it happen again. It's time for women to take over management of this planet. We must wrest control from the foolish forces of destruction, we must nurture the population as mothers care for their children, with compassion and ancient wisdom. History is evolving, getting – being *given* – the vote is just the first step to putting ultimate power where it belongs – in the hands of women.'

'Does anybody have any lotion?' Harriet says. 'My skin is so dry...'

All is quiet in the room for a moment. Louise breaks the silence. 'Dee, did you bring your journal?' although Dee is never without it.

'Yes!' Laetitia clasps her hands under her rounded chin. 'Read to us, like you used to!'

Dee peeps out from behind her silken tress. Seeing all faces turned her way she raises her petite bronze-and-copper diary and turns a page by the corner with one delicate finger.

'This is from last Monday... Mr. T. not as amusing as he used to be, before little Breckie was taken from us and Mrs. T. went to France. He seems graver now, and his stares are unfriendly and unwelcome. It's difficult to believe it's been more than a year since we lost our little treasure, so suddenly. The whole school was in tears for days, weeks. Our darling little boy, gone, just like that. All modern child-rearing methods futile. Death comes when it wants to.'

'Dangling preposition....' Laetitia glares at Agnes.

'Oh, who cares?' Louise is flexing one foot, watching her calf muscles move.

'And yet, I could swear I heard Breckie playing outside my door last night. I distinctly heard his ball, bouncing on the floor and walls all the way down the hallway. I got out of bed and opened my door. The sound of the ball stopped but I seemed to catch a glimpse of his pretty blond curls as he turned the corner by the back stairs. I was half asleep so perhaps what I saw was in my mind. And perhaps that is what ghosts consist of – powerful memories projected onto the outside world...'

'No. Not so.' Vera says. She stares into the candle flame. 'There are ghosts here at Crescent. I had an experience myself.'

'Vera! When?'

'Where?'

'Who was it?'

'Not *here*!' Agnes always looks slightly surprised, but tonight she seems excessively startled. 'In the College?'

'Oh, yes!' Vera lowers her voice. 'Out in the gardens...' She sits up.

Gasps of anticipation.

'Tell us!'

'Shall we blow out the candle?'

'Yes!'

'No!'

'We'd better anyway. It's after ten!'

Louise snuffs the candle with her fingertips. Harriet parts the curtains and opens the window. Moonlight pours in, though the moon is out of sight. When all the young ladies have arranged themselves so they can see and hear, Vera tucks her bare feet under her and begins, in a low voice as though afraid of being heard by someone unseen.

'It was one night near the end of last term. Remember how hot it was? Sweating all the time, lying around in our shifts? There was one night, I could not sleep at all. I was sharing with Jane Fellowes and I lay there looking at the shadows of the treetops on the windowpane and listening to her breathing – she could sleep through thunderstorms. But there was no wind that night, no sound at all except the building creaking occasionally. After a while I sat up and looked out through the window. The garden was all silver in the moonlight. Did I mention there was a full moon that night?'

'Strange things happen on full moon nights.'

'It's full tonight!'

'Shhh! Go on, Vera, did you see someone in the garden?'

'No. No one. At least –' She pauses. The girls hold their breaths. 'I saw shadows moving across the hedges. But I didn't think of anything... supernatural...'

Vera allows the word to hang in the air for a long time. She looks around at many pairs of wide eyes.

'I listened. No sounds. No one around. I slipped out of bed –'

'Vera...'

'I went to the door and opened it a crack, so I could peep out. Still no sounds. Just the long, empty hallway, with the light flickering. And before I knew what I was doing, I had slipped through the door.'

'Vera!'

'I closed it very carefully behind me. I tiptoed to the corner and stopped to listen. All quiet. I started down the stairs...'

'Vera – what were you wearing?'

65

'What do you wear in bed in midsummer, Harriet?'

'Vera!'

'I was wearing my slip, silly thing, even I wouldn't wander down the halls naked!'

Gasps and smothered giggles.

'All right, ladies, I think that's enough. Vera, you were telling us a ghost story as I recollect?'

'It's not a story, Agnes. It happened. Just as I'm telling you...'

'You went down the main stairs?' Louise wants details. 'What time was this?'

'It was a short while before three o'clock in the morning...'

A whisper passes around the room: *The witching hour...*

'The stairs creaked, so I crept down really slowly, with my heart in my mouth, listening all the time. My shadow on the wall was huge. I didn't breathe till I reached the bottom step.'

'But why did you leave your room? You would have been in such trouble if you were caught.' Laetitia bites her finger ends.

'Something was calling me. Something was compelling me. I was being drawn by something, some powerful force....'

'Some powerful force!' Dee scoffs and everyone looks at her, pained. 'Was it the Devil? A *vampire*...?'

'Shhh!''Vera, don't listen...'

But Vera is looking away, her face set, staring at the wall, her lips tightly closed.

'Vera....' they implore.

'Sor-ry!' Dee says, palms up, eyes cast down.

After a reproving glare Vera picks up the pace. 'By now my imagination was running wild. I kept thinking I saw figures out of the corner of my eye. Either someone living, or....'

'Stop!'

'I would have been so scared...' Latetitia clasps the back of her neck.

'I was! But somehow I knew I had to get outside, I had to get to the rose garden, I didn't know why – at the time...'

'The rose garden...'

'The haunted garden...'

'Where the murder –'

'Oh, Vera...'

'I ran across the dark lobby as fast as I could, just certain there was someone hiding behind every column. I tried the big back door, carefully. Locked. I wasn't going out the front. But I had to get outside...'

'You didn't go out a window?'

'Through the laundry?'

'Through the library to the shoo-fly walk?'

'No. I went down to where the staff rooms are...'

'Vera! Suppose -'

'I didn't care! I was being *summoned...* I crept past the porter's door and the gardener's door and the housekeeper's and cook's door and into the bowling alley... '

'It must have been pitch dark!'

'It was! But I could see the moonlight through the little window in the door at the end – '

Groans of excitement and sympathy.

'The next thing I remember... I was standing outside, looking up at the moon. Everything was completely still in the gardens. Like a painting, all blue and black with silver outlines on everything. There was no wind. But as I listened I heard the cry of some animal out there in the forest, killing or being killed. And I started to walk toward the rose garden.... I moved as though my limbs were not my own, like a person under hypnosis...'

'*Hypnosis...*' Squeals, as at a graphic vulgarity.

'I passed among the flowerbeds, and over the little bridge and through the rock garden and around the fountain and between the pine trees and through the box hedge into the rose garden...and there...'

Vera falls silent. She looks around at each face, pale in the moonlight from the window, holding each girl in her gaze as though to exact a vow of secrecy. After gazing out through the open widow for a long moment, she seems to gather herself.

'There in the shadows I saw... a man.'

Gasps of shock and trepidation.

'Now, Vera...'

'Agnes - he was old enough to be my *grandfather!* Handsome, though. Dashing. He had a beard and mustachios and he stood very straight – like a military man?'

She looks around again and the girls know that she is giving them a clue, a hint of revelation to come, possibly sinister.

'What was he doing?'

'Harriet!'

'I mean – was he standing, sitting, leaning, did he know you were there?'

'He was staring straight at me. With a very strange look on his face.'

'Was he a ghost? Could you see *through* him?'

'I don't know, I don't think so. He was all in dark clothes, and the moonlight threw shadows over him from the box hedge. He didn't move.'

'Just stood there?'

'Just – stood there.'

'Looking at you?'

'Staring at me. As though he had been waiting for me.'

'He sent for you!'

'That's what it felt like. I had been chosen.'

'Chosen? By whom?'

'Dee – let her tell it!'

'Did he – it – did it speak to you?'

'No. Not a word. He just stared at me with a strange expression on his face, as though he was happy for me but sad about something else. He appeared to me to be a man who had worked hard and fought and suffered for what he believed in, but held to his principals to the end.'

'You got all that from the way he was looking at you?'

'Dee! Shut up!'

Vera's voice is distant now, as though she is about to fall asleep, or faint. 'I stopped at the entrance to the Rose Garden. I didn't say anything. I waited for him to speak. The air was very still and the perfume from the roses was powerful. The only sound was the tinkling of the fountain.'

'And then -?'

'What happened?'

Eyes could not be wider, breath could not be held longer.

'Nothing. After a long moment he turned away and disappeared into the shadows.'

'Disappeared? You mean vanished?'

'I couldn't see him any more. That's all I'll say. '

'Maybe it was some townie.'

'No. The clothes he was wearing are no longer worn. And his hair was in the style of an age gone by.'

'Who do you think it was?'

'All I can say is – when he turned away from me, I observed that no hand emerged from his left coat sleeve…'

Muffled screams, from all but Louise.

'So Agnes,' Vera said. 'What do you think?'

'Powell Clayton! The Brigadier-General…'

'One hand lost in a hunting accident -'

'Dead these seven years.' Harriet says.

'The question is, what is he doing here?' Agnes might be solving a problem in geometry.

'Unfinished business?'

'Something he needs to reveal…?'

'After meeting Death in a foreign land, he returns to his castle on the mountaintop…' Dee stares out of the window into the darkness.

'A real ghost?' Laetitia is on the verge of tears, again. She chatters, breathless, 'Vera, what do you think? Did he summon you to give you a message?'

'All I know for sure is that I was there and he was there and – although I don't know how I know this – there was something he wanted to communicate.'

'But he did not?' Agnes says.

'Not any way that I understood. Maybe he decided against it.'

'He summoned you, personally in the middle of the night… So why didn't he reveal his secret to you?'

'He just faded into the shadows, taking his secret with him…:

'…leaving Vera in the garden in her *nightgown* -'

'At the witching hour…' Laetitia squeaks.

'Unless…'

'Unless you made it all up.'

'If that's what you prefer to think, Louise, your mind's your own.'

'Now why would Vera do that?'

'I was going to say,' Dee holds her pencil like a baton. 'Unless the message he brings is his very *presence.* Ghosts exist – that is his message. There is a world where the dead persist and mingle…'

'Just the sight of him proves it!'

'Words are unnecessary…'

They sit on in silence, shivering slightly in the wavering light from the candle, each lost in her own thoughts.

Dee opens her notebook and begins to write.

'I miss Breckie,' Laetitia says, quietly.

69

Author's note:

Mary Carson Breckenridge of Kentucky was granddaughter of a Vice-President (under Buchanan) and daughter of the Ambassador to Russia (under the Romanovs). After early education in Europe, she attended St. Luke's Hospital Training School for Nurses in New York City for four years. In 1913 she married Richard Thompson, President of Crescent College and Conservatory in Eureka Springs, Arkansas. Mary taught highly progressive child welfare methods and was sent around the nation to speak on the subject by President Taft. She had two children of her own, both of whom died: Polly after a few hours and Breckie, the darling of the school, suddenly at age four. A few months later Mary wrote:

It will help...to learn that...I have had good news of him through...a psychic of unusual gifts. That I should have this news will be no surprise to those who have been following the work of the Society for Psychical Research and especially the astonishing progress of the last few years.

It has been an inexpressible blessing to learn from old friends on the other side that Breckie is with his sister and impressing all who meet him over here, just as he did us, by the wonder of his expanding mind and the radiance reflected from his happy heart.

In addition I know that I am often with him when I sleep and that the passing months are not so much severing as uniting us.

Washington, D.C. August 1, 1918

Within a year, Mary left her husband and the school and traveled to Europe to assist the French recovery from World War One. In London she put herself through a course in Midwifery – a subject unavailable in America – and when she returned to her native Kentucky, she established the Frontier Nursing Service. In the 1920s Mary and her nurses traveled the Kentucky Mountains on horseback, often alone, assisting women in childbirth from pre-natal care through full recovery. The Frontier Nursing Service is still active today through the Frontier Nursing University and Mary is commemorated on the 77c postage stamp.

Chapter Seven:
Ghost Tour

Alas, where is the guide...
to supply the simple clue
that will give us courage
to face the Minotaur... ?

Joseph Campbell

CHAPTER SEVEN
Ghost Tour Guide

Davies welcomed the gathering crowd with platitudes that had once been sincere greetings, *Where are you folks from? Staying in the hotel? Your first time in Eureka Springs?* and wondering when the hell DreamCloud Detroit was going to show. The hallway was getting very crowded and the crowd was getting very cranky, staring first expectantly and soon impatiently at Davies.

The time to start seating the guests arrived. Davies, hoping that DreamCloud Detroit would yet get back in time to start on time, wondering what he would do if she didn't and why Billy Bull wasn't here to deal with this and realizing he could wait no longer, with an inner sigh, opened the door to the Faculty Lounge.

'Ladies and Gentlemen: This is where your voyage into the unknown will begin. All aboard, for the 1886 Crescent Hotel ghost tour! Please have your tickets ready, folks, numbered end toward me, so I can chop their little heads off – and ladies, if your husbands get scared, hold their hands real tight, okay?'

Flourishing his scissors, Davies made his customary jokes as he took tickets or, in the arcane patois of ghost tour guides, played Lovely Assistant to a parade of facial expressions rarely seen in other activities; from eager anticipation to cocky cynicism, the guests surrendered their tickets and their tour began.

What are they hoping for, those who look for ghosts? Is it empirical knowledge? Is it novelty? Is it proof of life after death? Reassurance that the darkness, when it comes, will not be absolute? Or is it merely the chill down the spine that they seek? If so - why?

As a pondering young man, Davies had spent interminable years in nocturnal internal debate, attempting to think himself to Paradise. For a while in his middle years he stopped thinking about what would come next in his life, let alone after his death, and his mental energy was mostly dissipated on calculations of which bills he could postpone in order to pay the rent, or squandered on insistent fantasies about the life he might have led if he had taken better care of his body and education in youth and so matured into a more attractive individual with greater career potentials. At a certain point, bored with his habitual distractions – mystery novels, adventure movies set in exotic locations - he developed a fascination with the Occult, and spent the years that most people devote to shoring up against their ruin trying to read himself to eternity.

In the waning of his years, still alone, still barely maintaining an apartment he did not care for, a diet with little nutrition or variety, a growing resume of low-skilled employment, and yet another unreliable vehicle, he fell into a job as a ghost tour guide – and found it unexpectedly interesting. More than anywhere he had worked he encountered people who had similar interests, had read the same books, puzzled over the same mysteries; and for the first time in his life, Davies found himself among people he impressed. Almost every night someone would treat him as a celebrity, want to shake his hand and share with him their own supernatural experiences, or their theories about orbs, or their screenplay. At first Davies' natural psychological carapace intervened and he shrugged off their admiration. But soon he realized his growing fan club wanted him otherwise, they wanted him remote and mysterious, not down to earth and just like them, they wanted to believe he had knowledge they did not and could not have, they wanted a Magus. And so Davies gave them what they wanted.

Provided the opportunity by a theatrical supply shop going out of business, Davies obtained a costume that he felt represented the direction he would like to progress in his personal development. On websites and Facebook and YouTube, tourists posted pictures of themselves standing beside Davies in the haunted halls of the Crescent Hotel: the Vacationers and the Hierophant. And night after night, pondering their questions and offering responses from Plato or Paracelsus or Carl Jung that gave the impression he knew more of the works of those venerable gentlemen than quotes found on dust jackets, Davies urged his followers to think ever more deeply about the Greatest Mystery of All. It seemed that, toward the end of a haphazard life, Davies was finally perfectly realized as the bearer of arcane knowledge and perfectly situated to pass his modest wisdom onto others; he had found his inner Hermes.

And for a few years Davies experienced something like content at last, all ambition quelled, all or at least most dissatisfaction with himself shrugged away. A recurrent nightmare, in which he scrabbled at the sides of a muddy, bottomless pit as the light above receded, troubled his nights less often. His days hummed along unhurried and he looked forward to going to work each evening in lively anticipation of interesting exchanges with people, like himself, curious about What Comes Next. And then it changed again, but so gradually he barely noticed the alteration in himself.

It began to seem to Davies that every evening the same couples came from various states with different names and faces: wife, barely keeping her excitement under control, eye-rolling husband in a football shirt; fun-loving couples on a dirty weekend who seemed to think the tour guide didn't notice them reaching into each other's clothing; small groups of friends, oddly dressed without seeming vanity, collectively familiar with every ghost tour in the country; reverential seekers into other worlds, or local history; whole families, here because the kids all watch those ghost hunter shows, they're mad for the whole ghost thing, what's that show called that came here, didn't they get an apparition with a thermal-imaging camera? Groups that made the decision to take the tour hours ago because it seemed like a good idea at the time, have been drinking ever since and enjoying themselves too much to quit now; not a few without a clue as to why they allowed themselves to be dragged into this fiasco; and sometimes but not often, a solitary individual, very sad – they crossed the threshold of the room called the Faculty Lounge, although it never was, where Davies waited to lead them on their journey through halls and stories to the dank little room known as the Morgue.

And after seven years of conversations with thousands of guests, most of whom believed exactly what they were brought up to believe, his nights started to lose their novelty and his tours to blend into each other in his memory. He gave up trying to open anyone else's mind about anything, and finally stopped caring what anybody thought about what he was telling them. And right around the time that Davies was losing interest in other people, he lost his belief in the supernatural.

After seven years walking the shadowy corridors of the most haunted hotel in America without experiencing any phenomena that absolutely could not be explained by rational means, Davies no longer waited to be tapped on the shoulder in the morgue, no longer listened for footsteps walking behind him through the basement late at night, no longer felt the hairs on his neck go up at every unfamiliar sound when alone in the dark. On the tours he no longer felt different wearing his long black cloak than he did when he arrived for work in his old windcheater and blue jeans; at home he flipped through his esoteric library without expectation of learning anything new.

Davies, in fact, became soporifically bored with the subject of life after death. He did not read ghost stories or go to fright night movies and he certainly did not watch whispering, flashlit paranormal investigators on television. When not at work he assiduously avoided all reference to whatever might lie beyond the grave. Which is not to say that the final distinction: Afterlife or Lights Out, lost importance to him; but little now remained of his youthful anguish, his drifting perplexity or obsessive curiosity, he was left with that which he was born to along with the rest of humanity – the fear of Death. The nightmares returned.

But Davies did not consider finding other employment because he could not contemplate a return to greasy kitchens, loud factories, schedule–ridden delivery routes, sunburned days in lumpy fields or insecticide-drenched orchards; and so he forced himself to do his job as well as he could, never arriving late for his shift, never refusing to fill in for a sick or otherwise distracted colleague, counting his hours and depending on his tips. Which was a life, of sorts, preferable to many; and his supervisor, the beloved Keith, was patient, uncritical and grateful to have him. But when Keith mysteriously vanished one night on his way to the fireplace theatre to light the fire for the storytelling program, Billy Bull was hired to take his place. And a livelihood that had been at least congenial became suddenly far too stressful for a man Davies' age. And so the Magus retired from the world into himself, nightly performing his melodious tour, so carefully crafted in more enthusiastic days, and asking nothing more from his guests than that he be allowed to perform without interruption, and they don't sneak out the side door without leaving at least a token of their appreciation.

*

'I'm so excited!' Short, well-grounded, yellowish blonde hair in cornrows, she made punching moves in the air. 'I've been saving up all year for this, I took all my sick leave at once...'

Her companion, short, heavy, tattooed, in boots, leather jacket and Mohawk haircut painted black, testified to her friend's enthusiasm with much nodding of the head and sentences that started, 'She's….' and rarely got much further.

A young and very affectionate couple wearing identical eyeglasses let slip they were on honeymoon. Davies had long since ceased to wonder why people would choose to spend their first night as a married couple on a ghost tour. It happened fairly frequently. For this young couple with twin glasses, the first night of declared public union, the night of the honey'd moon, to be remembered always, would be a search for proof of life after death, an approach to the last and constant frontier still waiting for its Vasco da Gama, it's Lewis and Clark, its Armstrong and Aldrin. Twenty-two fifty plus tax, 365 days a year at the Crescent Hotel, Eureka Springs.

'Are you ready for this?' Davies asked in a playful whisper, as he handed a ticket stub down to a little girl with her fingers in her mouth. She looked away. He moved on to her sister, a few inches taller, in a T-shirt that bore the face of a little kitten and read, *Cuddle me, I'm cute*. Eyeing Davies's scissors, she held the ticket as close to the end as possible. 'What you gonna do if you see a ghost?' Davies said. That usually got a response. Davies liked kids – of a certain age – he felt he communicated with them, and that if his life had come together differently he would have made a good father. The little girl shrugged and pushed her sister into the Faculty Lounge. As they passed behind him he heard one say, 'That guy freaks me out,' and her sister agree: 'Weirdo.' Their mother, who looked ready to drop from fatigue, said, 'They love all this supernatural… stuff.'

A man on the tour alone, short, quick, uncommonly friendly, wearing a silver jacket emblazoned with the emblem of NASA, offered his ticket right way round to Davies, saying, 'I am *really* looking forward to this…'

'NASA?' Davies said, intrigued at last.

'Launch technician at Kennedy – one of the ones at the computers, sending up the rockets…'

'Ah – wow! What a privilege to have you here!'

'Privilege to be here!' He passed jauntily into the Faculty Lounge, and Davies turned his attention to three giggling and colorful young ladies, clutching onto each other and writhing like electric eels.

'Sorry, but I need to ask your age…'

'Sixteen!' came the prompt response from all three at once. More giggles, showing braces. Torn between holding up the line to extract The Truth and the longing for a peaceful life, Davies gave them a close look and muttered, 'Whatever. No screaming,' grateful they were not on his tour. They spluttered and struggled awkwardly through the door arm in arm, blowing gum bubbles.

A small army of young ad execs came pouring out of the Sky High Pizza Palace and Lounge Bar across the hall, falling over frequently, shouting 'Margarita!' and laughing helplessly as though tickled. They had trouble finding their way from one side of the hall to the other, could not locate their tickets and dispersed in search of the department head in charge of reservations, mostly back into the bar or the men's room.

Davies cut another single, from an older woman in a cowboy hat wearing a lot of rings, her skin wind-burned under a trace of makeup, her neckerchief tucked into a bleached-blue light denim shirt, with rhinestones. She did not smile. But as Davies handed her the ticket stub - 'For your scrapbook!' - she took his arm.

'Listen, can you help me?' she said, turning him away from the others in line. 'Isn't it a fact that when a body dies, if that person has left some important unfinished business undone, that person can't move on until it gets tooken care of? And that's the best time to communicate, right after they pass and before they lose interest? I need to speak just one more time with my dearly departed and deeply missed late husband...'

'Ma'am, I'm not a medium, I just tell stories...'

'You're a ghost tour guide at the most haunted hotel in America, you know how to get in touch. Won't you help me? I am so desperate, I come here all the way from Amarillo, I can make it worth your while...'

When a guest makes a request of a staff person, that staff person shall be responsible to ensure said request is fulfilled. This includes ghost tour guides.

'I'll be in the lobby for a few minutes after the tour to answer questions. Or try to...'

'Thank you, bless your heart, I knew you wouldn't let me down, I had that feeling about you as soon as I saw you, you're a good man, your aura is completely white, did you know that? I hope it stays that way....' And with a last conspiratorial clasp of the forearm and a long stare into his eyes, she entered the Faculty Lounge.

Come on, DreamCloud... Davies chanted in his mind, chopping the little heads off the last few tickets. But when all twenty-two guests had been accounted for, including the absent ad execs, there was still no sign of DreamCloud Detroit.

Davies took one last long look each way along the hall, hoping for a rainbow-colored fairy on a moonbeam or at least Billy Bull to appear. *No chance.* Davies was going to have to talk to the group and keep them entertained until DreamCloud arrived, kids, teenagers and the widow from Amarillo included. So soon after wrecking his car with no time to adjust and enduring Billy Bull's ominous threats to his livelihood, he was really not in the mood.   At least the tipsy tyros had not returned.

But just as he was reluctantly loosening the door stop on the Faculty Lounge door, Billy Bull came bustling around the corner from the elevator. *Great!* At least Billy Bull was going to do his job; even if he did make intelligent or even sensible discussion impossible, Billy Bull could be relied upon to fulfill the function of supervisor; the pressure was off.

Davies stood with his hand on the handle of the almost-closed Faculty Lounge door. 'Where's DreamCloud?'

Billy Bull motioned to Davies to bring his ear down a little closer. 'Disappeared!' he whispered, 'Vanished! Nowhere to be found! It's a minute after, why haven't you started?'

'This is not my tour – '

'It is now!'

'I'm supposed to be doing the next tour...'

'There is no next tour. This is the only tour tonight and you're doing it. Hop to it!'

'No more tours? All cancelled?'

'What's the matter, don't you check your e-mails?'

'All the time – I didn't see anything changing tonight's schedule....'

'Whose fault is that? You're on your own tonight. Give a good tour, clean up, close up and don't milk the clock, okay? Let's go, dummy, people are waiting!'

Davies leapt suddenly onto Billy Bull's torso and savagely bit his face, over and over, tearing off great hunks of cheek and chin as his immediate supervisor reeled screaming about the Faculty Lounge. In years to come, other ghost tour guides will be standing in this room, telling a horrified audience the gory details of the day a ghost tour guide went mad and ate his supervisor's face. In this very room. They will probably describe poor Billy Bull as a harmless victim, and Davies as a violent pervert.

The pleasant fantasy passed, Davies adjusted his hat, cloak and talisman, drew a deep breath, and let it out again.

'So where is everybody? All gone home? Suppose something happens, who do I call? And, and, my car won't start – '

'Listen – what part of You Are On Your Own don't you understand?' Billy Bull snapped his fingers under Davies' nose. 'Let's go – sparkle, bubble, cue-pickup! Showtime!' And with that he physically shoved Davies into the Faculty Lounge and closed the door tight shut behind him.

As the spooky music tape came to an end, silence fell and a whole room full of people stared at Davies, expressionless. He walked up the center aisle to the platform and, feeling a little like a

Templar addressing his inquisitors, began, with dogged enthusiasm, 'Ladies and Gentlemen! Welcome to the 1886 Crescent Hotel ghost tour! Your voyage into the unknown is about to begin!' which, since he had already used that line, earned him no new fans.

This is going to be the ghost tour from hell... Davies warned himself.

And, though no seer or prophet, Davies would prove absolutely correct.

INTERLUDE:

In the Gardens

Things flit. That is all that can be stated with accuracy. Sitting in the gardens outside the Crescent Hotel, on a bench in the shadows by a pond where frogs sing in clearly orchestrated chorus, you let your gaze wander around the paths lined with bushes and scattered shrubs, over the lawns, the tiny amphitheatre where the bizarre stories of the antique Ozarks are still told, to the scrub grass farther down the hill, the small stone walls that were flowerbeds once and beyond, the Stations of the Cross modeled in marble on the wall beside the path that leads to the big bronze doors of the old stone chapel; the road below winds down into darkness.

Every so often something moves in the corner of your eye, too swift and fleeting to identify, a movement, little more. Did someone just slip behind that tree? Is that a shadow on the moonlit path, cast by no living person? Do you see where the grass blades are bending, is that the feet of unseen people crossing the lawn? What just disappeared on the other side of the fountain? Is someone standing behind you?

Is that a tall man made taller by his top hat, turning the corner of the Shoofly Walk? What kind of animal just streaked between two elms, and is something sitting up in the branches or is it the reflection of the lobby lights on the leaves, stirred by the breeze? Is that a cloud of mist floating down from an upper balcony, or a girl in a white nightdress that billows as she falls? Who is the one leaning on the railing, in a white suit, one hand in his pocket, chuckling, puffing on a cigar, or is it just a lightning bug, flashing intermittently like a lighthouse? Here comes a small boy bouncing a huge ball though it makes no sound and now he's gone. There is the man in the top hat again, walking straight and stiff as though reviewing a regiment, one arm behind his back, an empty sleeve where a hand should be, dissolving into the trellis.

The roses remain, there is no doubt they are there, they are real, they can be touched and their fragrance breathed in, though you're not so sure about the giggling girl in the gym slip, apparently hiding from her friends among the rosebushes. Is it their voices that you can hear on the wind? What name are they calling? You can almost make out the syllables but the frogs are suddenly very loud, in response to some unknown perception of their own.

What if every time it happened, instead of being a trick of the light or the wind or an insect hovering around your head, there really was an entity, flitting at the edge of your peripheral vision? Do you hear someone sobbing? Merry laughter deep in the trees? A death rattle? What if all those things you thought you saw and dismissed as imagination or projection, are really there? And not just the ones you chance to glimpse. What if the fringe of perception is the only place the Others can be perceived? And suppose this park is filled with them, they are everywhere, all around you, all the time? And not just after dark?

What if?

PART TWO:
THE LAST GHOST TOUR

All that we see or seem
is but a dream
within a dream.

Edgar Allen Poe

Chapter Eight
Townbuilders

...it is a ghost's right,
His element is so fine
Being sharpened by his death,
To drink from the wine-breath
While our gross palates drink from the whole wine.

W. B. Yeats

CHAPTER EIGHT
Townbuilders

The hidden valley where the healing waters flowed had been sacred to the Osage tribe for centuries; with their removal the location of the spring was lost, though its magical properties were remembered in legend. In the summer of 1878 an epidemic of yellow fever took twenty thousand lives in Tennessee and Louisiana, and the state of Arkansas quarantined itself against its neighbors to the south and east, severely crippling cotton trade and plunging the state into poverty. The winter cold eradicated the source of the plague – mosquitoes. But the following spring, news of the rediscovery of the miraculous Indian Spring in the Ozark hills tore across the land like wildfire in a whirlwind.

The rush to partake of magic waters that could heal any wound or weakness – or to take advantage of those who rushed - created almost overnight a higgledy-piggledy, rickety-rackety scatter of tents and shacks and boarded-in overhangs, each with its tales to tell, dotting the hillsides wherever a space could be found and cleared, spreading outward from the spring, along the valley floor and up the steep hillsides, an unplanned community of the afflicted bound together by hope and daily recourse to the waters of the Indian spring.

One eye-witness declared, 'Many who were not able to walk would use the water and be able to move in two or three weeks to climb the mountains...' As more people announced themselves cured, more flocked to the miraculous spring to taste and test the waters for themselves. The quiet forest was filled with 'the screams and groans from the suffering as the wagons bounce and jostle over the rocks and ill made roads. They carry them down the mountain on stretchers, in chairs, in their arms and every other way imaginable... There is no let up – they come by day and by night...'

By that summer, the empty valley was crammed with makeshift camps. On July the fourth the settlement was officially named Eureka Springs; next day the first store was built and the following Valentine's Day the rough and ready, wildly proliferating assortment of primitive dwellings, randomly strewn on unhelpful terrain, miles from anywhere, was officially incorporated as a city. Eureka Springs became instantly, internationally famous as the Miracle City in the Wilderness, The Town Built on Water, the Shangri-la of Arkansas, Lourdes in America.

The traveler desiring to reach this Mecca of health and personal reincarnation was confronted with the problem of merely getting there. Northwest Arkansas, at that time, did not have one mile of hard-surfaced road. The only access to Eureka Springs, often impossible in rain or snow, was on foot or mule-back or, with great difficulty, ox-drawn wagon – or by way of a back-breaking, nine hour stagecoach ride from Pierce City, Missouri. And yet newcomers continued to arrive at the rate of two hundred a day, legions of the ailing, bringing with them infection and disease.

Not all who came were invalids or caregivers. Eureka Springs was a boom town like any in the goldfields of California, though the rush in Arkansas was not for gold but for water, not wealth but health. Tradespeople and storekeepers, lawyers and carpenters, looking to create a living where they could partake daily of the restorative waters of life; opportunists and proselytizers; drifters and grifters, down and outs and ne'er-do-wells, runaways and renegades and the not-quite-all-there, found their way to the sudden city.

In less than a year '...the residents numbered some 3,000, the transient population stayed around 15,000... Living conditions were unbelievably crude...no water works, no sewer system, no paved streets, no street cars... and a lot of horses and mules.... The many saloons attracted characters desiring to raise a little hell, accompanied by yells and pistol shots. ... nights were real noisy with some kind of entertainment going on in every block. Pianos and orchestras tried to outdo each other with noise... the two most common arrests were for drunkenness and discharge of firearms within the city limits.'

By her second birthday, July 4th 1881, Eureka Springs boasted: 'a post office with telegraph, 57 boarding houses and hotels, one bank, 33 groceries, 12 saloons, 22 doctors, one undertaker, 12 real estate agents, 1,511 children of school age and 50 boot shine boys. And at least 8 churches.' Eureka Springs had become a city of the first class, the fourth largest in Arkansas, 'the Wonder City of America.'

However, there were no formal medical services apart from the capricious springs, no burial grounds for those the waters did not reprieve, no educational opportunities for the young brought here by unwell parents, no facilities to help bring the next generation into the world. Newcomers were building above the springs, compromising the purity of the water. Every part of the city of close-packed wooden dwellings was destroyed by fire at one time or another. But the reputation of the springs was unquestioned: health was to be found at Eureka Springs, for all the sick and afflicted who could make the journey.

The elected city officials did their best to control land-clearing, sanitation, safety, business practices and fair access to the springs, as well as provide some semblance of redress of crime, abuse and exploitation; but the primitive and overcrowded conditions, imported infectious diseases, corruption and civic chaos and the never–ending stream of arrivals threatened to destroy the community of the faithful huddled around the healing spring.

It would take an authoritarian leader with imagination, connections and knowledge of civil engineering to stabilize the burgeoning town. Enter ex-governor Powell Clayton, a northerner who had distinguished himself as a Union forces commander in Helena, Pine Bluff and Little Rock, and was elected by the newly enfranchised citizens to govern the state during the critical years of the period known as Reconstruction. As might have been expected, Clayton was not popular with the officially disbanded Confederacy.

*

1865. Helena, Arkansas. Society belle Miss Adeline McGraw is arrested by Union Brigadier General Powell Clayton. Espionage occurs. At war's end he and Adeline marry, remaining in the south to serve and protect the state Clayton helped vanquish. The war is declared over but violence continues and Governor Clayton has to make some hard decisions. There were two sides in that war, and what came after. Clayton is on the ruling side, the side of the future; but his power is constantly under threat, under pressure and under-supplied. It is Adeline's task to maintain the civility of the house - always open to scrutiny - and to support her husband in his daily struggle.

After one bloody term demanding iron rule, Clayton retired from the Governor's office to a plantation along the Mississippi with his younger half-brothers, twins John and William and their families. The Clayton house was always filled with guests from every walk of life, especially the railroads and Congress. Bankers and thinkers, politicians and old union soldiers enjoyed good dinners, brandy, cigars and high-stakes card games far into the night. The neighboring plantation was the property of one Clifton Rodes Breckinridge. Son of a U.S. vice-president, Clifton had been ambassador to Russia under the Romanovs.

Adeline Clayton was too fully occupied with her obligations as hostess and chatelaine to experience discontent, except perhaps in odd moments when she found herself wondering what her life might be like if she had not committed to the current arrangement. Powell Clayton is credited with installing free education statewide, founding the Arkansas Industrial University that became the University of Arkansas and opening schools for the blind and deaf; the world little knows how many of those crusades the Governor was persuaded to undertake by the governor's wife.

Came the day Clayton took a notion to visit Eureka Springs, since it was so much in the news and generated so many conflicting stories. He rode all the way, accompanied by a small contingency of companions. When he finally found the place, he was fairly disgusted by what he saw: disaster coming apace.

Perhaps the old soldier sat his horse on a hilltop overlooking the spring and the shanty town stretching along the valley floor and leaning up the precipitous hillsides, wondering what it would take to save the rudderless community from inevitable disaster, when the idea came into his mind: in those days, 'taking the waters' was a very popular recreation among the wealthier classes...

Clayton assembled a group of investors and set about converting the unsavory, anarchic firetrap in the Ozark hills into a health resort. In characteristic, autocratic fashion Clayton imposed sanitation and social services on the volatile community. From the point of view of the devotees and profiteers who had made Eureka Springs their home, a Yankee carpetbagger had come charging in and taken over without an invitation, and the Brigadier General met with more local opposition than cooperation. But Powell Clayton was a pile-driver; when he wanted to get things done he drove right on through any obstacles in his way.

Clayton and his associates gave Eureka Springs a water supply, waste disposal, streets and streetcars and street lights, electricity, the telegraph and stone from a new quarry downriver. Most significantly, the Eureka Improvement Company, as they were officially called, facilitated access for the outside world with a new railroad line. Cutting twenty-six miles through the wilderness, crossing rivers and ravines, blasting through hillsides, thick forest and over limestone bluffs, it was the most expensive stretch of railroad to that time.

The train station was built on the north edge of town at the bottom of a crescent-shaped hill, the highest point in the region. Clayton found alternative housing for the families that were legally squatting on that hilltop, and replaced a handful of rudimentary wood cabins with the finest hotel west of the Mississippi.

Designed by the architect responsible for the grander buildings of St Louis, constructed by specialist Irish stonemasons using the finest limestone, the imposing Crescent Hotel, rising out of the endless Ozark forest, was built to last for centuries. The times were turbulent and the future uncertain. It's no accident that Powell Clayton's own Camp David resembles a hilltop fortress. Within those impenetrable walls Clayton established a comfortable headquarters
for his activities in the political and economic spheres, entertaining in grand style, gambling and drinking all the way.

A new and wealthier population, riding in Pullman luxury, made their way to Eureka Springs, widely advertised as a fashionable spa resort. Those who came to the boom town in the wilderness in hopes of health and those who came in search of wealth built their own homes on any available space, it did not even have to be horizontal; and soon the valley where once a lush forest of white oak, pine and hickory had flourished was filled with examples of architecture from just about everywhere. In a few short years the disorderly, inconvenient and unsanitary collection of mostly temporary shelters would be transformed into a city of gracious dwellings, wide boulevards and well-kept parks, a thriving business community – but an increasing social divide between the prosperous 'Silk Stockings' who occupied the mansions on West Mountain, and the workers, most of whom were here first, living in much more modest circumstances on the other side of the valley. Watchful and protective, visible from miles around, The Crescent Hotel towered above the community, and the future of the region was forged within her walls.

*

Adeline was always her husband's companion, but less of a confidant to him as the years went by. She spent more time assisting the great numbers barely surviving in the very shadow of Clayton's lavish entertainments. She formed the Ladies United Relief Auxiliary, an organization composed of women like herself, the wealthy wives of Eureka Springs. They scoured the streets during the day for children with no shoes, and shod them. After dark they accosted the ladies of the night, fed them a good meal and dropped them off at the edge of town. They worked so hard for the poor that the destitute of towns all around the county made their way to Eureka Springs.

Debutante, spy, society lady, chatelaine, charity worker, wife and mother and briefly, widow: from Helena, Arkansas to Mexico as an Ambassador's wife, Adeline spent the First World War in England and died there at the end of it. Her husband's passing at the beginning of the war had weakened her; her son's death in 1917, falling from a young horse, put an end to her.

*

It's said the dead cannot cross great waters. But people have seen someone who might be Adeline Clayton gracefully descending the south stairs into the lobby, holding up her skirts with one hand, fluttering a fan, to the applause of the guests gathered in the lobby waiting for her to lead them into the great hall. And perhaps it is also she who enters the Crescent through the almost secret door at the end of the bowling alley, hauling a dirty child by the hand, to hide him in the servant's quarters? And is she the one who goes into the kitchen in the middle of the night and hurls pots and pans?

Today the Indian trails that followed animal tracks are winding streets lined with gift shops and galleries, hotels and gathering places, swirling with visitors from all over the south and increasingly from much farther away. On the upper ridges, tree-lined boulevards of Victorian dwellings look remarkably as they did in the early years of the Miracle City in the Wilderness. Eureka Springs is still hard to get to, and still unruly. The population is smaller now, hovering around two thousand independent-minded individuals with powerful opinions. Local city council meetings are notoriously contentious; but the divisions within the city were once even greater than they are today.

Author's Note:

The text quoted on occasion in this chapter is from *The Healing Fountain: Eureka Springs, Arkansas - - A Complete History, with a Description of the Surrounding Country, and the Local Curiositites* by L. J. Kalklosch, published in Eureka Springs in 1881.

Chapter Nine
Mohawk

Now o'er the one halfworld
Nature seems dead, and withered Murder,
...moves like a ghost...

Shakespeare
Macbeth

9

CHAPTER NINE
Mohawk

Summer, 1889

i

The great stone palace on the hilltop was alight and alive. Looking up from the shadows on Spring Street, a thousand steps below, I could see groups of revelers strolling the moonlit gardens, drifting across several levels of gas-lit verandas, gathering on the promenade. Frequent bursts of laughter grew louder every time. Clearly, some important event was in progress. But what was the occasion these wealthy and therefore powerful people, Northerners all I had no doubt, were celebrating? And why had I, a resident since the incorporation of the town, a city council member and editor of the *Eureka Springs Advocate*, not been informed that such a gathering would be taking place? I climbed the long wooden staircase, keeping to the unlit side.

The revelers were numerous and richly adorned and mostly merry. I slipped around the perimeter in the shadows, listening for clues but hearing little except over-enthusiastic greetings and flirtation. The ladies swayed and touched the gentlemen on their lapels with lace-adorned, down-turned fingertips, the men stood proudly in their toppers and tails, swirling their drinks. Somewhere inside the hotel an orchestra played tunes I had never heard. The smells of perfume and whisky, scented candles and early summer flowers drifted through the gardens, the smell of roasting flesh emanated from the dining room.

I heard voices of two men arguing, coming in my direction, and withdrew further into the bushes. As they passed, waving their cigars in emphasis, I heard a fragment of their disagreement.

'Victory on Tuesday,' a tall thin man with a dangling white silk scarf was saying, 'will put these fellows in their place, and prove, once and for all that the majority of the people in Conway County want to be represented by Mister John Clayton – '

'*Majority* - if you don't include the disenfranchised Confederates and sympathizers,' his short, portly companion objected. 'They don't give up easily in these parts, general.'

'They will.'

'You fellers got your own way in the matter of slaves having rights, but now the masters have none, that's hard on them ...

'*They* are no longer part of the decision making process.' The tall man in the white scarf stopped a few feet from where I was lurking in the darkness. 'That's what defeat means.'

'They are still dangerous... '

'As am I.'

'Let's pray this affair does not degenerate into violence...'

'We all pray, Richard, every night, to different gods. Let's get a drink and play some cards. Business tomorrow.' The tall man set off again, his portly companion trotting to keep up with him. 'Any time you take the vote away from one group and give it to another, and I don't care red, black, green, white or Indian, you're going to have a rocky transition. A period of turbulence. Integration of new forms of social organization usually takes *one* full generation to accomplish, one! The old ways and allegiances wither away, a new configuration emerges, unified by new challenges. And by God we're almost there...' The orchestra struck up again and I heard no more.

John Clayton, the Brigadier's younger brother... I had run the story a few days before. John Clayton was contesting the conduct of an election in Conway County that had lost him a seat in Congress. The investigation was due to commence in Plumerville next Tuesday. But what was the purpose of this huge celebration, here in Eureka Springs, three days before the tribunal had even taken their seats? I stepped out of the bushes and lingered in the shadows as long as I dared, hoping to learn more, but then I noticed one of the servants, grizzled white hair round a dark brown dome, squinting in my direction. I moved out of the gaslight into the gardens, where bush-lined pathways and ornamental pools were silvery in the moonlight, hoping to gain the trees and slip back down the hill before anyone came looking for the gate-crasher. I passed under an arch of twisted branches into a small, dark clearing bounded and canopied by hawthorn, and stopped.

ii

Two carved wooden benches faced each other in the darkness, one of them occupied. After a moment I distinguished a man in

100

evening dress, his face in shadow. He acknowledged my presence with a nod, put back his head and looked up at the racing clouds.

The accident of the two of us meeting in a moonlit glade in the gardens of the Crescent Hotel was unlikely and incongruous - he, in his frock coat and starched white shirt, well-fed and self-satisfied, his indolent ways supported by the labors of those like me, born hungry and still skinny. I could have nodded back and gone on through the glade, but here was a slight chance of discovering more about the goings-on at the hotel this evening. Given the opportunity I took a gamble and ventured an opener.

'Evening, mister. Didn't mean to come up on you, didn't see you there in the dark. Doing all right?'

He lowered his head to look at me full face, with a kind of puzzled inquisitiveness as though I were an example of some species hitherto unknown in his world, which I probably was. No doubt he was wondering if I was there to trim the bushes. Or if he might be in some kind of danger.

'Nice party!' I offered, which was another wrong thing to say because it was pretty obvious from my every-day-of-the-week-go-to-work clothes that I was not on that guest list.

He smiled, faintly and briefly. 'Yes,' he said. 'Nice party...' and went back to looking up at the night sky, which felt to me like I was being dismissed. But I have a talent for grabbing bulls by their horns in pursuit of a story, that's what makes me a good journalist; and it could have been argued that as a public servant I had every right to be making inquiries, even without a tailcoat.

'Having a good time?' I pursued.

'I was,' he said, distantly, without lowering his gaze.

Now, what would you have supposed that comment to mean? Until I came along. What else was he saying? Until local yokels started showing up, spoiling the private extravagances of the smooth and privileged with our uneducated, unwashed and uninvited presences. I talked to him right back, in my head.

Don't you worry yourself, mister, I said, I am not here to gobble down your delicacies like a wild hog, I have no interest in attending your fancy gathering. But I like to know what's going on in my town. I don't live in a mansion on Yankee Boulevard and wear silk stockings. I have a little house on East Mountain and I go to work every day and get my hands dirty, holding this town together, so forgive me for offending your sensibilities with my presence, I'll be only too happy to remove myself as soon as I find out what you people are up to. You folks don't throw this kind of party for someone's birthday, all you politicians and financiers and railroad developers, you're here to make decisions without even consulting the people living and working in the town at the bottom of the hill. Whatever you folks are finagling, you won't get away with it for long. History shows that. English Civil War, French Revolution, Ireland... it's going to happen in Russia and it's happening here now, so drink your champagne while you can, chum, pretty soon you'll be working right alongside me and my neighbors, getting your hands dirty, too.

I didn't say it, I just got it ready to say if I found myself sufficiently aggrieved. Because, technically, without a press invitation I was an uninvited guest at a private affair, and legally an intruder. Even though I almost married into the Fortner family that cut down the trees to build a cabin on this spot and raised kids in it before the Brigadier General and his pals moved them out so he could build his fancy party palace; what they call the Governor's Suite is situated on the exact same spot as the old outhouse.

I waited, knowing he was aware of me, deliberately insolent. 'Bunch of folks from out of town, I'm guessing?' I said, meaning, *Who are all these big shots and what's the occasion?*

He lowered his gaze and regarded me, expressionless. After a moment, 'Do you believe in ghosts?' he said.

Okay. 'I believe in spirits,' I said.

'You think I'm drunk. No, sir, I am not drunk, far from it. Is that an affirmative?'

I was willing to play his little game, to go along with the charade of interclass politeness, until one or the other of us revealed his true self and treated the other exactly the way he wanted to all along.

'Sir, I do not believe anything I cannot test. I have yet to see a ghost with my own eyes. But I have heard stories.'

'You will hear more. Ghosts are everywhere.'

'There's a lot of people in this part of the world would agree with you. But if they're here, I sure don't see them, and until I do, I'm not about to give myself the heebie jeebies thinking about them.'

'Good man,' he said, unexpectedly. Then, 'I didn't mean you,' he said. 'You're not the reason I'm not enjoying the party. Newspaperman?' Maybe he saw ink on my fingers.

'I put out the *Advocate*, every week. One page, one man operation.'

'And you are wondering what is going on in the Crescent Hotel this evening?'

'Where there's news you'll find a reporter.'

'Looking for a story, an angle. To sell advertising.'

I felt like slapping the guy. But that would have brought me more problems than satisfaction so I contented myself with an exit, to retain my dignity at the expense of his. I said, as polite and formal as I could manage, 'The *Advocate* is a free publication. My mission is to keep the citizens of Eureka Springs informed of developments within the city and provide a forum for comment. I don't carry advertising, only news and editorials and I do not endorse. This is a poor town, I'm a poor man and integrity is all I got. I guess I'll just take my leave at this point, sorry to have disturbed you.' I started to walk away.

'What do you want to know?' He sounded almost like he was about to tell me a joke.

I turned back.

He indicated the bench. 'If you decide to sit back down, I have a story for you that concerns the entire region, but which you will not hear elsewhere. The veracity of my report will be confirmed as events unfold in the weeks ahead. But you will be the first to know and understand certain facts that will bewilder and confuse all others. You want to know what's going on in your town? Sit back down, I'll tell you. Or, you can go on home to East Mountain and we'll forget the whole thing.' He put his head back and stared again at the moon.

'I'd like to know everything,' I said, and sat back down. I heard a round of applause as a dance tune came to an end.

He took a moment, like he was trying to find the best place to start his story; then he seemed to relax, or to decide he had nothing to lose. 'I do not understand – yet – how or why it should happen that a man should come across another man in a secluded garden, and be prepared to listen to his story – at precisely the moment that story must be told, or lost forever...'

Leaning back on the bench with his legs straight out before him, a figure blue and black in the moonlight, he began to talk.

'There were three brothers: twins, one in politics, one in law; and their older brother - a man of the highest accomplishments, a war hero in the eyes of the North and an insufferable carpetbagger to the South, who governed this state through Reconstruction. He survived, the state survived, and he went on to marry a girl from Helena, rescue

Eureka Springs, and build this fine hotel.'

'I have laid eyes on the Brigadier General,' I said. 'He has never spoken to me.'

'Powell Clayton does not speak to many people. But he cares for humanity at large and has done many good works for this state: a railroad system, free education for all, a state university, schools for the blind and deaf ...'

'We're grateful to him for all of that.'

'But he's not from here, is that it?'

'No, sir, he is not.'

'You think Eureka Springs was better off before Clayton took the town in hand?'

'Something had to be done.'

'Someone had to do it.'

'And the General did it. We all acknowledge that.'

'But the town hates him for it.'

'Sir, I would not choose so powerful a word to describe the sentiments of the townspeople toward General Clayton. Since he arrived I have watched the interests of this town go from healing spring to steam locomotive. That was all the General's doing, I guess, him and his friends. But while it's true he has used his resources and his almighty energy to build a city of the first class out of a slum, he does not go out of his way to befriend the citizens.'

'Nonetheless, he and his brothers declare themselves loyal to the new state of Arkansas, and they all work for the good of their chosen home. Agreed?'

'I know that William is the Prosecuting Attorney in Fort Smith. Isaac Parker passes sentence, but William Clayton secures the convictions.'

'William is here this evening, watching everything and everyone. But his twin brother John – you are aware of the skullduggery surrounding John Clayton's election in Conway County?'

'I know he is contesting the results.'

'With good reason! An entire ballot box of votes, mostly black votes for John, stolen in Morrilton by white men in masks waving guns?'

I was beginning to put the pieces together. 'Might John Clayton be here in Eureka Springs this evening?'

'Oh, yes, he is here. The investigating tribunal is scheduled to meet in Plumerville on Tuesday. Witnesses are being subpoenaed, revelations are expected and one possible, I should say probable verdict will be the reversal of the election decision, putting Northern invader John Clayton into the office he was rightfully elected to by majority vote, and sending Clifton Rodes Breckinridge back to his plantation. As I'm sure you appreciate, there are a number of individuals in a particular handful of counties, would hate to see that happen.'

'The men you are referring to still refuse to accept that the war is over.'

'Or that the rules have changed. It's time to move on, work together. Wouldn't you agree?'

'In principal, I would agree with the ideal.'

'Most of the state is looking forward to a new era of opportunity for everyone, not just the white folks.'

'But not everybody wants that,' I said. He looked away, suddenly silent. 'That's the problem,' I added, hastily.

He regarded me again, apparently relieved. 'There are a greater number, by far, of good folk that would prefer a peaceful life with possibilities for bettering themselves, and friendly trading relationships with neighbors, over a return to the days of whippings and manhunts and savagery in farmhouses. We must move on from those bad old days and work together for a new future, as a country, as a state, in every community! We are all human beings and we must look out for each other, the war is over.'

'Not in the minds of the kind of men you are talking about. They're not going to change.'

'You may be correct. But those men must not be allowed to prevail!'

'Is the Brigadier anticipating violence in Plumerville?'

'Do you ask me as a newspaperman or a citizen? Or a spy?'

'I'm a reporter. I tell stories as they unfold. It's the way I think.'

'I think it would be constructive if you could see your way, as a newspaperman, to indicate to your public that Powell Clayton's preference is to avoid violence.'

'Can I quote you on that?' I was hoping to hear his name without having to ask, but he deflected my question.

'Quote the man himself. He has said, on many occasions, 'We must have peace.''

'When he was governor he was not afraid to use force. But he's not the governor now, he's just a regular citizen. What if the Breckinridge faction turns violent?'

'Powell Clayton is a brilliant strategist. He studied warfare, and he won his battles. He was especially skillful at anticipating his enemy's every move. And intimidation from a distance. This weekend he has invited political allies from his days in the Senate, influential representatives of the railroad, banks, the Republican party, the telegraph, family members – all combining into a web of power stretching far beyond the borders of Arkansas - together with a certain number of retired but able-bodied veterans. They are here to show their support for John Clayton at the inquiry in Plumerville on Tuesday.'

'And to send a message.'

'To send whatever is necessary.'

I thought but did not say, Necessary to see Powell Clayton's brother safely installed in office in Conway County and on his way to bigger things. The Senate, not long from now? And maybe brother William will go into power politics, too. While the brilliant strategist relaxes in his mansion on the hill, his so-called hotel?

The stranger might almost have read my mind. 'The Claytons came here as conquerors,' he said. 'They remain here to help. The downtrodden of the earth shall be raised up. To the brothers, Powell and John, that means the poorest of the poor. Those who need help most should be helped first. And what William does in Fort Smith he does in the name of safety for ordinary citizens from ruthless desperados and brutal gunslingers and outright murderous psychopaths who like to call themselves renegades. What Powell Clayton did as governor always had the motive behind it of making things better for the dirt farmers, and also for the newly emancipated, untrained in the ways of social interaction among equals, help is needed there too. There is so much work to be done, in Conway County in particular. If we are ever going to learn to live in mutual respect and harmony in this world...'

He trailed off, staring at me in the shadows. The moonlight was filtering through the branches and for a moment his face was partly lit. Long waves of dark brown hair framed a sculpted face with high cheekbones and deep-set eyes, the color of which could not be distinguished in the half-light.

Music was playing and through the big windows I could see

people dancing. They chattered on the balconies and floated through the limestone pathways and croquet lawns, leaning on each other and laughing.

I had my information. I was ready to leave, I still had time to make my deadline. 'I appreciate the insights, sir. May I identify my sources?'

He chuckled. 'No, sir, you may not. This conversation cannot have happened. I was never here.'

'Understood. I look forward to watching this story play out, and describing it to my readers.'

'Your version.'

'It's the only version I have. I try to be objective. It may not be all the way possible, but I try. I should be able to get this all set up tonight, in time for tomorrow's edition. Thanks again for the story, I appreciate you.'

I rose and offered my hand, but he did not take it.

'I haven't given you the story yet,' he said.

iii

For a moment he seemed to be listening for something in the sounds of music and chatter from the hotel. Then he motioned for me to sit down again, leaned forward and spoke rapidly, almost in a whisper.

'Sir, stranger, friend as I would hope, I am about to reveal to you a piece of information of tremendous significance. Earlier this evening, all unnoticed in the midst of this gathering of illustrious citizens come together in the cause of justice, a callous murder was committed.'

I felt my blood run cold. 'How do you know?'

'I was present. To my eternal regret.'

And colder still. 'I should say – I'm a journalist. If something has happened and I know about it, I will report it.'

'There's the rub. Nothing has happened. A man has disappeared but his absence has not yet even been noticed.' He glanced over the hedge-tops at the verandas of the hotel, where small groups wandered. 'The man's abduction was a perfectly conducted exercise; his subsequent death was the final stage of a planned execution. The operation began during the lavish affair that is still going on. The man was lured into these gardens, set upon, quickly beaten senseless and removed from the premises. It took about ten minutes and was completely unobserved. And now, most of the parties involved in that piece of calculated brutality are back drinking champagne.

'When the victim is officially declared missing, it will be of more than passing interest to the voting public of this state. And when the people who put the politicians in office finally accept that he is gone for good, allegiances will shift, anger will have its day, power will dictate, and there is more than a possibility that this entire region could be plunged again into barbarism and chaos.

'They say that all's fair in love, war and politics. But political assassination is still a crime, first and foremost, of *murder.* And all agree, no matter who you vote for, that no man should be allowed to commit murder and walk away. It will be obvious to everyone exactly who it was that caused a rival to vanish forever during a swell affair in Eureka Springs. But - no body; no crime.'

He went on to tell me that the unconscious kidnap victim had been taken in an open buggy, propped between two of the conspirators, to the rear of a certain dry goods store on Mud Street; carried through the back door and down to the abandoned warren of tunnels beneath the town; and there made to breathe his last. They put the body in an obscure recess and piled rock in front to look like a wall.

'It will never be found,' my companion insisted, 'unless a search is initiated. But it must be found! Those who would kill to preserve their privileges must not be allowed to prevail. Seek the dead, find the horror in the tunnel, display the decomposing corpse, discredit those who brought John Clayton's life and all the good works he was planning to a sudden end, bring the murderers to justice!'

iv

I heard voices from within the hotel, calling.

The man stopped and listened. 'Sir, I suggest that you take to your heels, any stranger found – '

The shouts were getting closer. 'Clayton! Mr. Clayton, are you out here?'

The music wound to a sudden stop and the merriment fell to a hush.

'Clayton!' Voices called throughout the grounds.

Figures were wandering the gardens. 'Mr. Clayton!'

One voice came from immediately beyond the hedge, 'John, we are concerned for your welfare...'

108

'Go, man!' the stranger hissed.

But I knew better than to run and draw attention to myself. I stood stock still under a twisted hawthorn as good as invisible, unless the man on the bench decided to give me away. The calls for Clayton were coming closer.

Two men entered the little garden and peered around. 'Not here,' one shouted.

I watched them go on through into the trees beyond. But why hadn't they spoken to the man on the bench? And then I saw the bench was empty. Perhaps he was hiding in the shadows, too.

The searchers were coming closer yet, more voices joining in, calling out the missing person's name. Then came the sudden report of a pistol, fired from an upper balcony, and a man's shouting voice urged anyone aware of the whereabouts of Mr. John Clayton to please notify the concierge. Possible indications of foul play had been discovered.

Knowing that if I were caught in the middle of this turmoil no matter which side apprehended me I would soon be just another ghost wandering the Crescent Hotel I slipped through the orchard, ran across the moonlit upper lawn and rushed, leaping and stumbling, down the old stairs.

I heard a shout, 'Who's that? Clayton is that you? Hey! Stop that man!' Other voices shouted: 'There! That man! Stop him!' Someone fired a gun, several men shouted commands at each other, but I was already across the track and scrambling down the bluff. In the moonlight I could see just well enough to find, behind bushes, the hidden entrance to the same tunnels that apparently contained the body of a man recently murdered. I could hear shouts from above, but doubted any of the Silk Stockings knew of the existence of this part of the tunnel system or would venture into this darkness, even if they found the opening. A natural tube in the limestone, widened and supported with human engineering, this section of tunnel would take me far enough away from the Crescent to reach home safely tonight - if I could remember the way in the pitch dark.

I stooped down and felt my way through crumbling rock walls and soaking wood arches, sloshing loudly so the rats and water moccasins would get out of the way, repeating to myself over and again the story I had just heard and filling in the details the stranger had not given.

It was now clear why he had been reluctant to identify himself – he had been present at the kidnap, he said. Playing a double game, perhaps, and now filled with remorse, he needed to reveal the assassination without implicating himself. My feet were soaking and I banged my head and grazed my elbows painfully, but at least I was no longer alone in a darkened glade with a killer.

I was familiar with the dry goods store he spoke of, the owner was well known from Missouri to the Arkansas rivers. I had heard him express his political beliefs and brag about his prejudices; and I knew he had family in Morrilton. And a tunnel under his store. I had put in my time working on the tunnels below Mud Street, building the second level. I had a pretty good idea where to look for the body.

As I blundered painfully through the darkness my mind was filled with wild images of the possibilities for the immediate future, burdened as I now was with facts I wished I had never learned.

I was a newspaperman, with responsibilities to the public as a citizen, and to justice - in possession of dangerous knowledge about a very bad man with several violent brother**s**. I lived with my wife and small daughter above a print shop filled with flammable materials. What was I to do with my knowledge? Jeopardize my family's safety and my own in support of privileged carpetbaggers? Expose the crime, put the very bad man where he could do no more harm and risk the consequences? Or keep my knowledge to myself and wait to report the news of Clayton's disappearance till I heard it from someone else? Could I somehow engineer the discovery of the putrefying evidence beneath the pavement?

Devise, devise, I told myself, crashing and splashing through the filthy waters in the labyrinth of dark, dank tunnels that lie beneath the pretty city of Eureka Springs.

The events of the night on which this story takes place are the author's invention and have no basis in history. The background situation, however, is historical fact. John Clayton was robbed of his majority in the 1888 election for the second congressional district in Conway County, when a ballot box full of votes in his favor was stolen in broad daylight by four armed white men wearing masks. John contested the conduct of the election and an inquiry was scheduled to take place on Tuesday, January 30, 1889 in Plumerville. John lived on the family plantation near Pine Bluff; perhaps it's not too wild a speculation that he might have stayed with his wise and powerful older brother the weekend before the inquiry. But he was not murdered at the Crescent hotel. Someone standing outside the boarding house where John Clayton was staying in Plumerville blew his head off with a shotgun blast through the window, the night before the inquiry.

John was forty-eight years old when he died, the widowed father of six. His brothers Powell and William each took in three of John's children. Powell Clayton dispatched Pinkerton men to investigate his brother's murder. Obstructed by the close and hostile community with violence and murder, the detectives retired from the chase. Although it is known that the men who stole the ballot box and plotted the murder included the Mayor, the town marshal, the sheriff, his deputy and other notable citizens of Plumerville, John Clayton's assassin was never brought to justice.

The inquiry into misconduct at the polls was held in the absence of John Clayton and a verdict returned in his favor. John's opponent in the race had been Clifton Rodes Breckinridge, who owned a neighboring plantation outside Pine Bluff. Breckinridge was unseated, but the position remained empty for the rest of the term. At the next election, Breckinridge was returned to office.

His daughter, Mary, married Richard R. Thompson, the president of Crescent College and Conservatory for Women housed at the Crescent Hotel. By then, Powell Clayton was serving as the first U.S. ambassador to Mexico. Shortly after Powell Clayton's death in 1914, Clifton Rodes Breckinridge was living in the Crescent Hotel teaching Political Economics at the College.

Chapter Ten:
In the Corridors
at Night

There are things known
and things unknown
and in between are the Doors.

Jim Morrison

CHAPTER TEN
The Corridors at Night

'Good evening, ladies and gentlemen,' Davies began, thinking, *that sounds stupid. Start again.* 'Welcome. To you and to whatever ghosts may be sharing this room with us, right now–' which occasioned the first shriek of the night from the three girls with braces but without chaperone that he had so generously allowed in a few minutes before.

'I'd like to welcome you to the 1886 Crescent Hotel Ghost Tour...' at which the Faculty Lounge door crashed open and the party of ad execs came falling through like a band of drunken marauders, throwing their tickets down, sitting heavily all about the room and shouting over the other guests' heads at each other, usually one or two-word phrases that detonated hoarse but hearty guffaws from all of them at once. 'Hey, Mitch!' one of the exalted yelled from the front row to the back. 'New Orleans!' and the walls of the room almost bulged with the force released by the middle-management chorus: *'New Orleans!'*

'So? What are you going to do?' The Amarillo widow said to Davies, as though waiting for him to tame an ornery bronco, pointing her fingers like six-guns at the invading Armani-clad tribe of ambitious but hysterical young execs.

Mentally throttling DreamCloud Detroit, 'Gentlemen, gentlemen, gentlemen!' Davies raised his arms above his head, an alchemist conjuring frolicking devils, and when at last he had their attention: 'Guys, I just want to let you know – this is not a party, it's a ghost tour, the party is across the hall, if that's what you're looking for...'

'We have to do the tour...' one said, as though eliciting sympathy, 'it's a team-building exercise...' at which they all guffawed some more.

'Who's in charge of your group?'

'He passed out in his room.'

'Margarita!' Cackles and howls.

'Guys, I'm going to have to ask you to leave – '

'No, no!' One - tall, balding, exploding with authority, probably the always-last-standing favorite for VP - took charge. 'We'll be good. Fellas! Cut it out! Hear me? You want your bonus for taking this trip? Show some respect!'

Thoroughly chastened, all the young men in dark suits and bright ties sat with knees together, staring at the floor.

Davies waited to see if the capitulation was genuine - a moment too long.

'Get on with the show!' A top-heavy older guest with sunburned skin and a face like a mountain top, whom Davies immediately dubbed Aging Rocky, stared at him as through a telescopic sight. His tiny wife rolled her eyes and pantomimed silent apologies for her old man.

'Wow – love your enthusiasm!' Davies had used that one a number of times. It didn't always work.

'Enthusiasm? For what?'

'For the 1886 Crescent Hotel ghost - '

'Ghosts? Gimme a break," Aging Rocky said, searching the ceiling for incoming.

Davies tried an allegiance development tactic, turning to the mortified wife. 'He doesn't believe in ghosts?'

She hunched her shoulders and tittered. 'He is a ghost,' she said, and at last the ice broke and the group burst into friendly laughter.

But Aging Rocky rose, like Neptune or a nuclear submarine from the sea. His, 'Quiet!' was effective. When the whole room was thoroughly quelled he pinned Davies in a Desert Warrior gaze. 'All right, soldier,' he said, 'Let's get this crap over with.'

'Hey!' Cornrows was impressively indignant. 'This is the most haunted hotel in America, do you understand what a privilege that is?'

Her companion supported her protest with much agitated shaking of her head and resultant jangling of the rings hanging from many parts of it. 'She's – '

'I wanna hear this, ' Cornrows said to Aging Rocky, indicating Davies.

The heads of the slack-jawed ad execs swiveled from Rocky to Cornrows to Davies and back.

'You wanna hear it?' Rocky bellowed, apparently under the impression he was on a parade ground.

'Yeah, I wanna hear it!' Cornrows responded, louder.

116

'All right, hear it,' he said, and sat down.

'The City of Eureka Springs was incorporated in 1879 – ' Davies began.

The smaller of the two little girls began to cry. 'Look what you did,' her sister said to Davies, 'I'm going to hit you.'

'Keep that child quiet,' Aging Rocky commanded. His wife disowned him.

'You shut up,' said the child in question.

The child's mother began to cry.

One of the girls with braces, looking sideways at Davies, whispered something behind her hand and all three shrieked at once.

Employee Manual and Hotel Creed: When faced with difficulties, obstacles, challenges or physical catastrophe the staff including ghost tour guides shall remain at their posts until all guests' needs have been satisfactorily met.

Deep breath... 'Folks, I am here to tell you tonight the fascinating story surrounding the discovery of a magic spring in a hidden valley, the straaaange little village that sprang up around it and the spirits of the ages that are said to haunt this building...' he offered and, to his complete surprise, before he reached the end of the line, he had them. Except for the younger of the two girls, and at least she was a recognizable threat, they were all listening. Davies could weave his spell...

'Untold centuries ago -' he began.

'Be right back,' said the tall, bald ad exec and opened the door. 'Just going for a -' whereupon all but one of the young men in suits and florid faces followed, leaving the door open. Davies, as he closed it, could see them all falling about giggling in the doorway to the SkyHigh Pizza Palace. Davies' tour was down from twenty-two to seventeen - including one lone, snoring ad exec - before even leaving the Faculty Lounge.

The remaining guests were watching Davies, stone-faced.

"So anyway – long before the settlers arrived..."

'Excuse me!' A plump, not to say porcine individual stood up to allow himself to be seen by the entire audience and cleared his nose as loudly as any rooting boar. Shadows from the overhead fans passed unhurriedly across the man's doughy face, shiny with greasy sweat. 'On behalf of everyone in the room, I have some questions for you, yourself, our guide, regarding the, quote, experience, unquote that we just paid twenty-two-fifty plus tax for. We would like to know' – snort,

117

snort - 'What is your title? How long have you worked here? Have you, yourself, ever experienced the paranormal, here or elsewhere?' Snort. Task accomplished, he resumed his seat and leaned back, arms folded, his tiny, beady eyes shining from within folds of ham.

Davies had a good idea where this was going. Mr. Pork's catechism was a prelude to a well-rehearsed recitation of his own personal engagements with the supernatural, proving - to his own satisfaction - that he, Mr. Pork, was a greater expert in the paranormal than the tour guide at the most haunted hotel in America. Just what Davies' evening was lacking – a challenge to defend something he no longer believed. It was not, however, Davies' first encounter with self-appointed experts in the Unknown.

'I have not personally experienced anything I would offer as hard evidence,' he said, 'but I'm only one guy: me. There are reports throughout history, in every culture in the world. There has never been a time or place that the existence of life after death was not accepted as fact. I'm not going to argue with that.'

'Oh, very good!' The man from NASA nodded his head as gleefully as any gnome sitting on his hands on a fence.

'Are you a ghost?' the little girl on her mother's lap in the front row stopped squirming long enough to ask. She was rewarded with a kiss on the top of her angelic hair-do from her mother and a sharp poke in the side from her big sister.

Giving a fair imitation of an unruffled tour guide, Davies attempted to resume: 'For example, the Osage Indians came to this valley to conduct healing ceremonies....'

But Mr. Pork had listened long enough and hastened on to his next trick question: 'All right, you're a ghost tour guide, you deal with paranormal phenomena all the time, you're the expert, right? Then how do you explain this?' All the people leaned in to hear the question. 'How come ghosts - wear *clothes*?'

'Yes. That's interesting – '

But Davies had no more opportunity to elaborate. His inquisitor was already sharing his own opinion with the world at large and it was now evident that he was not here just to show off or challenge - he was on the attack.

'My great, great, great, great uncle, for instance, the Laird Arbuthnot of Castle MacGannis always appears in a long cloak with a ruff around his neck – but it's a well-known fact that Laird Arbuthnot was drowned in his bath by a jealous manservant. So why doesn't he appear stark naked, dripping wet and blue in the face? Do you have opinions you would like to share? '

It was not in fact a completely new question to Davies. He had once posed it to a well-established paranormal investigator (by night, particle physicist by day) who appeared on his tour some years before and gave an explanation involving wave function collapse and telekinetic energy that Davies was not even going to try to repeat. But suddenly, with the single exception of the dangerously listing, snoring ad exec, the whole group - the lady in search of her dead husband; the three young ladies with braces, unexpectedly suddenly as well-behaved as nuns in an Irish convent; the sprightly man from NASA; the Amarillo widow; military man-mountain and dormouse wife; melancholy mother and two small daughters - were staring at him with intense interest, without revealing why.

Davies directed the answer he was making up on the spot to the audience at large. 'It's not generally accepted that the departed spirit retains the appearance it had at the moment of death. Which would make for a pretty frightful afterlife. It has even been suggested that ghosts might grow younger –' And at last he received a response from the noncommittal group he was attempting, since he was going to be responsible for their experience for the next hour and ten minutes, to befriend: a short bark of laughter that seemed to come from all of them at once; followed by a swift return to impassivity.   It was a curious, unidentifiable response, but it was enough: advantage, Davies.

However,   'What about all the people that take their last breaths in hospital gowns?' McPork continued, quickly. 'Where do apparitions obtain the outfits they appear in, some kind of otherworldly costume supply store?' Overcome by delight in his own sarcasm the pig went into a snorting fit, which probably lost him his edge with the crowd.

Since it was now obvious that Pork was also here to ridicule, Davies took aim at the core of the discussion. 'It depends what you mean by *ghost* – '

Intercept by McPork. 'Ghosts are the residue of human beings, souls that live on after the body dies, spirits surviving after death, that's a known fact. But what about ghosts' *clothing*? Are you saying fabric has a soul, too? Does a cotton shirt leave a residue, does an overcoat have a spirit self?   Does wool have an immortal soul? Gabardine, denim? How many souls does a pair of shoes get? You're the expert, you must have pondered these conundrums and have some theories of your own, why don't you share with us?'

'Well, I'm trying to – '

'Silk has a soul,' Cornrows said. The room, which had begun to buzz with murmurs during the unquenchable Arbuthnot's diatribes, fell silent. 'I feel it! '

'Leather,' her companion added. *'Definitely.'* She rattled her facial rings at the Laird's distant descendant, and he visibly blanched.

'Apparently *something* survives,' Davies granted, with charity developed on the job. 'On this tour we just tell the stories and let you make up your own minds, for instance, the handsome young Irish stonemason who liked the ladies... But once broached, the subject of ghostwear engaged the immediate interest of the group. Various fabrics were proposed by assorted theorists of the supernatural, and the likelihood or otherwise of those materials possessing immortality was accepted or rejected in varying proportion. The man from NASA followed the conversation closely, without comment. Tweed was thought to be dense, complex and resilient and was high on the list of soul-possessing fabrics. Cotton, and wool of course, received murmurs of approval. But when it came to manmade fibers, nylon, microfiber, spandex and Kevlar had few supporters. Polyester had none and, moved by contemplation of an entity that existed apparently without a soul at all, the crowd gradually hushed and fell silent, as though a well-coordinated swarm of hazy, indefinite forms had hovered over all their graves at once.

The moment of quiet was broken by the ad exec falling off his chair. He scrambled hastily to his feet, stared blearily around as though waking up shanghaied, lurched toward the door, threw it open, announced, 'This is bullshit!' and staggered out.

Taking careful advantage of the lull to refocus concentration on himself, a tour guide whose tour was already down by six and ten minutes late casting off, Davies threw his arms wide, head on side, and concluded with what he thought a brilliant recovery, 'The Fabric of Existence... *Who can explain the mystery?'*

His audience stared at him, expressionless and silent.

Chapter Eleven:
Ghosts Everywhere

Ghosts...like the stars at noonday
are there all the time
and it is we who cannot see them.

Oliver Onions
Credo

CHAPTER ELEVEN
Ghosts Everywhere

Between the Crescent Hotel and the town, on a geological bench halfway down the hill, stands a chapel, built by Richard Kerens, one of Powell Clayton's partners in the conversion of Eureka Springs from anarchy on the frontier to world-famous, fashionable health resort. Kerens' mother lived in the hotel. One day Richard, leaving on a trip, turned at the turn in the steps down to the town to share a wave with his mother, as was their invariable custom. He would not see her again.

Richard Kerens owned the hillside; he interrupted the stairway with a chapel built to his mother's memory, at the place he was standing the last time he saw her alive.

One hundred years later, a guest at a wild and whimsical wedding feast in the fountain garden awakes to find he has passed out on a bench in a gazebo. It is now quite dark and everybody else has apparently advanced to the conservatory. Through the open doors he can hear loud music thumping; jerking, gyrating shadows are thrown on the windows. But he is in no hurry to move. The air is warm, the breeze is fragrant and the full moon hangs like a greeting in the branches of the tall trees. He is in no mood for Mother, this evening of all evenings.

If I go in there and she starts telling the world and sundry - she's very loud with champagne - that Wisteria Pollock – *von Krump* as of this afternoon – broke my heart in college, I will dump her in the punch bowl. It wouldn't matter if it didn't bother me so much. *Him?* I know what she's like, I know what she likes, I know she hasn't changed, she's the same only more so and *he* is never going to keep up, why is she doing this, why? Well, I don't care, it's been years and she didn't break my heart, I was already putting the old devil-eye on a psych major in her sorority when we broke up. But here I am, a grown man, as successful as I want to be, I don't like work, being humiliated at a posh wedding at the Crescent Hotel, by his mother. I could kill her!

Being a man of great forethought and resourcefulness I never go anywhere without a flask of something excellent in my jacket pocket. I shall await Mother's swoon into snoreland, she'll be out cold in a tune or two, I'll just stay out here in the breeze, contemplating the moon and swigging on my Glenfiddich. He sits back, flask in his curled hand by his lapel, burps and blurts out: 'Mothers!'

His gaze shifts in and out of focus as he stares into the abundant foliage, the young flowering shrubs, the venerable pine and sycamore, trickling brooks and a fountain with horses and putti springing from the gushing fountainhead; little bridges, limestone paths, footprints of deer and armadillo.

Still mentally committing indignities upon Mother's ample person, he rests his eyes on a group of nearby bushes, bathed in slow moving moonlight. His vision blurs. Shapes appear. Faces come and go. Because he has no reason not to, he allows his fancy to elaborate on the shapes suggested by the leaves in the half light. Sitting slumped, unmoving, with his head on one side, he watches as the shapes resolve into living people.

He watches as their expressions change, follows a conversation he cannot hear: a man is leaning over a figure in an old fashioned bath chair. The man straightens, slowly, nods his head, slowly, turns and strides down the hill. He no longer stands out from the bush, he is gone. But the bath-chair is turning slightly and its occupant appears: an old, old lady, all in black, covered by a woven blanket despite the warmth of the evening. She has a little lacy cap on her head. Silver streams down her drawn and wrinkled cheeks where teardrops roll. One hand is raised, weakly, a handkerchief dangling, as she watches her son turn at the turn of the stairs for a final wave before he has gone completely. At length her arm drops, her smile fades, her tears cease to flow. Her breaths come slowly and with effort. Then the wind changes, the bushes bend a different way, and the bath chair and its occupant are no longer there.

He shakes his head, peers into the dark. Bushes, only bushes. 'I fell asleep with my eyes open,' he says. 'Dreaming awake. I guess. What do you know?'

He rises, stiffly, upends the flask, staggers, straightens his jacket and says, 'Mother. You had better not, you just had better not...' and notices that the music has stopped playing and the windows of the conservatory are dark.

'Slept for a while. I guess. What's my room number? Where's my key? Mother has it. Front desk will figure it out. That's what we're paying them for. I'll go find a bellman. In a minute. Just sit here. For a minute. Lay on this bench. Smells so good. Roses.'

Blessed darkness, out of time.

Dew on his face, the need to change positions, sunrise. Curled up on his side, he watches the light invade the clouds. Better get to bed. Mother will be up soon. Sneak past her room and get a nap before breakfast. Or I could take her coffee. She would love that. Or I could stay where I am for a bit longer. My heads hurts so bad.

*

Changing tactics to one that usually worked to engage even the most distracted, hostile or deliberately disruptive tour groups, Davies appealed to the whole room: 'So – million dollar question – how many people on this tour believe in life after death?'

Some hands shot up, some rose slowly, some shoulders were shrugged, some arms folded and a few eyes rolled. The genial little chap from NASA was bursting with enthusiasm.

'But before we can talk about death, we have to ask ourselves: What is Life? That's the real question, surely? And it's a question worth asking! Organic material emerged from collisions of inanimate particles and evolved - remarkably quickly! - into you and me. Living organisms are composed of the same atoms and organized by the same forces as water, light, rocks - and yet something causes some of those atoms to come together and complexify and grow and eventually - die. Why? Why does this process occur - birth, maturation, decay and death – followed by regeneration, the result of which is proliferant variety? It all looks so much more like a grand objective than just a scatter of random accidents. Don't you think?'

In the uncomfortable pause that followed, the man from NASA, his contribution to the discussion delivered, sat quietly with his hands folded in his lap, smiling delightedly. Feet shifted, throats were cleared, the Laird's wee bairn opened his jaw, closed it again. Davies was about to thank the man from NASA and go on from where he left off, which suddenly seemed rather slender material, when Aging Rocky's tiny wife shouted 'Go Hogs!' and the room filled with raucous laughter, into which the man from NASA joined.

And when the noise at last subsided and Davies was on the point of attempting yet again to re-take his tour, 'Go hogs!' the man from NASA cried and the room exploded again.

127

Davies had noticed a young woman sitting bolt upright in the front row to the left of the aisle, alone. She had freckles, and swaths of reddish hair framing a pale face; her eyes were also pale, almost translucent. Despite the comfortable temperature she was covered by many sweaters up to the chin, and down to the ankle-boots by a long, dark, woolen skirt, all wrapped up in a large plaid shawl. She stared at him, unsmiling. He gave her his friendly, we're all ordinary folks here look. When she did not respond he shone it likewise on the rest of the crowd seated before him, and realized they were all observing him, following closely his every move and gesture with that same acute yet oddly impassive attention which Davies, being prone to mild paranoia, interpreted as dislike.

The girl in the shawl watched Davies, her head held very erect and shaking slowly from side to side. Davies knew that he would have to get in quick and low, or the tour would be done for.

'So – how about you, going on the tour all by yourself - true believer, skeptic, on the fence?'

'I do not believe,' she said, pertly, easily loud enough for the back row to hear. 'I *know*.'

Appreciative murmurs hummed about the room, though the scornful sneer on the face of the Laird's wee bairn grew perceptibly broader.

'Oh-ho,' thought the part of Davies' brain that would have helped him survive in the jungle or the desert had he been abandoned there instead of the orphanage steps. He sized up the adversarial potential in the slightly mocking, straight-backed, deliberately unglamorous and curiously confident young woman: What was she about? 'Personal experience?' Davies encouraged her to come out in the open, where he could get a bead on her.

The direction most such conversations took at this point was a short list of reports of the presence of a ghost in the speaker's house, usually a person with some kind of notoriety but quite often a grandparent: unexplained sounds, calling voices, the movement of small objects during the night. But this young woman, as though dismissing a stupid question, said merely, 'All the time.'

Davies could sense a room full of chuckles waiting to be released. 'All the time!' He was not, as he tried to appear, repeating her response for the back row, but making time to strategize.

'Yes! It's...' she shrugged, slightly. 'It's who I am.'

The scornful lip in the buttery hogshead spoke. 'Oh. You see dead people!' Mr. Pork looked about him, waiting for the laugh.

'Don't make fun!' snapped Cornrows. Her companion's dangling rings jangled dangerously.

An older lady in a smart business suit, every hair in its precise place, said, 'It's true. This young lady has the Sight. I should know. I am an Empath.'

'Yes?' Pork said. 'What am I feeling right now, then?'

'Superior, cynical and cantankerous. But no psychic abilities are required to observe that.'

'Oh, yes?' he said again

Davies, ignored, hastily attempting to regain the focus of the room before he was forgotten altogether, employed careful timing and polite Socratic inquiry.

'Interesting!' He maintained the focus on the intriguing young woman in the shawl. 'Can I ask - if you see them all the time....' Pause, to make them hold their tongues and prick up their ears – 'do you see them...' *wait for it*... 'everywhere?'

The girl sighed her irritation at having to explain the obvious to a cretin. 'They *are* everywhere.'

Mr. Pork, apparently not skeptical of the existence of ghosts, just of anyone else's ability to perceive them, scoffed.

'Everywhere your mind can think of.'

'Oh, I gave up thinking a long time ago,' she said, and for some reason that escaped Davies, half the audience burst into laughter.

Some sort of tribal allegiance signal, he surmised, hopefully not a rallying cry or war-whoop, and went on pursuing his question and control of his tour. 'So when you say everywhere... you mean, right here, right now, in this room?'

She sank down inside her wooly shawl, but popped her face back out to say only, 'Well – what do you think?'

'All around us? Everywhere?'

The word was picked up and repeated. Louder the general agreement hummed, and louder yet, as the single word shuffled about the room....*Everywhere*...and perhaps the ghosts of the Faculty Lounge joined in the general cacophony, unnoticed.

Chapter Twelve:
Ghosts in the Mist

It seems we stood and talked like this before
We looked at each other in the same way then
But I can't remember where or when...

Richard Rogers
Babes in Arms

12

CHAPTER TWELVE
Ghosts in the Mist

At ten-thirty on an October night, on the third floor west veranda of Crescent College and Conservatory for Women, a student twists a lacy handkerchief between her fingers. A young man who should not be there at that hour is smoking, leaning on the rail. The Ozark fog lies thick in the valley, shrouding the gardens, trees, the church at the bottom of the hill, everything; the moon itself can only be glimpsed through the obscurity, watery and pale.

'Hello, Esme. You asked me to come so – here I am. I do have people waiting for me... are you okay?'

'Robert... Light me a cig, would you?'

Robert shakes out a cigarette, lights it and hands it to her. Her hand is shaking badly.

'Esme – you're not sick are you?

'No. Yes. No. Wait." She takes a draw on the cigarette.

He sighs. 'What is it, Esme? If you're having so much trouble speaking the thought I can't imagine it's all that important.'

'It's very important.'

'Waiting on you.' He lounges. She paces.

'Robert...'

'That's my name.'

'I am going to have a baby.'

'Oh.' He throws his cigarette into the fog, watches the glowing ember arc into the white haze, fade away. 'This is why you had me sneak in after hours, to tell me this?'

She inclines her head, but does not speak.

'So who's the father and don't say me.'

'I wish I had something else to tell you. But there it is.'

They stand apart, leaning on the same rail, gazing silently into the same mist. She turns to him. 'I apologize, Robert. I told myself I wouldn't get emotional...'

'What makes you so sure I'm the one?'

'There's no one else it could be.'

'Oh, you kid.'

She turns suddenly, trembling with anger.

'There has only ever been you – '

'I haven't even seen you for two months!'

'That's right. Two months!'

'I can't think of getting married, I've yet to make my mark!'

She stares at him.

'My family better not hear of this, my father would probably shoot... someone, no, this can't get out.'

She shrinks away. Neither speaks, neither watches the other, quiet in the mist on the top veranda.

Esme drops her cigarette into the mist. 'Robert – as inconvenient as it is for all concerned, you're going to be a father... I just assumed you would want to know.'

'And by the way I really don't have any money of my own, it's all the family money, I have to account for every...'

'Don't be trivial, Robert, not tonight!' Now she comes uncomfortably close and speaks fiercely but clearly, drilling the meaning of her words into the surprised young man. 'Your family owns a few properties in Arkansas. Have you any idea what my family owns in Texas? Compared to what faces me in Dallas the danger to your reputation in Eureka Springs is negligible. I haven't even come out yet! But I would rather deal with that than deal with you as a husband. I have no need, desire or stomach for marriage into the Ozarks!' She leans against the rail looking down. Somewhere far below, beneath the impenetrable mist, lie shrubs and lawns and limestone pavement. When she starts to speak again her voice is calmer. 'Robert. Whether it pleases you or not, I am going to raise this child. *Our* child. I don't need your money and I don't want to marry you. But I do need something from you. When this night is over I will begin to devote my life to the little thing your body produced in my body. My hope is that in years to come, when I look at the child's face and see yours, I will not hate that child. I must be able to love the new creature unreservedly, or how can I do what this year and the years after will demand? You see that, don't you? Just - give me good reason to name our child after you.'

'I don't see why you don't just pay someone to take it, that's the usual thing, isn't it?'

'The *usual* thing?'

'But if that's what you want – '

'What I want? What I *want*, Robert? I wanted to play my violin professionally, I wanted to work with major musicians who could teach me how to play better. I'll be six months at audition season. I'll be a year behind, with a baby to take care of that my family will pretend does not exist. *Your* baby.'

He reaches for another cigarette, the packet is empty. He crumples it and tosses it into the night.

'Look, Esme, I have to go now, the guys are waiting for me - what are you doing? Come down from there! Esme!'

She stands on the railing, hanging on with both hands to the awning above.

'You're going to fall if you're not careful.'

"Careful? You're advising me to be *careful?*" She lets go the awning with one hand.

'Here, Esme, give me one hand, now, let me help you down from there, come on, Esme...'

He reaches out a hand for her to clasp, she jerks away, and her body swings. She laughs. 'Now that I have your attention, I'm going to tell you something.'

'Esme, just get down, please?'

'Not till you've heard what I have to say – stay away!'

'All right, okay, I just wish you'd get down and tell me, but - Do what you want.' He makes a show of leaning casually on the rail.

'Listen! Last night I stood on this railing like this for half an hour, trying to pluck up the courage to let myself fall. But I changed my mind, because it would not only be my life that would be lost. At that moment I chose my baby over my music. I thought that you and I could part as friends, I thought you would be interested in the child's future. I thought at least it would be worth going on. But after talking to you, I'm not sure I still feel that way. I don't think I want to have your baby.'

"Well – jumping off the side of the conservatory won't solve the problem..."

"*Solve the problem?*' Holding onto the awning rail with both hands, she leans farther out, raises one foot off the railing, cautiously; then abruptly lets go of the awning with one hand, and swings.

'Look Robert! Your child, in danger...'

'Esme - look - don't be completely stupid.'

'All I have to do is let go –'

'Here – give me your hand. We can figure it out. Between us. Let's just sit quiet and talk, right here, about the future –'

He offers her his hand. She hesitates, then, 'All right.' She reaches to take his hand. He make a sudden grab for her wrist, she jerks back, her foot slips off the rail, he snatches at the cuff of her dress, it rips, she screams as she falls, her face turned to him in terror, disappearing into the engulfing mist. And then the thud.

Robert wrenches himself from the rail, cursing, hurtles headlong down the empty hall, stumbles all the way down the back stairs. A woman is shouting. 'In the *gardens...* Someone fell – *go!*' He peers around the corner at the bottom of the stairs. The lobby is empty, but through the big glass doors to the gardens he can see shapes in the mist beyond, people gathering. He moves swiftly, head down, across the lobby to the opposite doors, slips out and down the back steps and quickly into the darkness under the great stone wall of the building, where he stops, listening for voices to call out to him, fully expecting a crowd to pour through the glass doors in his pursuit.

Horror fills Robert, standing flattened in the shadows. His entire body is racked with the enormity of what happened a moment ago, his innards roil at the possibilities of what could happen next. A breeze stirs the mist; it begins to fragment into drifting swaths, like scarves, or wraiths. Adrenaline urges him to run from this place of danger, avoid discovery, get out, get away, forget it ever happened. But the desperate need to know what is happening on the flagstones at that moment and the urgency to foresee his future draw him along the side of the building to the corner, up the steps to the shoo-fly walk, quickly down the other side and into the shadows again. Through the drifting mist he can see an agitated knot of people and hear their cries of alarm.

He steps quickly across the path to the dark bushes where he can hide and see. He moves carefully, stooped, scratching his face on branches like whips, as close as he dares, troubled by an increasing urge to relieve himself. No one sees him, All are looking down at the flagstones, murmuring quietly.

Between their silhouettes he glimpses her, prone. Why is no one attending her?

Now the girls are arriving from the upper rooms, shivering with apprehension and President Thompson instructs them to stay back, to return to their rooms, they will receive information at the earliest possible opportunity. Other teachers are there now, physically urging the girls away from the ragged circle on the flagstones, backs turned outwards, heads bowed, murmuring.

Two men and two women, all in dressing gowns, struggle to lift the young girl, their task made more difficult by the companions of her dormitory attempting to help, crying now and loudly exclaiming. Between them all they manage to lift the young girl and stagger awkwardly with their limp burden to the steps, somehow up to the porch and after a pause for breath, in through the great bottle-glass-windowed double doors. The other students begin to clamor and panic and the teachers usher them all back to their rooms. There is Thompson, examining something he picked up from the path.

Now the garden is empty, but for a few last wafting strands of mist. Shadows deepen as the moonlight brightens. Robert pitches all his intelligent thought into arranging the pieces of his sudden predicament into a scenario that will leave him as carefree as he was ten minutes before.

Esme is dead. She can't tell them what happened. No one else knows of their appointment, they had always met in secret. No witnesses. Which means she could have fallen, or thrown herself off the veranda, accident or suicide. And no connection with Robert's family necessary. Everything back to the way it was. He has only to slip away down the hill in the dark while everyone in the school is preoccupied and he might never have been here. But it must be now. The worst thing would be to get caught running away. His breathing is still constricted into gasps and already sweat is running into his eyes. He leans on his knees for a moment to catch his breath, calculating, decides his best bet is the long steps down to the town, dabs his brow with a kerchief, braces himself, and someone is there.

Dim and difficult to make out, she seems to be floating inside a cloud, undamaged, or perhaps the cloud is Esme. She opens her arms to him, appealing, promising, saying words he cannot quite hear.

His fear bursts from him as an inarticulate shout. One of the solarium doors opens. Esme is gone. Was she ever there?

'Who's there? Who is that?' Robert knows the voice: 'Don't move, I'll come to you.'

Mopping his brow, attempting to breathe normally, Robert watches the silhouette of college president Richard Thompson approach across the shoo-fly walk and down the steps, carrying a pistol in plain sight. He stops a few feet off, motions with the gun barrel for Robert to move into the light.

'Is that –? Master Robert! I am surprised to find you here.'

'I ah was ah passing, thought I'd ah drop in, see who was around, just passing, out for a walk, nice night, foggy, I suppose....'

Richard Thompson lowers the gun. 'Not a very good time to visit, I'm afraid, Master Robert, there's been an accident – '

Why does he stop talking? Why is he staring at Robert's kerchief? Robert stops mopping his neck and looks at the kerchief, too. He is holding the lace from Esme's cuff.

Thompson stands back and looks carefully at Robert. With the moon-bright sky at Thompson's back all Robert can see is darkness in the shape of a man. Thompson holds out his hand. Robert surrenders the scrap of lace.

'My regards to your father, Master Robert. We'll see you another day. You know your way home, I'm sure.' He turns to go, turns back, 'Say - I'm out of smokes. I don't suppose you'd have a Camel about your person?'

Robert rummages through pockets, stops. 'Sorry, Mr. ah Thompson, all out.'

'Bad habit anyway. Good night, young sir.' He pockets the cuff of Esme's dress and walks quickly back up the steps and into the solarium, closing the door behind him.

And Esme is there again, a mist within a mist speaking with a voice that seemed to come from everywhere at once, or might have been inside his own head:

'You see what you have done, Robert? You have put your family in Richard Thompson's hands, and you will bring about your father's death as surely as you ended my life, so sadly, so early. I had everything in life until the day we met. But your child was no more meant to be than my career. Two deaths in one, Robert. And because of that, I now can never leave you. I shall always be here, walking behind you, watching everything you do – and I will not be keeping my opinions to myself - until the moment of your death when we can escape each other at last. Your carefree days are over.'

Author's Note:

Almost any night you will find groups of believers gathered in the east gardens of the Crescent Hotel, telephones and cameras pointed up to the balconies. Sometimes, but not always, at 10:30 p.m. a cloud of mist may be seen descending from the balcony. And within that cloud some have claimed to see a figure: a young girl in the uniform of the Conservatory falling, terribly slowly, to the limestone pavement. And sometimes, turning away from the place on the balcony from which the mist is falling, the figure of a man has been glimpsed.

The story of a ghostly figure descending in a cloud of mist has been told for decades; we find references to her appearance floating down from the upper balcony at ten-thirty at night, in articles and magazines published at least fifty years ago. Never a name or even a year, but always the same, distinctive story: the girl going over the railing, a man on the balcony whose face cannot be seen, the subsequent apparitions of a falling figure in a cloud of mist. It is what is known as a residual haunting.

But if the young student we refer to as the Girl in the Mist ever existed, she has been erased from all records, hidden too deeply to be found; after extensive research we decided that if it was so important to the family to keep it within the family, we should respect the family's wishes; and consigned her to Mystery.

We have no evidence, to date, for the story of the Girl in the Mist, what we don't know about her far outweighs what we do. However, as material for a tragic love story, the plot fits the historical time and place uncannily satisfactorily; the probability factor is not beneath regard; and whatever narrative we each develop – yours is yours and mine is mine - from those few sad, indelible images, none are, as all the physicists agree, impossible; so if your version did not happen in the Crescent Hotel the way you imagine it in this reality, it surely did in some other. There's comfort in that, in the sheer, unimaginable complexity of it all.

Meanwhile, we tell the story of the Girl in the Mist because it might be true. We all wonder what happened on the balcony that foggy night; did she fall, did she throw herself over the railing, was she pushed? Or did something else happen? We all picture that night for ourselves, we harbor our own ghost stories in our heads, all as insubstantial as apparitions, and as real. A story is a ghost; and ghost stories generate the ghostly worlds, which are different for each of us.

Chapter Thirteen:
Upper Balcony, West

We don't just perceive
the world around us,
we actually generate it...

Anil Seth,
Professor of Cognitive
and Computational
Neuroscience at
Sussex University, U.K.

CHAPTER THIRTEEN
Upper Balcony, West

The Sky High Pizza Palace on the fourth floor used to be called Baker's Lounge - until it was realized what a disgusting individual was behind the macabre legends about the phony cancer hospital that occupied the building in the late thirties. No sadistic psychopath, murdering his patients and burying them in the walls and beneath the floorboards, as urban legend would have it, Norman Baker was nothing more interesting than a deceitful pariah feeding on the last hopes of the ailing - an excrescence too despicable to name a bar after.

There was a ghost named Charlie in that bar, decades ago, known for pushing glasses off the edges of tables, but he seems to have left. Far below, two dimensional shadow men flit across certain walls of the racketing laundry room. In the Morgue someone unseen will, on occasion, engage in conversation with the tour guide and members of the group, through a meter on the floor flashing red at varying speeds and rhythms, different each time but uncannily on topic.

The stories and sightings, remembered and renewed, seem to present glimpses of things that someone, somewhere, wants understood...

A sudden wave of woozliness passed through Davies' consciousness; not just space but time receded into regions unknown where everything was oddly shaped and the air was filled with continuous but unidentifiable chatter. When he regained focus the girl was still staring at him and the man from NASA was saying: 'Let's go! Enough sitting around, let's embark on our voyage into the Unknown!' and again unprovoked laughter burst briefly from several in the group.

'Ah, sure –' Davis agreed, unheard. 'I was just going to tell you a couple of things – well, we can catch up on the way – yes, why not, let's go – ' But the group was already moving out through the door. Like a school of fish that knows where it's going, they turned to the right and gathered at the top of the south staircase.

Davies had lost control of tours before, to violent drunks, hysterical children, fainting sensitives or veterans of ghost tours nationwide who stole all the punch lines, but it was usually possible to overcome those attempted hijackings with the finesse the profession refines. On this night, he would find himself swept along by an unlikely mix of chattering enthusiasts rushing him on to the next location. Seemingly even-tempered but impossible to divine, they laughed in concert at the oddest moments in his narrative; all seemed to think they knew more about the paranormal than he, their guide; and yet they all encouraged him to tell his stories, sometimes twice, and gave him such rapt attention that he gave up any thought of bringing the tour in on time and resigned himself to still being in the morgue at midnight. Their concentration when still, their unpredictability when on the move and the presence of the girl in the shawl - always close, one translucent eye peeping through her hair, looking straight at him, always - had the effect of elevating his storytelling to previously unachieved heights; all the fortuitous phrases that he had developed over seven years of telling the same stories rolled off his tongue, he hit all his marks without rushing and his renditions of the Tales of the Crescent were as colorful, coherent and evocative as though he were telling them for the last time.

At the top of the stairs where the little girl fell Davies pointed out, as usual, the unexpectedly low level of the balustrade and invited them to look cautiously over and down, as usual; but on this night when he leaned over the rail to point to where the little girl would have landed, far below, he felt for a moment almost as though he were falling, spinning slowly in that void between the staircases, floating down floor by floor like Alice. When he recovered, concentrating on the feeling of the solid fourth floor landing beneath his feet, he saw that his guests were all watching him, dispassionately, as though he were not really a man experiencing vertigo at a dangerous height but an image on a screen somewhere, of something happening somewhere else at some time in the past, or in a writer's imagination.

The increasing oddness of this night's tour, which so far had nothing in common with any of the tours he had given over the last seven years except perhaps that one New Year's Day when he was still hung-over from an ill-advised over-indulgence in absinthe the night before, intensified when he took his group onto the fourth floor east observation deck.

He held the door to the deck open for his guests and endeavored to make eye contact with each passing face; but they seemed interested only in each other, murmuring quietly, occasionally exclaiming, until it was time to be told the story, when their collective scrutiny of Davies was so intense it was impossible to tell if they were actually hearing his words.

Assuming the spot from which to relate the mystery of the Girl in the Mist he noticed he had lost two of his three teenagers, who had spent most of the time texting and snapping selfies anyway.

Down to fourteen. The third teenager, who remained, had also been taking pictures with a mood-killing flash during his narrations, but now switched to documentary film-making complete with occasional editorial comment, while he was giving the best bits.

'Did she fall, did she jump, was she pushed? All we are able to say is, It's a mystery! We call her the Girl in the Mist...' As he was speaking he noticed in his peripheral vision the teenage movie maker walking backward toward the railing which, when she reached it, she abruptly tipped over. The scream seemed to go on for a long time. Thump.

Thirteen.

Davies could not prevent his shout of 'Oh, my god!' as he rushed toward the railing. After two or three steps he realized that not one person on the tour was even turned in that direction, they were all still looking at Davies, expressionless.

There are moments in everyone's life when it seems that elements from all different times, and sources, focus down onto some deep place in the back of the mind and the entire perception of the world around shifts, just a little, never to go back. This was such a moment for Davies. It was suddenly and irrefutably obvious - like an image appearing in an ink-blot or the clouds or on a time-wrinkled mountainside, once seen impossible to un-see - that Davies was standing between two worlds, two realities, two possible interpretations of a mystery that a split second ago did not exist, and therefore between two possible futures. In one world, the body of one of the hotel guests entrusted to his care was lying groaning or deathly still on the path below; in the other, guests would be wandering from spa to swimming pool, arms round each other's waists, inhaling the scents of flowers in the moonlight, and Davies had just hallucinated. And all that that implied for his usefulness or otherwise to society, for the duration.   One of two futures was about to begin, and Davies would know which, the moment he looked over the balcony. And bleak as either outcome appeared, avoidance was not an option. Davies needs must continue on his path to the edge, there to look over.

He urged his way through the crowd. They shrank away at his approach. *Could I be the only one who saw the girl fall? Was it all in my mind?*

Davies grasped the railings, took a breath and thrust his neck over the balcony.

She lay on the limestone below, ungainly in death, twisted like a discarded cigarette. People were hurrying across the lawns toward her.

Overcompensating possibly, but suddenly very concerned for their sensibilities, Davies turned to the guests remaining on his tour, with his back to the rail. They all stared at him in silence. 'I would not look over the balcony,' he said, 'unless you are a doctor.'

'Well, let's see for ourselves, shall we?' The Laird of Arbuthnot's offspring strode, that is almost the right word, let's say he tried to stride to the balcony, more like a waddle, really, and looked down.

'What?' he said. 'What's down there you don't want us to see?'

Half a dozen others looked over the railings, to general cries of disappointment.

'What are you trying to pull?' Aging Rocky demanded, as though someone in a dusty marketplace were attempting to peddle him false intelligence.

Davies forced himself to look down again.

People were wandering the lawns and flowerbeds, heads on each other's shoulders, breathing the perfumes of the evening; the full moon hung in empty space between strands of cloud, the cicadas chattered. No dead girls. *Had me going for a moment there. I thought we were in the reality where random accidents occur, but no, we are in the one where my mind is going. And I am standing here talking to a dozen people, supposedly making sense and they are looking at me like they know I'm crazy...* Happily, inspiration struck. 'You didn't see the girl in the bikini?'

'Bikini?'

'I guess that's what you'd call it. She must have been headed to the hot tub.'

'Hot tub!' Cornrow's excitement almost matched that of her enthusiasm for the dead.

'She's – no, really – '

'Party!' exclaimed the young bride, and her husband started to dance.

'What's next?' The young woman in the shawl spoke, apparently, for the group.

It wasn't much, but it was enough to let Davies know he had not lost them, he still had time to win them over and get some good tips. Even if his mind was beginning to betray him.

'Step this way, folks,' he said, holding the observation deck door open with his usual olde worlde tilt of the hips and head. 'Our next location is Room 419, *Theodora's room!* Turn right out of the hallway and all the way to the end of the corridor, and when everybody's ready I have someone very interesting to introduce to you!'

Despite his encouragement to move it along the guests lingered, whispering among themselves. Davies stood politely holding the door open and carefully not looking in the direction of the balcony over which he had just watched someone fall backwards. In his imagination.

The last to pass through the door was the well-groomed, gray-haired lady in a business suit who had identified herself as an empath. She glanced at Davies with a knowing look, as though they who had not yet been introduced shared secrets of which the multitude was unaware, and whispered in his ear: 'I saw her, too...'

'Ah – cool!' Davies said. A nutcase had identified him as one of her own. He waited till she had turned the corner into the corridor, then dashed back to the railing. All was peaceful in the gardens. Not so in his mind. He found himself very short of breath and again experienced a brief blurring of his vision, as though the world he lived in had shifted momentarily slightly out of focus.

When he emerged from the little hall leading to the fourth floor south, the group was nowhere to be seen. Had they all decided to decamp, at once? No tips at all? But a burst of laughter from the north end of the fourth floor hall told him that his remaining guests were all around the corner, outside Theodora's room, waiting for him. Hurrying along the corridor, he rattled his head to clear his brain. By the time he reached the corner he had cramp in his toes and a sharp pain in his left side as though winded. Catching his breath, he noticed that the unpleasant Mr. Pork was no longer with the group. *Fine.*

'Okay,' he began, with an evident gasp for air, 'you will notice the door handles are lower than they would be today – '

'Tell us about Theodora,' the girl in the shawl demanded. The name was repeated in low tones: *Theodora...*

'Our favorite ghost!' Davies complied, glad to be obliged to think about anything besides his own apparently dissolving sanity. 'Everybody's grandma! Very caring. But very particular! It's been said, if you are staying in her room and she thinks you are not behaving with proper decorum, she will pack your bags for you...'

The crowd listened closely, without a single interruption, even from the two little sisters, standing in the hall outside Room 419.

*

Theodora admires herself in the long oval glass, smiling with a summer Sunday morning charm, just because that is something she never gets to do any more. Like slaves, servants, hunter-gatherers and the devout of the ages, Theodora rises at the same time every day and performs her duties until it is time to sleep again. But every night when her daily service to others is finally suspended for a few hours, just before she sleeps she steals a glance in the long oval mirror and remembers herself in younger days.

In the universe of her mind are many universes: early family memories, books and moving pictures, the remembrances of being in love, the romance that comes to everyone at least once but sometimes, as in Theodora's case, only once and then but briefly. That short-lived youthful love-affair occupies as many rooms in the mansions of her memory as the years of devotion and sacrifice that followed. Always a nurse, at first to endless wounded soldiers and later the accidents of peace or local turmoil; always grateful for the opportunity to do some real good for others; now she finds herself, as her reflection in the long oval mirror acknowledges with a gradual diminishing of her after-church gaiety, an accomplice to chicanery.

Theodora's summer turned to dark winter the day she began to work for Norman Baker. Somehow it happened: circumstance brought Theodora, in the autumn of her life, to Norman Baker's Cancer Curable Hospital, and to personal responsibility for the day-to-day operation of a healing facility built on lies.

Something placed her here. And all the power she has left lies in the choice to do her best to do good in any and all circumstances, or at least to do no harm. Why does she stay? Why doesn't she run away one night, notify authorities, go to ground in a legitimate clinic or mission? Every day she resolves that she will start tying the sheets together that very evening and every morning she stays, for the patients: the poor suffering individuals lured to this mockery of a hospital as a last and final resort, all the hope they have left bestowed on a deliberate falsehood; so many, arriving every day. How can a person even take a day off?

After ensuring that every object in the room is in its allotted location, Theodora kneels briefly at the side of the bed before turning out the lamp and climbing between the starch-stiff sheets.

*

'...and this is the most touching part of the story, in my opinion; it has been suggested, by mediums apparently in contact with the spirit of Theodora, that she is not obliged to remain on this plane of existence, but for some reason she chooses not to move on, and my question is, why? Once out of this life, why continue to haunt the old neighborhood?'

'She stays to help others find their way Home,' the Empath said. 'That's who she is.'

'Interesting thought!' the man from NASA said. 'Enormous implications...'

Suddenly the door of Room 419 burst open and Mr. Pork came bustling out, swinging an overnight bag from which odd items of clothing were escaping, and shouting hysterically. Davies almost jumped out of his skin, though the guests did not appear unduly perturbed.

'I *know* where I left my keys! The Arbuthnots have a history of O.C.D. and I am very careful about things like that, I don't make that kind of mistake, I'm too retentive and I *know* I left my keys on the bedside table and when I got back they were *hanging in the door!* My socks were all mixed up, and that's not me! My air purifier had been *turned off...*' Arbuthnot thrust his way through the crowd like an early morning shopper on Black Friday or a protestor spotting the horses. 'I have to leave. I'm not unfamiliar with the spirit world, I've been on hundreds of ghost tours, I enjoy bursting people's bubbles, but there is something very weird going on here and I just want to find a brand new Holiday Inn or Best Western and get a good night's sleep!' And he was gone.

Twelve.

Relieved not to have to deal with the conceited moron any longer Davies checked in with his crowd. They were all staring at him, seemingly studying their tour guide with the concentration of particle physicists colliding protons, and paying no attention whatever to the receding Jabba with lairds for ancestors.

'Tell us about Norman Baker.'

Chapter Fourteen: Mastermind

Ghoul: legendary evil being
that robs graves and feeds on corpses.
          Merriam-Webster
          Incorporated

CHAPTER FOURTEEN
Mastermind

'Nineteen-thirty-seven. The region was suffering as much as any in the country from the Depression, preceded by the worst floods in memory, followed by drought. People were starving or leaving. Crescent College had closed. The summer operation as a hotel had been fruitless. The building sat virtually empty for three years, nothing up here on the hilltop but birds, and silence, and a few ghosts.

'But one day there came roaring up the hill a sight unfamiliar to struggling rural Arkansawyers: a chauffeur-driven, orchid-colored Cord convertible, carrying a man in a white suit and purple shirt: a man whose *voice* was familiar to anyone with a radio from Mexico to the Aleutian Islands - Norman Baker, broadcasting pioneer, former vaudevillian and mesmerist, inventor, brilliant entrepreneur, public relations wizard and visionary opportunist, come to the City of Healing Waters to buy the Crescent Hotel and convert the building into a cancer hospital.

'The town welcomed the voice of KTNT, Know The Naked Truth radio, broadcasting from south of the border in beautiful Nuevo Laredo. The willing citizens assisted in every way with the conversion of the hotel and sometime College. Six months later, June 1938, the doors to the Baker Cancer Curable Hospital opened... and Eureka Springs entered a dark phase of the moon.

'Norman Baker - who never set foot in medical school - had made several fortunes before he discovered the thriving field of quack medicine - in which he made himself richer than ever before, to the equivalent in today's money of sixty-five million dollars – that we know about – all from terminal cancer victims, whom he promised outright to cure with his secret remedies, in six weeks, in this building.

'Norman Baker was a handsome, eccentric, daring, creative, brilliant, thoroughly despicable con artist and charlatan – preying with terrifying skill on the weakness and last, desperate hope of those near death, to line his own pockets. What happened next in this building deserves a movie all its own.'

HEARTBREAK HOSPITAL

Film Noir

Starring:

James Cagney *as*   Norman Baker!
Lauren Bacall *as*   Thelma Yount!
Peter Lorre *as*   Doctor Statler!
Billy Bob Thornton *as*   Rennie Bellows!

Directed by Orson Welles

In moody black and white

SCENE: *Third floor hallway. Open doorframes, tattered walls, garish lighting.*

THE PATIENTS *of the Cancer Curable Baker Hospital, all in or approaching terminal stages of various cancers, sit outside the rooms, fanning themselves, mostly silent except for occasional expressions of discomfort. A scream is heard from offstage. The cancer victims do not respond.*

NORMAN BAKER, *attractive, portly, energetic, a short man who fills every room he enters, appears at the far end of the hall in white suit, purple shirt and lavender tie, enhanced by gold and diamond personal jewelry including an extravagant horseshoe tie-pin. Small rimless glasses contribute to an impression of warmth and wisdom.*

BAKER (*in his best radio voice*) Howdy folks! Here's Norman Baker, checking in! *(Imitates a jolly calliaphone)* K – TNT! KNOW - THE -NAKED TRUTH! Norman Baker is here – for *you!*

BAKER *progresses the length of the hall, greeting every patient by name, with a quiet word and an occasional encouraging light touch on the shoulder.*

BAKER   Mr. Hearn! Keeping up with the exercises? You are? You are! And it shows! Mrs. English, my goodness you are positively radiant this morning - good thing we're not alone! I hear you're a little off your feed, Mrs. Manis – bit of a tummy upset? ... Slop? Did you say - slop? Well, I'm sorry you feel that way. It may not look like a roast beef sandwich or a hot dog, but my patented Baker dietary regimen is prepared from the finest ingredients, especially formulated, by experts, to cleanse the bloodstream. Once your internal plumbing is up and running we can set about flushing that awful growth out of your abdomen okay?

Good morning Mr. Box, how are you? What? Would you repeat that, please? You're hurting where? No, no, that's all right, I believe you, I'll send Doctor Statler to check on you in the morning - What? Doctor Statler calls it slop? Well, I look forward to setting him straight!

Miss Haley, my regards to your father - You think it's slop, too? And you, Mrs. Ott? How many of would say that the food at the Baker Cancer Curable Hospital is... All of you.

My friends. My *family* - that's how I think of you - I want to explain something to you. We, you and I, all of us here, are locked in deadly combat with a fierce and intractable enemy. And I am not talking about the tax collector! Or the AMA! I'm talking about the ghastly cancers, eating away at your internal organs even as we stand here, arguing the toss.

I would never have built up the unsullied rcputation that I have, I would never have attracted audiences in the tens of thousands, I would never have accumulated my personal fortune – which I am happy to put at the service of the healing arts - if I allowed my chefs to serve a single meal to my patients that was not first class cuisine, just like it says in my brochure!

I suspect some of you are still suffering from the effects

of your radium treatment, it does tend to distort the flavor buds, but I can promise you, Mrs. Manis, that bad taste in your mouth will not bother you for much longer.   You will soon become accustomed to the flavors of the Baker diet, and begin to recognize the subtleties that my culinary artistes derive from the simplest natural ingredients. Right now you miss the salt and the sugar. And the meat. And the tobacco and the alcohol. None of those are going to help us in the struggle for health - but you will not have to fight those addictions formed in early youth for too long, I can promise you that.   That's where the Baker Mental Therapeutical System comes in. Mind over body. Mind over body.

My friends, you don't need me, you don't need Doctor Statler or even Nurse Theodora, you are each your own physician! I cannot heal you, I am not a divine being, no matter what some have said about me, but *you* can heal yourself, you and only you. Whether you get well or not depends on what's going on *in your mind*. If you think you are going to die, you will. But if you will stick to my natural food diet and don't go sneaking off downtown looking for food with grease in it; if you will take your shots without fussing; and if you will diligently practice the Mental Therapeutics exercises that you have been shown - you *can* get better.   I've seen it happen. I know it works, as long as everybody does their part - giving some things up, making some effort, paying attention. As you agreed to do, on the day we were so happy to welcome you to this place of refuge and hope and darn good sense, your treatment includes radical changes to your lifestyle, your daily habits, yes, and your diet, too.   You tell me it's hard. You came here with serious health issues - did you think eradicating them would be easy?

There are those who come here knowing the expectations, but unwilling to make the changes.   And for those people - there is nothing even Norman

Baker's Secret Remedy #5 can do, those people gave up before they left home. Norman Baker does *everything t*hat is within my power. I can create a place for you to be that supports the major life changes that fighting this hideous monster requires. I can give you the resources, I can show you what to do. But I cannot do it for you.

Yes, Mr. Bailey, you had a quick question? Pain killer? As it was explained to you when you were admitted, Baker hospitals operate according to natural healing procedures, as opposed to the invasive techniques employed in commercial medical establishments, which we consider to be worse than the diseases they treat and don't even cure – because they don't want to! If everybody was to get better the entire medical profession would be on the soup line!

But here at Baker's hospital we care about you, we want you to get better, to get well, to go back to your families and your hobbies and pastimes just like your old selves, that is reward enough for us, the doctors and myself are happy when we are able to turn a poor suffering individual right around and send them home healthier than they arrived, and therefore we do not resort to x-ray, radium or surgery – you will not find many knives in this hospital - and we repudiate the use of opiates, which only deaden the very senses we need to stimulate.

It is your pain killers that hasten the ends of those poor victims of the American Medical Association. I call them the American Meatcutters Association, drugs and the butchery of innocent bodies, that's all the AMA wants us to believe in, because they're in league with pill-makers! Slice and slash with the knife, pour in the chemicals... barbaric and asinine! That is not the Baker hospital way; we know that the greatest drug is not some pill or weed that grows in the dust of the wayside; the most potent medicine on this planet is not liquid, nor solid - it is *your mind!*

You know what to do. I have given you instructions. Keep up the exercises, and if you feel you're not making progress as fast as you would like, do the exercises more often! Between your willpower and my secret remedies, we'll have you back out there on the golf course in no time...'

Keep up the good work everyone – I will be by to see you all again sometime tomorrow! This is Norman Baker – signing off!

BAKER *stops to light a cigar as the lights in the hallway begin to fade. He exits into the 3rd floor annex, singing, 'I'm tying the leaves...'*

Blackout

*

'Norman Baker could never have enough money. He always had to be making more, getting richer, developing other businesses around town, playing the stock market. But one thing is often forgotten: everybody in town was making money, too; Baker brought wealth to the City of Eureka Springs at the height of the Depression. And a lot of people worked for Norman Baker, a few were with him for a lot of years, although there was no love lost between them by the end.
    'It was the 1930's. At a time when the national economy was at its lowest ebb there was untold money to be made in quack medicine and the people who were making it were gangsters. Norman Baker carried Tommy guns with him everywhere he went. His mistress, Thelma, ran suitcases of cash down to Laredo every two weeks. He was an outlaw, he never accounted for his money, never declared it, never banked it, he hid it, and all the guesses that have been made about how much cash he distributed in various secret hiding places are probably way too low. No one knows what happened to all that money. There are fortune hunters out there looking for it today, in Laredo, Nuevo Laredo and Muscatine, Iowa. And the most likely place for at least some of the missing millions to be hidden, the week he was suddenly busted? Right here in Eureka!'

Davies finished his story with perfect timing as the group reached the last turn in the third stair down to the second floor north. The twelve seemed to consult together, reach consensus and appoint the man from NASA as spokesperson, all without speech.

'You're right,' he said, 'It's a movie waiting to be made.'

Chapter Fifteen:
Heartbreak Hospital

When you look at the dark side,
careful you must be,
For the dark side looks back.

Yoda

CHAPTER FIFTEEN
Heartbreak Hospital

Scene Two
Crescent Hotel, Governor's Suite, 101
August, 1939

RENNIE BELLOWS, *Baker's expediter, tall, thin and watchful*; DR. STATLER, *resident medical consultant, nervous and unhappy with himself; and Baker's mistress* THELMA YOUNT, *groomed and aloof, still beautiful, are smoking in silence.*

A ceiling fan revolves slowly overhead.   Cigarette smoke floating.

Distant jolly calliaphone music.

BELLOWS *watches* THELMA *wielding a cigarette holder.*

Silence.

THELMA (*to* BELLOWS) What are you looking at?

BELLOWS   Who's looking?   I don't look nowhere, I don't see nothing, I just do what the boss says. Right, doc?

STATLER, *staring at the floor, does not respond.*

THELMA   Because you know what happens if you don't.

BELLOWS   I'm just sitting.   Waiting for the boss.

Silence

NORMAN BAKER *is heard approaching, singing:*
            I'm tying the leaves so they won't come down,

165

So the wind won't blow them away,
For the best little girl in the whole wide world,
Is lying so ill today.
Her young life must go when the first leaves fall.
I'm fixing them tight so they'll stay.

BAKER *enters grandly, in time to his song*
I'm tying the leaves so they won't come down,
So Nellie won't go away…

THELMA *(throwing her arms around him)* Oh, Norman!

BAKER (*to* Thelma) What are you doing here?

THELMA   Honey – I can't do this any more...

BAKER   Don't tell me –

THELMA/BELLOWS It happened again!

BAKER   *Again!* Thelma...

BELLOWS   Same stretch of road, same bunch of banditos.

THELMA   You came this close to losing me, *this close,* I thought I
               was never, ever going to see my Norman again, I was so
               frightened...!

BAKER   *Again?* How much did they get?

THELMA   … they were on the verge of killing me!

BELLOWS   Looks like they got it all.

BAKER   Both suitcases?

BELLOWS   That's what it looks like.

THELMA   I'm so lucky to be here…

BAKER   Twenty-five thousand bucks?

THELMA   I had a knife at my throat, look, you can see -

BELLOWS *(nods)* Twenty-five gees.

BAKER   All gone?

STATLER   Just like that! *(Snaps his fingers, laughs briefly, looks back at the floor.)*

Pause

BAKER stares at THELMA

THELMA   It may not be quite that much.

BELLOWS   There's a suitcase in the car.

BAKER   Which suitcase?

BELLOWS   The one with the strap.

THELMA   That's my clothes.

BAKER   Strap – the big bills?

THELMA   They loaded all the bills into their saddlebags.

BAKER   They did! So the question becomes - where are those saddlebags now?

THELMA   Over the border! He'll spread the money around his village, we'll never track it down. No one down there is going to give him up, his people will do anything for him. It's understandable, he's Robin Hood with Errol Flynn's looks and he fights for the people. They call him El Sombre Hombre, Man of the Shadows - -

BAKER	And you let that bastard get away with twenty-five thousand bucks of my money? You know how much a family of eight can live on for a month in Mexico?
THELMA	And what about what they got away with from me? Huh?
BAKER	Thelma, please! – What do you mean, from you?
THELMA *(Weeping into her handkerchief)*	All for a measly thirty... twenty-five thousand –
BAKER	Measly?
THELMA	I don't know what they were planning to do with me first –
BAKER	Twenty-five thousand bucks is not measly!
THELMA	Senators transport a lot more cash than that, every day, bankers...
BELLOWS	Twenty-five Gs is twenty-five Gs...
THELMA	Brilliant, Bellows. Your Gs almost cost me my face, look, you can see where he scratched me with his knife...
BAKER	Where? Show me.
BELLOWS	Nineteen-five last time.
BAKER	Forty-five thousand dollars - that's a lot of guacamole! Show it to the doc.
THELMA	I've known guys throw that away on the tables in an hour - -
BAKER	- and you let that bastard get away with it!

THELMA   Well, now. I didn't say that...

Pause

BAKER   What are you saying?

THELMA   Nothing you need to hear about, Mr. Hospital
              Administrator. *(quietly)* I know where to find him.

STATLER *(to THELMA, examining her face)* You'll survive.

THELMA   Nobody steals from Norman Baker.

STATLER   What are you going to do?

THELMA *and* BAKER *exchange a glance.*

BAKER   Why – take him to court, of course!

BAKER *and* THELMA *laugh.*

STATLER *(abruptly)*   It's chicken feed to you - two week's take!

BAKER   How would you know? The old lady been talking?

STATLER   I can do arithmetic!

BAKER   Alright, try this: two week's income from my secret
              remedy #5, multiplied by the street value of dollar bills
              in Mexico City, invested in some nice Canadians I
              happen to have an inside track on - does that add up to
              chicken feed? (*To* Thelma) It happened where? Same
              place as last time - exactly?

THELMA   Close – few miles nearer the border.

BAKER   You were supposed to take a different route...

169

THELMA	I did! I went through San Antonio, that's an extra hour on the road for me – but when you get on the last stretch into Laredo there's only one road.
BAKER	They were waiting for you?
THELMA	Yes.
BAKER	They knew you were coming.
THELMA	Yes! They forced me off the road, I thought I was going to roll over...
BAKER	Forced you off the road... But you went a day earlier than usual. So who knew?
THELMA	No one! Just me and you. And Rennie.
BAKER	Did you mention the change to anyone?
BELLOWS *(shrugs)*	The Doc. The old lady knew. Weems got the car ready. Maybe they told someone.
BAKER	Forget my sister, she wouldn't put the take in jeopardy, why would she? And Weems didn't know in time to get the word to those sons of bitches ahead of Thelma... Doc? Been talking out of turn?
STATLER	Who am I going to tell? The patients? Who else do I see?
BAKER	I am attempting to determine how the bandits happened to be in the right place at the *right time!*
STATLER	They're highwaymen! They could have been there for days, waiting for anything that came along...
THELMA	They were expecting me alright. They had rope to tie me up. And a blindfold.
BAKER	They found out somehow!

170

BELLOWS   Not from me!

THELMA   Honey, can I have a drink, I'm still shaking, I drove straight through to be with you.

Silence. BAKER *stares at each of the three in turn.*

BAKER   Yes. Good idea. Let's all have a drink. *(Sits)* You too, *Doctor.*

STATLER *watches* BELLOWS *pour whiskey for all.* BAKER *watches* THELMA *weakly grooming.*

THELMA *(brightly brave)* So – first anniversary coming up, a year since you opened the doors. What are we doing to celebrate? Norman, we should throw a party!

BAKER   What's to celebrate? Losing forty-five thousand dollars in two months? Fuller's dragging his feet in the senate, the AMA has spies everywhere, the town is becoming downright insolent to me –

THELMA   Norman, honey, you could buy and sell Eureka Springs, this is your town, it's about time they realized that. Do they even *have* radios? You need to let them know who you really are, outside this dump.

BAKER   Dump? I love it here. This Crescent Hotel is Norman Baker's castle. *Castle Crescent. Where Cancer is Cured.* Hey! What do you think?

BELLOWS   I like it!

THELMA *(applauds)* Genius!

STATLER *throws back his whiskey.*

BAKER   No. It has to say Baker.

BELLOWS   How about *Baker's Hospital at Castle Crescent where Cancer is Cured?*

171

STATLER   *Might* be cured!

THELMA   Give me a break.   Way too long. Always stay a step
               ahead of the suckers, right honey?   *(She sits on
               BAKER's knee.)* Who else could make so much money
               out of this ratty old hotel?

BAKER   It's not so ratty in the lobby, it's bright and cheerful and
               modern. And for those who have eyes to see there are
               hidden symbolisms in the designs.

BELLOWS   Hidden what?

BAKER   Don't waste your time trying to figure it out, Bellows,
               you'll only hurt your head, I'm having an idea, bring
               that bottle over here, I think we should throw a party!
               We'll get all the bigwigs from the county, and the
               Muscatine contingent, I know I have a few friends left
               up there and we'll invite a few of our enemies too, so
               they can see what they're missing.   We'll spare no
               expense, we'll put on the party of the century! Aha! You
               see the way I am?

               Now that's Norman Baker! This, *this* is Norman Baker!
               We'll keep the guests on the   ground   level   -   dining
               room, lobby, gardens - seal off the upper floors, Statler,
               that'll be your job, Bellows, you do the party, you're
               going to have to get going on this one right away, we
               can accommodate up to five hundred - better make up
               twenty-five hundred invitations... best of everything for
               every VIP in Arkansas, and while we have them here,
               Norman Baker will rub their noses in it! I'll give them
               an evening Eureka Springs will never forget! Hey – the
               lady's ready for another drink – fresh glass! The
               question is, Do I invite the honorable senator from
               Arkansas or not? If I do, it gives him the opportunity to
               turn me down.   Making Norman Baker look like a
               nobody.   But if I don't, it looks like I'm giving him the
               cold shoulder.

172

BELLOWS *replenishes their drinks. He pauses at* STATLER*'s glass, checks with Baker, who nods, then refills it. He does not refill his own.*

BELLOWS   He's got it in for you, boss. One of the guys heard him talking to his brother in the post office.   'He needs taking down,' he said. 'We'll get him,' he said.

BAKER   That's what you heard.

BELLOWS   It's what I heard.

THELMA   That's what he said?

BELLOWS   That's what I was told he said.

BAKER   Ungrateful, treacherous bastards! You notice he's all smiles when we see him? But what does he say when we're not there?

STATLER *(slurring his words)* He ceased to support you the day he visited this facility in his official capacity.

BAKER   *Unannounced!* You see how they try to trap me? Any phony AMA hospital would get warning of an inspection but not Norman Baker! It's an opportunity to interfere, it's a weapon! That was a surprise attack, they tried to ambush me! But I have plenty of people willing to stand up in court and testify to Norman Baker's outstanding commitment to the health and well-being of each and every one of my patients, that piece of bureaucratic buckshot will backfire right up their rectums –

THELMA   Norman... *(she gets up off his knee.)*

BAKER   *(Standing)* Screw Fuller! That's it, no invite for him. We'll see who wins the popularity contest when Norman Baker runs against him.   He's too big for his boots. There is no room for him in Eureka Springs. Most of his real estate is farmland, I own as much downtown commercial as he does, almost. He may have been here since they found the damned spring but Norman Baker is here now and I intend to stay, this is just the beginning!

STATLER   Why do you have to piss people off so bad, Norman? Everywhere you go –

BAKER   I stand up for what's right! And I know what I'm doing so keep your opinions to yourself. *Doctor.*

THELMA   Yeah – like he keeps secrets?

BELLOWS   All he's saying, don't underestimate these people, just because we're in Arkansas.

STATLER   Sometimes you need to tread a little lightly, test the waters -

BELLOWS   - know who your friends are... who to trust...

BAKER   You got your fingers in everything, Rennie Bellows and you'd like to think you know what's going on but you don't and that's why this is my hospital, not yours! They will never try to arrest Norman Baker! After what I've done for this town? Everybody is making money, thanks to the Baker Hospital! I'm the goose that lays the golden eggs.... Why would they arrest me? On what charge? There's nothing they could make stick. Why do you think we're a cash-only hospital?

STATLER   The forty-five grand would still be in the bank if you'd put it there...

BAKER   Banks? Banks? Don't get me started.

STATLER   The Senator, the radio commission, the AMA...

BAKER   The American Medical Association cannot stomach

Norman Baker because I call them out: they can't cure cancer and they don't want anybody else to, while they're raking in the profits.

THELMA *(applying make up)* They have the voice, Norman, how many thousand members...?

BAKER   Not once I get my radio station back up and running! Brought to you from the highest point in the Ozark mountains, the very battlements of a castle in the sky, KTNT, KNOW. THE. NAKED. TRUTH! Your host, the friend of the working man, the laborer and the farmer in the field! Norman Baker wants you to...

ALL *(Baker conducting)* ...Know The Naked Truth!

BAKER   There will be no stopping Norman Baker, I won't *have* a voice, I will *be* the Voice of the South: *Norman Baker – a force to be reckoned with!* Bellows, write that down...

STATLER   They are *all* working to see you closed down, Norman! They're putting the screws to Brinkley, they're forcing Hoxsey out, you know we'll be next...

BAKER   Listen! The only way they could close this operation would be for them to prove that the Baker Method does not work -

STATLER   It doesn't work!

BAKER   It works as well as x-ray, radium or surgery!

STATLER   But you've never cured anybody!

BAKER   What about Mrs. Ferzackerly from Muskogee?

STATLER   That wasn't cancer, that was warts.

BAKER   Which were going to turn into melanomas, I prevented it! And what about Mandus Johnson?

175

BELLOWS   I forgot to tell you - he died.

BAKER   Everybody dies sooner or later! That's what terminal
             means!

STATLER   What it means is, your Secret Remedy Number Five is –
             ineffective –

BAKER *(standing over* STATLER*)* They can't prove that!

STATLER *(cowering)* But you can't prove it works!

BAKER   I, don't, *have to!* And they know that. They know better
             than to try to outwit Norman Baker.   (*Suddenly, to*
             THELMA)   Twice on the same road? That's pretty
             strange…

THELMA   What's strange about it? It worked the first time, didn't
             it?

BELLOWS   You wouldn't think a person would pull the same gag
             twice in a month.

THELMA   What are you suggesting?   Norman, what is he
             suggesting?

BAKER   You said they took everything? And you turned around
             and came straight back, didn't stop in at Laredo? What
             did you use for gas money to get back to Eureka?

THELMA *(Striking a pose)* El Hombre Sombre is a hidalgo!   A
             gentleman. As he was untying me he said, 'My quarrel
             is with ugly gringos, not with beautiful women,' and
             with a flourish of his cape and a deep bow, he handed
             me a C-note. I could see he was attracted to me.

BELLOWS   I thought you said he was going to cut your face off.

They stare. BAKER *watches.* STATLER *is growing maudlin.*

THELMA   He exercised self-control... Just like you're always saying, Norman! Take me to dinner, honey, I'm starving.

STATLER   You don't want to eat here?

THELMA   Are you being funny?

BELLOWS   He don't mean nothing.

BAKER   Statler – watch it! The lady's been through an ordeal. Poor baby! I'm taking you to the Roof Garden at the Basin Park!

THELMA   My favorite! You're so good to me...

BAKER   Bellows! Let them know we're on the way, I want my *special* table.

As THELMA *and* BAKER *prepare to exit:*

THELMA (*to* BELLOWS) You better get to work on the party!

BAKER *(at the door)*   I have a strong feeling we have a rattlesnake in our nest. But no one fools Norman Baker for long. After you, sweetheart...

Exit BAKER *and* THELMA

STATLER   I don't like the way things are going, Rennie. Not at all... what the boss says to do...

LIGHTS fade on the office of the Baker Cancer Curable Hospital

*

177

Every night on the ghost tour someone will ask the guide the question: 'Have __you__ ever seen anything... paranormal?' A useful reply for those guides for whom It's just a job for crying out loud, is: it's a very rare thing for anyone to actually see a ghost. They are felt, sensed, heard or their presence indicated by movement of objects in the physical world, but visual sightings are extremely unusual and the only recorded accounts describe fleeting glimpses of things ambiguous. But a lot happens in cameras. Orbs, flying rods, blurs, faces emerging from abstract shapes and, strangest of all, sometimes the picture seen is not the picture taken, but appears to be of the same place at some other time. A photograph of the corridor when examined will show a different carpet, or paint color, or current signs and fixtures will not appear in the photograph. How does this happen?

Can it be that there is still in existence, on some other plane or unidentified dimension, previous or alternative versions of the entire hotel? Residua of an earlier time, but not of living creatures now dead, rather of inanimate objects somehow caught through an atemporal lens, the walls and floors and furniture of the past still there, haunting the present? And who is to say that the halls the hotel guests walk and the rooms they rest in are in the present? Might it not be possible that the entire hotel is a revenant, a relic of times gone by, a ghost of itself, lingering still on the majestic hilltop?

*

HEARTBREAK HOSPITAL
Scene 3
Third Floor Ward

NEWCOMER   My husband wanted to pay up front but Mr. Baker wouldn't take it! He wants us to pay by the week until I'm well enough to go home, I might not be here long, he said. It's a miracle. We had given up. X- ray, radium, surgery – nothing worked. And he guessed that, when he saw me. He took one look under my eyelids, that's all it took, and then he and that nice Doctor Statler went out of the room to talk, while we waited. It seemed like forever. I was ready to tell Jeb to go home, there would be nothing more to do but watch

178

me die and I would be in good hands... but then they came back in and Mr. Baker was smiling and we just knew! I have never had a moment of happiness like that, Jeb was in tears too and he never cries. Listen to me, jabbering away, I'm just so excited that's all, to think it's finally going to be over, we can go back to living our life again. He's probably just getting back to the house about now, telling the kids they don't have to worry any more...

CANCER VICTIM That's your bed. We're allowed to sit out in the hall during the day. Lights out at nine.

A muffled cry from the end of the hall.

NEWCOMER My god! What's happening?

CANCER VICTIM Mr. Baker says pain killer weakens the system. We have to teach the mind to fight the cancer. The patients who are unsuccessful are put in the ward at the end of the hall, where they can't be heard, mostly. Sometimes you might be woken up at night. And if you hear a squeaking wheel outside in the hall it means the night nurse and the porter are coming for someone, with a gurney. It comes along the hall, real slow, squeal, silence, squeal, silence, squeal again... Where will it stop? Outside your room? Is that scratching on your door? Pass on, pass on, you say...

NEWCOMER *clasps her hands and lowers her head in prayer.*

As the lights fade, the cry is heard again from the end of the hall.

Chapter Sixteen:
The Ghost of Thelma's Arm

listen:
there's a hell of a
good universe next door,
let's go.

e. e. cummings

CHAPTER SIXTEEN
The Ghost of Thelma's Arm

'This area of the hotel – the notorious *annex* - was reserved for those in the greatest suffering. Baker called it his Asylum, to explain the sounds coming from what was essentially a pain ward. People on this hallway sometimes hear a squeaking wheel outside their door and sightings have been reported, in the early hours of the morning, of a nurse pushing a gurney bearing a person under a sheet, from the last bed they will ever sleep in, to the elevator at the other end of the building, and thence down to the morgue, where we will be ending up tonight... temporarily, of course.'

And at last they laughed at one of his jokes.

'Morgue...' The word rumbled through the group, and faded.

Davies led the tour in the direction of the down staircase, with his most beguiling material. 'Next floor down, the second, long considered the most active, is known for repeated experiences and dramatic background stories...' But as they were leaving the annex, currently the location of the honeymoon suites, Davies looked back and saw a pile of bodies heaped in the far corner of the corridor. He froze.

As they had been all evening, his group was staring at him, giving nothing away. No one seemed aware of the gruesome heap behind them from which Davies, walking backwards, could not keep his eyes. 'Hold on,' he said, and started to walk in the direction of the bodies, making up a reason to be abandoning his tour group – looking for his pen, perhaps? – should the corpses prove to be products of his own mind.

But Cornrows and Jangles overtook him in the hall and crouched by the bodies, shaking shoulders. Other helpful and caring individuals joined in and pretty soon the mother and her two little girls, who had lain down for a short nap during the last story, revived. The smallest began to cry. So did mom. 'Come on,' said the sister with kittens on her tee-shirt, 'bed.' And she dragged them both, protesting all the way, along the hall to their room.

Nine.

*

Most ghosts of the Crescent Hotel are never really seen; a few are glimpsed and that but rarely. So we tend to think of them as insubstantial. But when we can no longer see them, where are they? In a world as populous as our own? Or do they have existence only during those seconds in which we behold them, is what we glimpse all there is, do they wink in and out of existence like certain subatomic particles? Whence and what art thou?

What about those others, who are said to pass among the living unobserved because they do not appear to be dead? How many have you passed by today?

Or those Noisy Ones mounted on Mad Horse of Mischief, who throw pots and pans, snatch away the bedclothes, hide grandma's false teeth, turn your shower to freezing?

The Residua, caught in loops, repeating the same exact intense experience with deadly regularity, and presumably living through it all over again, every time.

Or the ones you hear but don't see; or feel only; or those whose presence is perceived only through waves of nameless fear.

And if they can startle us, perhaps it's they who amuse us or arouse us at inappropriate moments; perhaps they are in fact the wellsprings of all our floods of moods. When we get mad or sad or filled with pity or gladness beyond description on a hilltop somewhere or just before the deepest sleep of the night, does all arise from happenings in the Otherworld, among the dead - or whatever they are?

Presences as real as us; or so subtle we only know they are there by inference, by their cloud chamber trails – and is there a point, a somewhere, a boundary beyond which we cease to refer to ghosts as 'they'?

Or is there one special Presence waiting for each of us at the entrance to the long, dark tunnel that leads to the Bright Light; and should we have cause for fear at the moment of the final farewell?

*

Wondering if the fact that the dead bodies turned out to be Bawling Mom and her two girls, and not products of his unhappy imagination, was a sign that his seemingly weakening ability to distinguish reality from waking dream was on the mend; or if the fact

184

that he did not immediately see mom and two girls but something much more distressing was a warning that it was time to take this hallucination bit seriously, Davies led his group from the third floor landing down three flights of stairs to the second floor, where most of the ghosts are said to hang out.

At the first turn of the stairs Davies found the widow from Amarillo at his side. She tucked her arm in his and whispered, 'See, the thing is, there is something I need to ask my husband about, he couldn't hardly talk at the end there, or wouldn't and believe me I tried everything but he just clammed up on me, I expect it won't be long before we can pick up where we left off, my bowels have been acting up something terrible, Buck his name is, was, when his hearing started to go I used to call him butt, he couldn't tell. Yes Butt, no Butt, when are we going to start spending some of that money, Butt?'

Near the bottom of the steps from the last turn to the landing, Davies attempted to politely disengage lest his other guests should feel abandoned or get the wrong idea, but the widow from Amarillo gripped his upper arm as firmly as a full grown python. 'Point is, he left – something – hidden away somewhere. Probably on our ranch but that's a lot of land. Or maybe he put it in a bank vault in New Orleans. Or Seattle, he went there a lot, too. And the Far East. But he took the secret with him to the grave. I know he meant for me to have - it - but he died so sudden, I didn't think he was hurt that bad but it *was* a shovel, I never denied that it was, but it all depends what you mean by 'struck,' my lawyer couldn't seem to see that. Anyway that's all over now and I'm out finally and I would really like to know what the old bastard done with – something. If you do what you promised and put me in touch I'll be in a position to make it worth your while, just put me in touch that's all I'm asking...'

In her universe, Thelma Yount checks her blood-red fingernail polish at arm's length, waggling her fingers, especially the one wrapped in an extravagant, multi-carat diamond engagement ring. *Norman Baker, screw you. You're all washed up. I'm going into politics. A certain senator's son in Texasss... So long, Eureka Springs. I'll miss the big house across the street, I could probably sue you for that and get a good part of it too but I'll just take what I got out of the hotel and be on my way. Stay out of jail, Norman, it doesn't look good on you, you look ten years older not four. Me? I'm ready for a cowboy...* She turns to take a drag from her cigarette holder, unaware that her other arm has slipped up to the elbow into another time.

'Room 228, very pleasant room, very popular with our returning guests. But you wake up in the small hours, not knowing why. And you may begin to hear sounds, sporadic and consistent, which you eventually recognize as a ball, bouncing. They say that's little Breckie, who passed out of this life in this building, all too soon, and sometimes, they say, you can hear his voice, crying, 'It's not fair! It's not fair!' Although that could be his mother, the fierce and fearless friend to mothers everywhere, who could not have loved him more, courageous, compassionate Mary Carson Breckinridge, the wife of the president of Crescent College and Conservatory and founder of the Frontier Nursing Service. You can see her face on the seventy-seven cent stamp today.

'On my left, your right, it's a peculiarity of the architecture of the Crescent Hotel that only on this floor will you find an alcove beside the stairs. This alcove is reputed to be a gathering place for orbs, great place to take pictures.' No one did.

'And if you would follow me around the corner and down three steps, our next stop is the most requested room in the Hotel: Room 218!' He led the way, his group following like a gang of store detectives who had his number.

A rare but recognizable anomaly in the space-time near-continuum precipitates a brief interpenetration of discreet realities and Thelma's forearm, slender wrist and blood-tipped waggling fingers emerge more than seven decades into her future through what would be by then a solid wall into the 2nd floor corridor of the 1886 Crescent Hotel where, moments before, Davies' tour group had stood. The tiniest wobble in the anomaly and the apparition would have given almost a dozen tourists and one tour guide an unforgettable experience; but in Davies's location in time and space, at the moment of penetration of the wall by Thelma's forearm, the tour group had turned the corner and was descending from the third to the first turning of the stairs, leaving the bloody fingernails to waggle in the empty hall, unseen. Except by the unfortunate bride.

The only guests who were not watching Davies as intently as snipers were the newlyweds in identical eyewear, who had been glued at the hips and everywhere else throughout the tour, and now hung back around the corner for a quick couple of feels in the alcove. He was all over her, she was all over him, looking over his shoulder in case anyone came down the stairs or around the corner and suddenly she screamed, loud enough to send her brand-new groom reeling away down the hall. Bellmen came sprinting up from the lobby and the tour guide put the tour on pause while he took a moment to call someone to call someone.

Unobserved by anyone but the bride, the lower arm emerging through the wall of Room 226 waggled its blood-red fingertips and withdrew.

They had to apply wet towels to bring the bride around. The groom knitted his brows and chewed his inner lip, watching every flutter of her eyelids, obedient to the instructions of Hotel Security.

In her universe, Thelma Yount blows on her nails, adds a touch more varnish and turns to check them in the light from the window.

In hers, the young bride surfaced to find a circle of faces staring down at her from above. Voices asked her if she was OK and pleaded with her to drink some water. One demanded to know what the screaming was all about.

'Screaming?'

It was Security, bravely holding the crowd of gawkers at bay with one arm. 'Ma'am, did this man attack you? You're afraid to say it while he's standing there, is that right? Don't you worry, ma'am, I was a combat instructor in the United States Marines till I got my hernia, he ain't gonna try nothing, you just go ahead and describe what happened, you're in safe hands. Did this man force his attentions against your will? Was he stalking you, like prey? Do you remember ever having seen this man before?'

'That's my husband.'

'Oh. Your husband? So what the heck is all the screaming for, pardon my French?

'Screaming?'

'Yes, ma'am, you screamed before you passed out. Did you ever!'

'I did?'

She allowed them to help her to her feet, keeping her eyes down. After a moment and a deep breath, she stole a look back along the corridor, remembered what had caused her to faint and almost screamed again.

'Honey, can you tell us what happened?' Her husband steered her away from Hotel Security. 'Honey, what made you scream like that?'

'I thought... I saw...'

'What? Honey – what? What did you see? Someone doing something? And don't tell me you saw a ghost.'

'I don't – no, I don't know what I saw, I don't remember, whatever it was, I don't know! I'm fine now, sorry everyone, thanks for helping me... Honey, I really need to go back to our room, right now!'

'Feel free to join us in the morgue...' Davies offered.

'Oh, I don't think so,' said the bride. She gathered her skirts and started up the stairs, two at a time, her groom a step behind.

Davies stared at his group, down from twenty-two to seven.

In all his years as a ghost tour guide, that rate of attrition was unprecedented. *What's wrong here? Am I different tonight? Can they tell I'm hallucinating?*

They were all staring at him. Waiting, he realized, for him to explain. In the conspicuous absence of inspiration, he used the tried and true: 'Some very strange things happen in this hotel...' and hastily returned to the story of Michael, the impertinent stonemason.

Outside Room 218, if it has not already happened on the tour, a group of strangers will become acquaintances, even friends for a time as they reveal their own proclivities through their reactions to the reports of interpenetrating shenanigans between this world and the next, inside Michael's room. But on this night, Davies' told his lightly suggestive stories to shock-and-humor-proof faces staring back at him, his saucy jokes fell on indifferent ears.

'There have been accounts of experiences, sometimes quite vivid, in Room 218 apparently for as long as people have been sleeping in it - or not sleeping! But most of those stories are not appropriate to be told on public tours... So if you want to know more you'll have to stay here overnight. Best to make your reservations early, Michael's room is usually booked up months ahead of time by.... You guessed it: women!' *Laugh, you bastards.* And when he reached his punchline: 'So ladies - I'm not saying don't take a shower while you're here. But don't be surprised if Michael shows up...' No response. At all. Just the impassive stare.

'Next,' Aging Rocky said.

At that point in the tour, since nothing had dropped from the ceiling or emerged wiggling from a tourist's ear, he had not suddenly begun to curse in Urdu and nobody had vanished completely for at least ten minutes, Davies' predominant emotions were relief regarding his possibly deteriorating sanity, accompanied by the as-yet unresolved dilemma: how to mention the tip jar?

'The next stop on the way will be the office of one of the heroes of Eureka Springs, a principal member of the Improvement Company assembled by ex-governor Powell Clayton to turn a shanty town into a world-class health resort. Dr. John Freemont Ellis, homeopath, was the Crescent Hotel house physician *and* a hydraulic engineer, who arranged for a house-by-house fresh water system and city-wide waste disposal, among other accomplishments. And old Doc Ellis left us a unique legacy: a greeting from whatever realm the good doctor now inhabits, to our sense of *smell*: an aroma of cherry pipe tobacco... Anyone? Cherry pipe tobacco, anybody get a whiff?'

It was a rare tour when at least one person did not claim to have experienced the cherry pipe tobacco, either at that moment or some time previously in the day before they had even heard of Dr. Ellis. But tonight, there were no takers.

The crowd watched him seemingly forensically, murmuring quietly among themselves. From the mixture of sounds, he was able to pick out, several times, the word *Morgue...*

But they had paid for a full tour and Davies was not about to give them any less, their apparent catatonia notwithstanding. Like a mountaineer who climbs best when angry, Davies gave his narratives the works. 'Now, we believe that the dreadful charlatan Norman Baker is long gone, but that good-hearted Dr. Ellis is still here. There have been many reports, over the years, of a tall man in a dark suit with top hat and mutton chops, on the lower landing of the south stairs. There is always a cold spot where the stairs make the first turn, which is where the tall man has been seen, going up the steps and disappearing at the next turn. He is seen elsewhere, too, although mostly sitting, in the lobby or in guest rooms or on the stage in the Faculty Lounge. It's said that if you look closely you will observe that down from the knees he becomes increasingly less substantial... and actually displays no feet at all. But most people don't notice other peoples' ankles and the good doctor's lack of them goes unremarked.' *Pause for at least a chuckle.*

'Morgue?'

Davies started down the stairs to the lobby, 'Anyone staying here tonight? Sleep well... Anyone having breakfast in the Crystal Dining Room? Don't forget to look over to your right as you go in, you'll see a table for two in a corner with tall windows on two sides. That's Joseph's table....'

'MORGUE!'

Chapter Seventeen:
Ghost, Waiting

Tell me where is Fancy bred,
Or in the heart or in the head...

William Shakespeare
The Merchant of Venice

CHAPTER SEVENTEEN
Ghost, Waiting

Jacob sits at his regular table in the window corner, watching the glass-paned dining-room doors open and close, waiting for Avril to arrive. He sees everyone who comes and goes. Each time the door opens his heart rises in expectation, and each time he sees it is not Avril, his heart sinks a little lower. He has been waiting for over a hundred years. He is seen in brown pinstripes and spats with a small brown bowler on his head, a bow tie and gold watch chain dangling, fingering the timepiece in his waistcoat pocket as he waits and watches, ready to leap to his feet in joyous welcome the moment his beloved steps through the dining room doors.

1906

He came in the early spring, when the winter was quite over, buds breaking open, birds returning, flowers taking turns to put on a show in honor of the sun's recovery from darkness once again. He sat for three weeks at that window table, by special arrangement with the maitre d'hotel. Each day the lilac bushes outside his window grew more abundant. The sprays of blossoms, purple and white, flourished for their brief but annual existence, crowding closer and filling the windows around him, so close, and abruptly withered. That same day, a Wednesday, Jacob paid his bill in full, walked down the steps, across the park into a grove of trees, and shot himself.

The evening before the day that Avril was due to arrive, Jacob checked into the Crescent Hotel, overflowing with loving-kindness for the world. The cabman, the concierge, the bellhops and the waiters all experienced his bonhomie and said what a nice man he was, and generous, too. He retired early and spent the next morning unpacking, humming, returning to the mirror every so often to be sure of his coiffure, drumming his fingers on the credenza. He forced himself to wait till five minutes before the hour of noon before he dashed a little musk oil on his cheeks and hands, checked the mirror one last time and proceeded down two flights of stairs and across the spacious lobby to the opulent Dining Room.

They had agreed, at her insistence, not to meet at the station amid smoke and bustle, potential delays and the business of baggage and cabs. Better meet at the hotel, but not yet in either of the rooms they had reserved in their own names; rather in formal fashion, among a hundred other anonymous diners.

They made their sudden decision to abscond, under the big willow at the end of her gardens when the branches were yet bare, though buds were beginning to fatten on the tips of twigs. Jacob and Avril lingered behind a group of chattering guests, mostly business acquaintances of her husband taking the air after lunch. At table, her husband had been even more insufferable than usual, humiliating his wife with his thoughtless mockery of her personal vanity, her lack of common sense, her ridiculously sentimental affection for small animals. Jacob had barely restrained himself from attacking the oaf, huge and battle-scarred though he was. He determined at that very dining table to accede to Avril's wistful fantasy of the last few weeks, that he and she might go away to some far distant place and be together forever, in happy defiance of her boorish husband, his tyranny at home, his concern for propriety. What would it matter what their social circle thought and said, once she and Jacob were out of sight, out of hearing, out of mind?

Under the willow, 'Leave him,' Jacob had whispered, watching the backs of the smokers strolling the paths leading back to the house.

'When?'

'Now! This minute! We'll run away and never come back!'

Her eyes were bright with excitement and tears, her lower lip trembling. She hid for a moment under the brim of her straw hat. 'But - how will I tell him?'

'Tell him nothing! We'll just go! Write to everybody later... or don't.'

'There are so many guests in the house, we will be seen leaving...'

'Meet me somewhere!'

'Where?'

'Eureka Springs!'

'Eureka – why there?'

'I don't know, it came into my head. There's a grand hotel....'

'The Crescent! It's famous!'

'The Crescent. We'll meet there. When?'

But before she could reply, the group farther along the sandy path stopped to chat and some turned to look back. Jacob and Avril moved as one, stepping forward casually as though the gap between themselves and the smoking party was a trivial accident.

'You have a very capable gardening staff...' Jacob said loudly and as inconsequentially as he could feign.

'We are fond of old Silas and his sons, they do fine work, very conscientious...'

'Keep 'em busy! Put 'em to work!' One of the guests, drink in hand, joined their conversation, and they all drifted in the direction of the great house for more refreshments and no doubt more boastful big-game hunting stories from Avril's husband, standing legs spread wide, the dead staring heads of his conquests adorning the walls behind him.

Once the group had achieved the drawing room, 'I think this is an occasion for champagne!' Avril said, without looking at Jacob. Her husband grunted twice, once in apparent approval of her wifely hospitality and again when she downed the glass of champagne at a gulp and reached for another. Aware of his glare, Avril merely wrinkled her nose as though tickled by the bubbles in the champagne and gave a merry little laugh that seemed to say, 'I am of a frivolous disposition, you say so yourself...'

Jacob was light-headed with anticipation. He dared not catch Avril's eye, since no look that passed between them that afternoon could possibly be casual. He made an excuse to leave early. Avril brought him his cape. When he fished in his pocket for a coin for the cab man he found a small square of lavender paper, folded twice. In the light of the cab lantern he read: *March 23. Crescent Hotel Dining Room.*

The days of waiting in vain for Avril mounted, March gave place to April and Jacob began to fear the worst. Every morning he would check at the front desk for messages or individuals who might be inquiring after him. Every day, until the dining room opened he sat on the balcony outside his suite watching the roads, from the train station, winding up one side of the hill, or from Eureka Springs on the other; and every evening after the dining room closed he returned to the balcony and sat staring out into darkness, trying to understand. Could something have happened to her on the journey? A sudden illness? Could her husband have discovered their plan and done her an injury?

Jacob sent a cable to his brother, asking him to hire a Pinkerton man to make discreet inquiries into the whereabouts and welfare of Mrs. Avril Hearthstone. The detective, a retired U.S. Marshal with many years in Indian Territory under his belt, negotiating the Cookson hills for hideouts, was out of his depth in the thickets of wealthy St. Louis society. The best he could do was crash a party. He was quickly discovered, but not before he spotted Avril.

Two days later a cable came to the hotel for Jacob. The person in question had been seen at a ball, elegantly dressed, hanging onto her husband's arm, drinking champagne and laughing excessively.

Jacob gave it one more day, sitting staring at the shiny dining room doors, in case the world gone mad might yet come right again. The lilac blossoms behind him curled and dropped from their stems. And that afternoon Jacob developed the determination to tolerate his desertion and betrayal, the absence of the object of his happiness, and the emptiness of a life made even emptier than it had been before the whispered words under the willow tree, not a day longer. At the closing of the big dining room that evening, Jacob left an extra large tip under his untouched coffee cup, nodded a sad goodbye to all the staff, climbed stiffly the stairs to his room, took the revolver from his travelling bag, descended the service stairs and went out the back door of the hotel, across the tramlines and into the trees.

Jacob's story, told from the only point of view available to him, his own, is one in which true love could have triumphed over the strictures of convention, but love proved treacherous. That story so saddened him that he lost interest in going on.

And yet the story as imagined by Jacob after sitting at the window table for three weeks among the lilacs is incomplete, a version only, lacking an important detail which he did not discover before he pulled the trigger. The same story from Avril's point of view is very different.

Jacob sits on, in the window overlooking the west lawn, fingering the timepiece in his waistcoat pocket, watching every person who comes through the dining room doors, waiting for his heart's desire, waiting for resolution, for a satisfactory end to a story based on an unacceptable contradiction: the love he felt from Avril for himself was at one and the same time real and unreal.

Chapter Eighteen:
On the Way to the Morgue

All we know is that
no one who has ventured
into the Valley Obscured by Clouds
has ever returned...

La Vallée
written and directed
by Barbet Schroeder

CHAPTER EIGHTEEN
On the Way to the Morgue

Davies shepherded the little group across the lobby, through the double doors and down the steps out to the bright moonlit night and the serenading cicadas. On the way across the parking lot to the morgue he pointed out the chimney stacks, which in daylight are bright purple, courtesy of Norman Baker, and showed them a rare photo-op: the full moon behind the ominous annex. Still no one took pictures.

'Sometimes, especially on nights like tonight, when the moon is full, we see bats...'

Davies kept talking, but his attention was suddenly riveted on a sight just beyond the crowd he was addressing – a pick-up truck parked in the shadows and, climbing up to the passenger seat, a filmy vision from the realm of fairy tale: DreamCloud Detroit. And although it seemed unlikely, Davies thought he knew who drove that pickup. 'Sometimes you see bats, especially on full moon nights,' he said, as the moon was eclipsed by a large black cloud and the silver pick-up engine and headlights roared into life.

Screeching tires rendered Davies' much-practiced evocations inaudible as Billy Bull's truck peeled out across the parking lot, to the accompaniment of loud squeals and giggles from the passenger side. Davies watched till nothing remained of the truck but a shapeless cloud of drifting dust.

'Sometimes you see bats,' he said, 'especially on full moon nights – '

'You said that,' the haughty girl in the shawl pointed out. 'You need to wake up!'

'You're probably receiving a message from my darlin' husband...'

'No, he's not,' the Empath said, 'I'm getting agitation."

'Morgue?' Mrs. Aging Rocky suggested.

'And now,' the man from NASA said, anticipating Davies, 'The moment we've all been waiting for...!'

'Lead on, *Mac Beth!*' Aging Rocky laid his oversized arm lightly about Davies' shoulders, 'Come on, guy, let's get on with it...'

'I'm sooo looking forward to this!' Cornrows was a coiled spring; her companion's comments were lost under the jangling of her facial jewelry.

Down the sloping tarmac, under the great oak tree whose limbs all reach in the direction of the Crescent Hotel, around the wide steel sliding door, through an alley walled with corrugated tin, Davies led his few remaining guests to the concealed doorway on which hangs the picture of a hollow skull and the words, *Morgue. Authorized Personnel Only.*

*

HEARTBREAK HOSPITAL
Scene 3
Pitch Darkness

The face of NORMAN BAKER *appears, staring out.*

BAKER   Do you know how many dead people I've seen?

The face of RENNIE BELLOWS *appears out the blackness, behind and above* NORMAN BAKER, *staring out.*

BELLOWS   Not many! You hate to look at 'em.

BAKER   It's true. They bother me. Lying there decomposing. Watching you sometimes. And let's face it - dead people stink! I have a very sensitive nose.

BELLOWS   You can smell money a mile away!

BAKER   That's true, too.

BELLOWS   I was never good at that. Have to hand it to you.

BAKER   That why you always stuck around, Rennie?

BELLOWS   Thick and thin.

202

BAKER   Till you turned around and sued me. You and Statler
               both.

The face of Dr. STATLER *appears out the blackness, above and behind*
BAKER, *staring out.*

STATLER   There comes a point, Norman.

BAKER   You hurt my feelings. After everything I did for you.

STATLER   I didn't need you to do anything for me. I had what I
               wanted. I was a doctor. Helping the sick...
BAKER   You took the job!

STATLER   And you broke up my family, got me struck off the list
               and run out of town, turned me into a liar and a thief
               and an alcoholic and got me a year and a day in jail!

BAKER   Could have been worse. Could have been two years,
               like Bellows.

BELLOWS   Two years out of a person's life – you can't blame us for
               trying to get what you promised us.

BAKER   Didn't turn out to be two years though, did it?

BELLOWS   Only because I died.

BAKER   And saved me a job!

Both laugh

STATLER   Suing you proved fruitless, anyway...

BELLOWS   Norman Baker, two steps ahead as always...

BAKER   So I thought, when I put everything in Thelma's name...
               She already knew where all the bucks were buried, she
               was Thelma, she adored me, I trusted her with all my

property in Muscatine and Laredo, Nuevo Laredo, Eureka Springs, including the Avarana Mansion, the Crescent Hotel -

The face of THELMA *appears out of the blackness, above* BAKER.

THELMA   The Crescent Hotel? A falling-down, leaky scrap-heap in the middle of nowhere, filled with beat-up medical equipment and a room full of body parts in what passed for a morgue? I had to wait till the war was over to cash it in. You were out of jail and in a rage. But by then I was married to the son of a senator in Texas and according to state law, my fortune belonged to him. Everything that had my name on it. The profits went to a good cause. Into his campaign, on a ticket that would have had you running for the microphone if you hadn't been in prison and all. Sorry, Norman.

THELMA *begins to fade, returns.*

              Don't bother coming around, Norman. We don't like strangers hanging around our property.

THELMA *fades.*

BELLOWS   Sorry Bellows. My wife didn't give up though, and she made out all right. In a little house on Vaughan street that we bought for a hundred dollars from a madwoman on the courthouse steps.

BELLOWS *fades.*

STATLER   At least I made it through my jail time. Lived on what I had saved, lost both legs to diabetes. Died of alcoholic poisoning over a grocery store on Spring Street.

STATLER *fades.*

BAKER   Four years in Leavenworth, almost wasted. I taught myself about power stations. Came out of prison to an empty street. I rallied. I tried. And from this vantage point I see I had been on the rise, I was a force to reckon with, I had a plan to climb the political tree and my plan included winning an election for President of the United States, and Norman Baker would have been remembered as a great statesman. But my trajectory was arrested here in Eureka Springs, or Norman Baker would have gone down in history as the man who made America great again.

BAKER *remains, staring, for a long time.*

BLACKOUT.

INTERLUDE:

Uncertainty

Not everybody sees ghosts, not everyone can. Most don't want to, anyway - only those for whom this universe is not enough, who must have others alongside, invisible and intangible but there, because this can't be all there is. But the question remains: why are some people more perceptive of the Beyond than others? And further: why don't we all perceive the same reality? Why don't we all read the same book, experience art, or a grass blade or other people the same way? Where is the solid ground? We all go along as if it was under our feet - but if Jack means one thing by Table or Teacup and Jill means another, how on earth do they manage to communicate, to cooperate? If Jack sees only the furniture of life, while Jill experiences waves of association evoking emotion, memory and desire; if for Jill the Table or Teacup resonates to the outer atmosphere, the air filled with story, her mind a swirl of traffic, seen, half seen; while Jack is only interested in the Tea – how is it that we understand each other even as well as we do?

We seem to share the same immediate actuality - yet it is different for each of us; I'm short sighted, everything in my distance is fuzzy; you're colorblind; someone is a ruthless profiteer, someone else is a musician – no two alike. We are similar enough that we can share space, yet each unique: therefore there are as many versions of What Is as there are minds - and if even that much is true, there are doubtless other orders of reality, countless possibilities, coexisting but barely interacting, aware of each other in varying degrees, through a multiplicity of modes of perception, all as different as may be; and so, therefore, all the ways to be dead that you can think of, as many kinds of ghost as there are beings in the universe. Some of them appear, occasionally, briefly, in the "real" world, the world we live in, and our world sits up and takes notice. A glimpse is all anyone gets: the corner of the curtain lifts and drops. But a glimpse of what waits at the other end of Being is all that is needed; once in the mind, all the mind from then on will be focused on the attempt to glimpse again, to raise the corner of the curtain further. Ghosts have to be good for something, right?

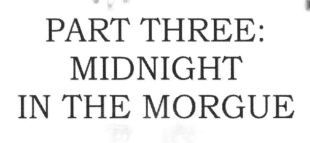

PART THREE: MIDNIGHT IN THE MORGUE

I can live with doubt and uncertainty
and not knowing. I think it's
much more interesting to live
not knowing than to have
answers which might be wrong...

Richard Feynman,
physicist,
Nobel Laureate

Chapter Nineteen: Tour's End

Crazy Horse died
and went into the world
where there is nothing
but the spirits of all things.
That is the real world that
is behind this one and
everything we see here is
something like a shadow
from that one.

Black Elk Speaks

CHAPTER NINETEEN
Tour's End

A moment after Davies had let the last guest into the morgue, a pain like a stab from a knife pierced through his chest and he almost collapsed, completely unnoticed. He leaned against the door jamb, waiting for the pressure to pass and tasting the cheese and mustard sandwich he had made himself for dinner. He straightened up and gulped air. *Ow. What's that all about? Figure it out later. Be strong. See it through. Finish the tour.* He entered the morgue and closed the door behind him.

The first room, old plaster walls and a tangle of pipes just below the low ceiling, was the mini-cinema where the ghost tour guests were shown a video clip of media-savvy ghost hunters investigating that very room. But the guests were not sitting before the screen; they had all gone straight to the third room, concrete floor and corrugated tin walls and ceiling, where autopsies were said to have been conducted by Baker's staff. The much-diminished tour group was milling around in the shafts of dim light, blue and black, murmuring, leaning against a pole or standing astride a drain in the floor, examining the rusty ceiling. Oddly, those who had met as strangers a scant hour before now seemed as if they had known each other forever.

Watching his tour group weave about in the space where once lay the remains of those unfortunate hopefuls for whom the guaranteed cure administered at Baker's Cancer Curable Hospital did nothing except increase discomfort, Davies lost time again, the actor became the audience. But then the scene he was watching turned its focus on him and he heard himself addressed by a voice he had heard once before, earlier that evening. Or was it later?

'Mr. Davies. Come in, why don't you?'

He passed along by the second room, the Parts Room, where one of the most famous apparition captures of modern-day paranormal investigation had been registered on the door of an old metal cabinet by a thermal imaging camera. In the autopsy room the man from NASA was sitting, curiously enough, up on the prep table, swinging his legs. 'There you are, still in the land of the living!' He greeted Davies cheerfully. The others expressed no such excitement. 'How are you feeling now?'

'Fine.' And there again came the brief but loud shout of group laughter that had bewildered him throughout the tour, as of many funny bones tickled at once by something Davies said that he was not even aware was amusing. And though his group was much smaller now, the bark of laughter let loose in the confines of the morgue was almost deafening, as was the silence that followed. *Billy Bull is right. I've lost my touch. I'm not even going to mention the tip jar.*

'If you'd like to take a seat in the viewing room – '

'We don't want to see any videos,' the girl in the shawl said.

'We want to see the meat locker,' Corporate Empath said, "where Norman Baker kept the bodies."

'Meat locker!!'

Clearly, consensus had been reached. 'Okay. I have a lot more to tell you, but okay…'

'You've told us enough,' the widow from Amarillo said.

'Meat locker, pal,' Aging Rocky said.

'If you're ready – 'Davies said, once again occasioning unintended, unexplained amusement. He unbolted and hauled open the great creaking door to the ice-room, once a kitchen cooler, later storage for the corpses of those whom Norman Baker failed. When it was open wide enough for the whole tour he turned back to invite his guests to step inside and found them all shimmering.

Davies blinked and squeezed his eyes; but the changing focus was not in his pupils, as became clear a moment later when the bright fuzziness that permeated his vision resolved and he could recognize each individual form again: the seven guests he had been leading through the labyrinthine halls were all suddenly wearing costumes. And changed in other ways. Dramatically.

The young girl with the mane of red hair had apparently cast aside the shawl and woolly overclothes to reveal a navy blue middy dress and jaunty sailor collar. Aging Rocky had lost about a foot-and-a -half in height and gained a brown suit and derby hat. The suntanned widow from Amarillo was now paler, thinner, minus rhinestones and denims, in a long, dark silk dress studded with pearls. The Empath was in a grimy nurse's uniform, carrying a bottle and a syringe.

212

Cornrows was wearing a stonemason's hat and Jangles had made the complete transposition into Billy Bob Thornton. The Gray Man from the room with no number sat on the autopsy table, swinging his legs, smiling at Davies, his eyes twinkling.

'This is all in my mind, right?' Davies said.

'All in your mind?' the Gray Man exclaimed. 'Who do you think you are, God?' That really cracked up the room.

Davies thought, *I shall be so glad when this tour is over.* 'At this moment, I don't know who I am. I don't know who any of you are, either. I started the tour in the Faculty Lounge with twenty-two guests. Now I'm alone in the morgue with seven people who all just changed into other people. At least, that's what I see. Or what I think I see.' Davies was more prepared to grieve for his lost sanity than embrace the evidence of his senses but, given his dull and repetitious existence, willing or at least resigned to make the best of a new and unfamiliar scenario. 'Okay,' he said. 'I'm reconciled to the fact that I cannot tell if you are all in my mind, in which case I am hallucinating, or if you have some kind of objective reality and would still be here if I were somewhere else. All of this is completely unexpected; but I can wait to figure out what's going on, probably when I wake up in a hospital somewhere on Methadone. I have no idea, and I do realize I may never know, how I got here or why or what happens next. In the meantime, since I seem to be down the rabbit hole and through the looking glass, I may as well explore this reality - as long as I'm not, in my usual one, wandering along the freeway at night.'

He stood with his back against the open cooler door, looking over the group. Each of his sudden acquaintances seemed as vivid as flesh when focused upon, but on the periphery of his vision it was difficult to tell the figures from the shadows. Voices responded.

No freeways...

No parallel universes...

No hallucinations...

Just us...

'Just *who*?'

Who do you think?

'I just gave up thinking.'

Might as well.

'I would like to know what's happening all the same – am I

213

about to have lovely hallucinations followed by stark terrors, like in the opium dens in Sherlock Holmes? Do I start to believe I can fly, and jump off an interstate bridge to prove it?'

Why would you do that?

'I've thought about it. And not to prove anything either.'

Don't be silly.

'I'm not worried about being silly, I'm worried about going crazy.'

Oh, you don't have time for that.

'What do you mean?'

You know what we mean.

'Why am I talking to you as if you were *not* in my mind?'

Get over it.

Relax.

You don't have anywhere to be.

'I think I should sit down.'

Give him some air.

In a morgue? Laughter, with prolonged reverb.

Give him some space!

It's time he's running out of! More laughter.

Won't be long now...

'What won't be long now?'

Nothing is going to be long, now.

Don't tell him!

'Don't tell me what?'

Nothing! they all said at once, and returned to the old maddeningly impassive porcelain faces.

'More mystery?' Davies sat on the only chair in the autopsy room, an old straight-back, his breath shallow and his heart pounding as though he were climbing a very steep flight of stairs and still had a long way to go. 'So, here in the Land of Delirium - am I supposed to give you folks the rest of the tour?'

'Don't you get it?' Gray Man said, 'We are the tour.'

And what you do not know is the only thing you know
And where you are is where you are not.

'Or a good part of it. The magnificent seven dwarfs, the ones who feel it's important to keep in touch with the Old Gal. There are more of us, but not everybody likes to show themselves. And of

214

course not all who were here at the Crescent Hotel feel compelled to return. But for each of *us*, significant events took place in this building when we were more substantial. And we each have reasons for keeping you company tonight, in the morgue.'

I think I read about this. Under the stress of severe mental conflict the mind begins to splinter into factions, which in turn are projected onto the world outside, and that's how we get pantheons. 'I'm making you all up as we go along, I get that. You are manifestations of my emotional impasses. The conflicted areas of my consciousness materialized. Anthropomorphized. You are projections and your purpose is to help me come to terms with myself. Got it. Thank you. I'm listening. '

The Gray Man crossed his legs and put his hands behind his head. Shadows moved.

'Let's start again. Mr. Tour Guide: teller of stories you do not know, cannot know, no matter how many books you read, how many hours you spend looking down from the Sunset Balcony trying to imagine how it felt to be Norman Baker or Richard Thompson or Powell Clayton surveying their domain. Their experience was not the same as yours, any more than it was each others'. How can you speak about any of them with authority? Let alone capture their lives in a few sentences spoken on the fly?'

Foreshortened Rocky in a derby passed in front of Davies, saying, 'We have been listening to your stories for years. And the best review we could give you is, you raise more questions than you answer. '

Cornrows in dungarees crossed the other way. 'At least you're not a fabricator, you don't pretend to know the real truth of any of the stories, history or mystery.'

'You try,' the empath in the blood-spattered nurse's uniform said, 'and we admire you for that and forgive you for getting us all wrong. '

The girl with the mane of red hair, now wearing the uniform of Crescent College, completed the information. 'Tonight we are going to tell *you* stories...'

215

Chapter Twenty:
Ghosts' Stories

You do yet taste
some subtleties o'the isle, that will not let you
believe things certain.

Shakespeare
The Tempest

CHAPTER TWENTY
Ghosts' Stories

Davies was glad to be sitting. His body hurt and he was very tired. Billy Bull had left, with DreamCloud Detroit; Davies was going to have to close down, was not going to make any tips and had yet to figure out how to get home, surrealistic hallucinations notwithstanding. The lights in the morgue kept shifting in color and the walls were lined with shadow people. The red-haired Crescent College student was speaking to him.

'The tour guides refer to me as the Girl in the Mist and some of you call me Annabelle. I'm not going to give you my real name, but it's not that! I'm not giving you his name either. I don't care what you say about me when you tell my story. It happened, almost the way you tell it. But if you're going to tell the story, you should tell it all. Your lurid suggestions are not inaccurate, but there is a detail that has never occurred to you that changes the story completely.

'I loved – my child's father - for the same qualities that destroyed his child and me: his carefree charm, his devil-take-tomorrow attitude; he seemed so daring, brave and adventurous, white teeth and ready laugh, generous with money I came to realize was not his at about the same time I realized his dashing gaiety came at the expense of others' peace of mind and his own conscience; at which point I ceased to love him, or even want him.

'As for my predicament and his part in it - he couldn't have cared less, he had other things to do. As did I! But there was no reason for him to be unkind. I simply tried to explain to him what was going on. His utter indifference drove me to the railing; the coldness in his words sent me over. But time was driving circumstance, we just did our best to keep up. A month earlier, or later, I do not think I would have risked our two lives.

'But what I would like to have people understand is that at the last minute, the moment of truth, after the betrayal and before the subterfuge, when I lost my balance on the railing of the third floor

balcony, my child's father did reach out and try to stop my fall; he tried to save my life. Our lives. And regretted his failure to the end of his days.

'Not yet twenty-one and steeped in shame, he found John Barleycorn not far away, ready to console a soul in torment and destroy his promise.'

'That's too *sad*...' Davies said. It was hard enough to keep the ghost tours light, without adding more disaster.

'You miss the point,' she said.

The Gray Man chuckled. 'Ghosts are people who are dead! Somehow they got that way, and that's what ghost stories like the ones you tell every night are about. No wonder you go home depressed sometimes.'

The girl whose name was not Annabelle smiled, surprisingly kindly. 'Cheer up, it won't be long now!'

'What won't?'

But a new voice spoke up from the shadows and a figure, tall, slender, elegant as a fencer yet unmistakably once Jangles, emerged, and tipped his fedora half an inch in Davies' direction.

'Rennie Bellows,' he said. *'Pleased to meetcha. Finally. You don't talk about me on the tour - or any of us working for Baker, except Theodora. Beautiful lady. Everybody loved her. And she never had anyone in her life, just the patients. But on your tours, the rest of us don't get a look in. You think Baker pulled off some of his stunts all by himself? He was the brains, I'll give you that, but I found this hotel for him, and it was always me dealing with the contractors, and the nosey-parkers. For twenty years I worked for him. At his beck and call, his wish my command: drive him someplace, keep the liquor cabinet filled, fire the help who bothered him, write the lying press releases and help load the bodies into the truck to be taken to the mortuary. And arm wrestling over what he owed me. He would always make a deal, a good deal, and he would always welsh on the deal and make it look like it was you that was trying to rob him!*

And it wasn't so bad to start with. Up in Muscatine we had some fun, in the early days of radio. We were breaking all the rules and raking it in and the people loved us. And Mexico was... there was plenty of everything in Mexico. Then he went on a trip to Michigan, saw the Battle Creek operation, and that was it, he had to go one better. He was going international. He sent me to look for a good headquarters: in a state that accepted eclectic medical degrees; good size building that could be made secure; outside the city; ready to move in; cheap.'

He raised his arms, proudly indicating the building rising above the rusted, corrugated tin ceiling.

'What a find! A one-hundred room hotel, antique-looking but solid as rock, forty thousand including the parks! On a mountain top where you can see who's coming from all directions. And a location that was once a famous health resort! Pure air and water; unspoiled nature all around, and a so-called magic spring – what a scam that must have been! - a town of seventeen hundred, desperate for someone from outside to create a little work for the locals. And I found it. We would never have been in Eureka Springs if it hadn't been for Rennie Bellows.

'Baker. You couldn't help but admire the guy, his energy, his guts, he would take on anybody and anything, he was like ten men all in one, and he would not quit, no one could keep up with Norman Baker, after being around Norman ordinary life was kind of humdrum.

'But by the time we got to Eureka Springs Norman had changed. He did not have the edge he had before Mexico. He was getting fat and fighting with everybody, angry all the time. But his dreams kept getting bigger. He really thought he was going to run for president some day. He loved all that campaign trail stuff, he loved giving speeches to huge crowds, which of course he didn't have in Eureka Springs. He lived in the penthouse straight up from where we are now except when he was across the street at the mansion he bought for Thelma, and all he ever talked about was money.

'I didn't like him anymore, and I never did feel right about the cancer scam. But my wife was not well. She was fragile, she wasn't good at managing things, she had to have real medical help and that cost real money. And this was in the Depression!

So how could I quit? When we came to Eureka Springs he bought us all houses to live in, nothing fancy, but four walls and a roof with a kitchen. I was able to make my wife comfortable, give her a good life. I would never have been able to do that as a barber, which is my training. Barbers are two a penny and they get paid in peanuts. Working for Baker I was able to satisfy her every whim, make things nice for her; she was in a lot of pain.

It wasn't so bad when he was just selling things, or expressing his opinions on the radio, or opening new businesses; but then he started dealing in people's lives – well, the manner of their death, let's put it that way.

'Baker sweet-talked the city, they were falling all over themselves to make us welcome. They gave us deals on power and water and helped us find whatever we needed, and within six months we were ready for patients. And this is when Norman went all out with his crazy ideas about how to make the patients think they're getting better - decorate the place like a funhouse and play calliaphone music all day, take the doors off their rooms so they have no privacy, feed them awful food and give them mind games to play.

'He never set out to kill anybody – no matter what has been said on the tours – he was not a murderer, he was just a con artist. But the people who came to him would have had a more peaceful passing, in a lot of cases, if they had stayed at home. It never fazed him. He'd shrug. 'Never saw anyone wanted so badly to die,' he said about one woman, to her husband's face.

I came to hate him so much I tried to kill him; he was trying to kill me at the time. But we were both so drunk – his sister came in with a pistol and threatened to shoot us both if we didn't quit. So we both let go and sat there, trying to get our breaths and then she pulled the trigger and it went click and we started to laugh and laugh and when we couldn't laugh any more, he gave me the key to the cabinet and told me to get another bottle.

'But Norman got uglier as he got older, that's a fact.   You can't make a living off other people's suffering, you can't ignore pain you are causing to others - and their families - and not have it affect you somewhere, somehow. His drinking got worse. And his hangovers! His bad moods... But when he was on about his third glass of that day's liquor of choice, he thought he was invulnerable.   Immortal. Indestructible. Idolized. No, he didn't just think it, he believed it.

'Till they came to get him. September First, 1939. The same day that Hitler invaded Poland and World War Two kicked off.   From the age of fifty-eight to sixty-two, Norman Baker's freedom was clamped down tight, in Leavenworth Prison, and no one cared. No one.

'Just wanted to give you a little... perspective.'

And with another slight tug on his hat brim, Rennie Bellows dissolved back into shadow.

'Ah, wow,' Davics said.   'I'm supposed to say all that in ten minutes on the tour?'

'Oh, forget about your old tour,' the girl who was not Annabelle said, suddenly at his elbow.

'That's all over now,' the voice of the widow from Amarillo said in his other ear. 'You're wondering – '

But the Gray Man intervened: 'Mr. Davies! I'd like you to meet Jacob, whom you call Joseph and describe as sitting by a window, checking his watch and staring disconsolately at the dining room door. Jacob, would you care to share with Mr. Davies your experience of the last hundred years or so?'

The short man in the brown suit and derby, whom Davies somehow recognized as Aging Rocky despite the addition of mutton chops and the loss of a quarter of his height, stood with his back to a mirror. Davies watched him from front and back as he talked about being a century dead and obliged to stay in one place.

'Sometimes I stick out my foot when a waiter goes past with a loaded tray, just to relieve the boredom. It doesn't work, I'm disembodied. But that doesn't mean I don't need a little distraction now and then. Once I tried popping in and out all around the dining room, appearing at different tables, disappearing again. No one noticed.

'I do enjoy watching people, seeing them change over the decades. I arrived a few years after the Brigadier General and all his pals had pulled up stakes. A few years later the Crescent began operations as a College during the off-season. That part was not quite so boring. I used to let one student per term catch a glimpse of me at my table, checking my pocket watch. The interesting thing is, when they made up stories about me they got some of it right, the part they still tell on the tours. Except my name. But there are parts of the story they do not know, could not guess; and some of the most important details were hidden from me, also, on the day I walked into the trees with my revolver in my inside pocket. Not that the story would have ended any more happily; the sad story of Jacob and Avril was not redeemed or justified at the final curtain.

'Why did I give up on Avril? And my own future? I loved her so absolutely. I adored her very faults. I was devoted to her nature. But the Avril that I knew would never have simply changed her mind and not even sent me a note. Not and be the Avril that I loved, it was an impossibility. And so I waited, watching the glass doors opening and closing and opening... and gradually wearing down my faith in my Avril, my own Avril. Then the telegram came from St Louis and I was faced with an incomprehensible fact: Avril was not coming. And had not

bothered to inform me of the fact. And therefore Avril was not Avril, there was no Avril, my Avril did not exist. And never had. I lost sight of my beloved; I could no longer keep faith even with her memory. I could not withstand the contradiction and so I went out and shot myself. Only then, once I was dead, could I see the truth at last...'

'Let me tell it, Jacob. It's always so hard for you to talk about.' The woman that a short time before Davies had thought of as the grieving Widow from Amarillo, now in a rustling silk dress with puff sleeves and high lace collar, took a place beside Jacob. 'I'm Avril,' she said.

The best comment Davies could muster was, 'Huh?'

She laughed, lightly. She was very pretty, fine-boned with a pert little nose and kiss curls in front of her tiny ears. 'You're wondering what happened to the cowboy hat. It's one of the few times you get to have fun as a ghost - apart from scaring those

arrogant enough to declare we don't exist - when you dress up and join in! Had you going there, didn't I? But no, I've never even been in Amarillo, I'm a St Louis girl, born, bred and died...'

Standing under the blue light in the morgue, Avril revealed to Davies the part of the story that the tour guides did not know.

She had planned her departure from her husband and St. Louis society very carefully. At 8.30 on the morning of Wednesday, March 23rd, she instructed her carriage to drop her and her valise off at the doctor's office, where she had a routine appointment, with the additional information that an acquaintance would be bringing her back to the house. This would leave her adequate time after nine a.m. to take a hansom to the train station and board the ten a.m. Frisco Pullman to Seligman, Missouri where she would transfer to the E.S and N.A train to Eureka Springs, arriving in the early afternoon. But when she came out of the doctor's office, the cab that Avril boarded did not take her to the train station but back to her husband's house, where she retired to her room with a bottle of brandy from the library, having left strict instructions that she was on no account to be disturbed before the following morning.

What Jacob never knew was that Avril was persuaded to change her plans and break faith with her lover by a few words spoken by her doctor. What Avril could not bring herself to communicate to Jacob, or

224

anyone else, was that she was pregnant; but owing to the unusually narrow construction of her pelvis it was unlikely either she or the baby would survive childbirth.

'And that's about as tragic a story as anybody would ever want to hear,' Davies said. 'But that's not the end, is that it, is that what you're telling me? You're together now. At last. Forever.'

Avril and Jacob shared a glance.

'Well – yes,' she hesitated. 'But...'

'What? Don't tell me something else went wrong?'

'Forever means forever,' the Gray Man said, from somewhere in the shadows.

'It's not the same,' Jacob said. 'When time ceases to matter, attachment to others ceases likewise.'

Avril said, 'When you find yourself on *this* side, you see everything and everyone, you know them all, you understand them all, they see you and through you – we are ghosts, after all – and as many of us as there are, because we are here and always will be, we are each alone.'

'Peace at last.' Jacob took Avrils's hand. 'Love is for the living.'

'Champagne too, sadly... It's nice to see you, Jacob, as always.'

'Lovely to see you, Av. How about a float around the corridors afterwards, for old time's sake? Witching hour approaches!'

'Delighted! My next appointment is not till sunrise. Mr. Davies, I understand you're to be joining us soon? Nice talking with you!'

'Till the next time...' Jacob said, with a cheery lift of his derby.

They faded back into the shadows.

Joining them?

Davies turned to the others, but they were no longer there.

'That's it for tonight,' the Gray Man said. 'Show's over. What you had is what you get. Any questions?'

'Is what I think is happening, happening?'

'Whatever that means!' The Gray Man seemed to be having a very good time, sitting cross-legged now on the autopsy table and playing with his bare toes. 'But, yes. This is where you change trains. Any minute now so – anything you want to know? '

'If they were ghosts – ghost, right? Am I saying it right? Spirits? I know now who they were – are - but who are you?'

The Gray Man fell over sideways laughing, maintaining the lotus pose. When he recovered his breath and the perpendicular again, he shook his head, still laughing.

'It really doesn't matter!'

Davies was not all at sure he enjoyed being made mock of by a phantom that might yet prove to be a product of his own imagination. 'You asked me what I want to know. I want to know how it works. The...' He struggled but eventually brought himself to say the word: 'Afterlife.'

And there it was again. Even though the morgue was empty but for Davies and the Gray Man, assuming he was in some sense an independent existence, the oppressive little room was suddenly racketing with a short, sharp bark of laughter from many guests, cut short. Davies looked around and now his flesh was beginning to creep, especially around the base of his skull and his upper back. Also his stomach muscles were doing weird things, and he could not tell if he was breathing or not.

'Are we alone now?' He asked the Gray Man, and immediately wondered if he had been tricked into giving up one of three wishes.

'Alone? In the 1886 Crescent Hotel morgue at midnight? Mr. Ghost Tour Guide?

'No, I just thought everyone had – left...'

'Left as far as you're concerned, right?'

'Huh?'

'Anyone in particular you wanted to see?'

'Well, is that girl in the shawl around?'

And her voice was in his ear, 'Yesssss....'

Two wishes...

'They're aware,' the Gray Man said, 'they and the others. They just don't need to be at this meeting. Ready?'

'Wait! I still don't understand! What's going to happen? Why is it all going on, any of it, what are we all here for? How does it work? Is there someone behind it all?'

'Alright, that's enough to be going on with. Let's see. You want to know how it works. How it all works? You think just because we're dead we're privy to that information? No one really understands particle physics, and that's just a crumb off the biggest banquet table you can imagine and imaginations have built-in limitations, the universe out there is, as they say, beyond imagining. Think about that. What does it mean? It means you can't think about that. It's too big to be thought about. Living human beings do not as individuals have the processing power to handle that much information, nor do they have - yet - the necessary understanding to have technology do it for them. Humanity has barely encountered a speck of the phenomena that swirl about in galaxies and parallel universes, human knowledge amounts to a millionth part of a grain of sand under the toes of the boy standing at the sea shore casting stones into the great ocean of the unknown. We figure out *what* happens sometimes, but not always how and rarely why. Good old fashioned empiricism, that's the best we've got. Anyway, why the rush to understand the universe? Just observing what's there is a magical mystery tour. I enjoy the ride, I'm in noooo hurry. And that's about all I can tell you. Is it taking us somewhere? You figure it out. Okay - it's time.'

The tour group re-emerged from the dark morgue corners and surged in his direction like billows of fog. The Fear that lurks in the morgue, fathomless, freezing, entered Davies at last as he backed away from the advancing phantoms, all the way into the meat locker. The heavy door swung shut with a groan of iron hinges and he heard the bolt on the outside being shot.

Pitch dark and dead silence.

Davies tried to breathe deeply but could not. He listened hard, he opened his eyes wide in the darkness but there was nothing, anywhere. He sank to the floor under the weight of crushing pain.

*

The moment the meat locker door is latched the autopsy room bursts into chatter, as of old acquaintances rarely met together, finally at ease and all trying to catch up at once.

So lovely to see you, you're looking well -

As well as can be expected!

When was the last time we were all together here? My memory is not what it was...

Morris' funeral! You remember that?

I don't think Morris does.

You never know with cats...

Was that really the last time we ran into each other here?

No murders, not a single suicide, no new apparition in decades, so - no get-togethers for us.

The ghost tours keep humming along, though.

You'd think they would find something better to do with their time – what little they have.

They've always been the same, we were too, always worrying about what comes next...
Fear for the future...
Regret for the past...
If only they knew...
They'd pay more attention!
Lucky for them we're here to wake them up every so often!

*

On the splintery wooden floor of the meat locker, Davies hears voices chattering, laughing and shouting cheery pleasantries or sarcastic barbs. He lies quiescent, listening, like a little boy in his bed in the corner under a shaded lamp listening to the older family members murmuring into the evening, the peaceful hour. And then he realizes that the voices are receding. And when they die away completely, there is nothing but silence. In the blackness there is no time. Davies is alone.

Chapter Twenty-One:
The Game of Alts

Everything that can happen does, somewhere.

Leonora Wandering

CHAPTER TWENTY-ONE
The Game of Alts

In this year of 2017, the international scientific community appears to have reached a consensus that seems extraordinary to the point of absurdity: there are, indeed there must be, an infinite number of universes in addition to the one of which we experience merely a fleeting fragment.

Put out a hand, we are told, and touch an Otherworld, divided from ours by something infinitely less substantial than the skin of a soap bubble, identical to ours except in miniscule details, connected to other almost exact replicas that repeat and repeat like bubbles in a bath, a tiny element changing with each repetition, on and on to eternal infinity; and eventually a parallel universe some branes away will not resemble our universe at all, monkeys will write plays. Many are the distortions and wonderful the creations that will develop in the permutations that must proliferate, given time without end. And perhaps the alternate versions ly even return eventually, to fit exactly over the one we now inhabit. Why not? Everything that can happen, we are told, will. Some visionaries even go so far as to predict a day when inter-verse travel agencies will be able to sell us tickets to anywhere, any time. But to our current perception there is no other universe apart from the one of buckets, bathtubs and wild boar that we know and often love.

We may use numbers to prove the existence of Otherworlds, but how do we get to There from Here, by what means may we pass from one reality into another?

Ask a ghost.

Or read a book.

The apparently completely unnecessary faculty for spinning yarns that we all possess in some degree, in the practice of which we spend a substantial proportion of the day, may be the passageway from our current cause-and-effect universe as understood in the Standard Model, out to or into the illimitable multi-versions beyond our buckets; the means of escape from the ordinary is the creative imagination, it's a

233

commonplace; the gateways in branes may be opened through Fantasy; but to actually go There, where story is, would be to actually leave Here – and not merely poetically.

As every reality has an infinite number of alternatives, so story has unlimited endings; in the world of Story, anything can happen. For example:

Some amount of time after Davies passes out in the meat locker, the great door might crack and creak open and a shaft of blue light fall in. The silence of the morgue is shattered by DreamCloud Detroit's's scream of horror.

'*Oh my God!* Goddess. Davis! What are you playing at? You gave me such a shock, it's a wonder I didn't have a heart attack, I thought you were dead! And you're in here *napping!* Really, you must find compassion in your heart for others, think about other people sometimes... Davis?' She runs through the laundry with her arms over her head screaming, '911! 911!'

Everyone in Eureka Springs except Davies hears the symphony of the emergency vehicles. Nor does he feel himself being lifted or any of the messy medical things that happen next. For Davies everything is very still and even the flashing lights behind his eyelids have faded. There is no time, there is no place.

And then out of the nothing, comes a sound: a regular thudding sound, as of plodding footsteps, or nails being hammered into a coffin, sods of earth being flung on top. Davies lies in the blackness waiting for it to stop but it does not stop and eventually he realizes he is hearing a heartbeat; and it is his own.

Something lightens. Light and dark emerge and intensify and resolve into shapes, glimmers, moving behind a translucent screen or frosted window, and coming from the shapes low formless sounds. It takes effort to even try to focus, the strain to hear exhausts what faint energy his body still commands; but when he gives up and allows himself to relax the misty shapes and murmuring sounds begin to fade and somewhere in the blackness at the back of his mind he understands that if he does not make the effort, now, it will be Lights Out, forever.

He narrows and aims all his concentration toward the shape immediately beyond the misty window, the smallest but most active shape. Slowly, all the areas in the fog begin to resolve; but the effort is almost too much, the inclination to just forget it and go back to sleep compelling; and yet something in him strives and he feels what must be his body snatch a gasping, shuddering intake of air. Sounds come from the shapes, loud and agitated; he takes another breath; one of the shapes is shouting at him and he sharpens his focus with all the willpower he can find and the loud shape clarifies and stills and resolves into Billy Bull.

'There you are, see, I told you! Faking it!' - shaking his head as at a hopeless case with only himself to blame - 'Listen. Do you ever think about other people? Do you? I don't think you do. Let me tell you something - are you listening to me?' Billy Bull's face comes closer, filling Davies' entire view of the world.' Hey! Wake up, I'm talking to you! I want to give you a piece of friendly advice...'

Not this time. Davies changes his mind, lets go and enters a dark and blessed place where wander others like himself and where he can see the world for what it is, and know contentment at last.

Or perhaps the meat locker door opens again.

'Happy birthday to you, happy birthday to you, happy birthday, Mister Davis, happy birthday to you!'

Billy Bull ended with a bravura high C, roughly, as DreamCloud Detroit held out a cupcake with a lit candle stuck in the cream, to Davies, her eyes pouring loving-kindness and her third eye flashing.

'I thought you guys left.'

'We went to get your cake, we told all the other guides it was your birthday and we took up a collection.'

'It's not my birthday,' Davies said.

'What? Not your birthday? Gimme that cupcake back! I'm kidding! I'm kidding!'

'We know it's not your birthday, Mr. Davis, but you have been looking so down in the mouth we wanted to do something nice for you to make you feel better about this wonderful pageant called life!'

'We care about ya, kid, we don't like to see you unhappy...'

'You said you were going to fire me...'

'You really believed all that back there, didn't ya? I know you did, because that's how good I am! That's what you call real acting - when you can get someone to believe you in a real life situation. Choose a reaction you want to get and get it. Like I had you really worried, right, really miserable because you thought you might be out of a job? That was how I wanted you, that was all *me*, making you feel depressed, under-confident, heavy-duty level of anxiety, that was me making you feel all that, that's how good an actor I am!'

'You can make me feel... any way you want me to?'

'That's right, and with me it's ninety percent inspiration, ten percent work, I was born good, what can I say?'

'So why did you choose to make me miserable?'

'Gullible, you're so gullible! Gullible! Because I wanted you to experience joy in your heart, happiness of the highest order, better than you get from beer, even, and in order to raise you up to that height, I had to get you way down in the dumps, it's the Messerschmidt theory of emotional manipulation onstage, I took a workshop. In the gutter with the blues, that's where I had to take you - so that when we surprise you with a birthday celebration you'll appreciate it, you'll remember who your friends are when their birthdays come around! That's how you feel now, right, glad to be alive, life is just a bowl of cherries, live it all the way up, right? You're happy, right?'

'Ah - yes, as a matter of fact, I am.'

'So am I good, or what? You have to admit it, right?'

'Anything you say. Thank you for the cake. It's been a long night. And my car won't start. And ghosts don't tip.'

'Don't worry! I'm giving you a ride, we'll worry about your car tomorrow – 'Tomorrow, tomorrow....' And tomorrow, creeps in life's pretty pace – you know that one?'

'This cake is really good! Have I got cream all over my face? I don't care! I thought I was dead, a minute ago. I never expected to see daylight again, let alone a cupcake!'

'Hey! Why don't you die now, and come back as a ghost every night on the special late late tour? We could make a lot of money!'

'Thanks, I don't want to be ghost.'

'Oh, Mr. Davis... See, that's what you still don't understand. You *are* a ghost. We're all ghosts here.'

'Are you saying I'm dead?'

'That's the part you don't get! I know you read all those books and quote Paracelery but what you missed is - you don't have to be dead to be a ghost.'

'That's what a ghost is, someone who's dead but still here.'

'Gimme a break...'

'See, you're still thinking Here, There. There is no there, there is no here, there is no dead or living, there are only ghosts and sometimes they have a body for a while, mostly they don't but they are here all the time, waiting for us to join them. The only thing that keeps us apart is Life, when we cross back over the beautiful river we revert to our natural state. '

'Natural state – crazy like a loon! Come on, I'll give you a ride as far as featherbrain's house and you can figure it out from there.'

'We can start off at my place, we'll get you cleaned up, you're going to love my shower, and unwind a little, we have to celebrate your un-birthday, we all run out of birthdays sooner or later, and we will all be ghosts someday – if not today, some other day.'

'Davis, you're a bigger man than me, don't need a slide rule to see that, and if you can put up with that woo-woo crap all night, you're a far, far better man than me, Gunga Doone! Let's go...' With that Billy Bull jigged out of the autopsy room backwards, one leg raised, waggling his straw hat like a fan.

'All night?' Davies said.

'We'll see...' she said, taking his arm. 'Let's get out of this morgue...' And she drew him toward the doors to the outside world.

Anything that can *happen...*

Perhaps in the universe that you are reading this in, Davies is still working as a tour guide at the Crescent Hotel, but now he sees ghosts everywhere, all the time. Floating in the gardens, slinking in shadowy corners, hovering near the ceiling like cobwebs, on the other side of every door, on the stairs, peeping from bushes, lurking at dining room tables, disappearing into elevators or dropping past the window, usually urgently trying to get his attention. The gentleman in derby hat and silk cravat, gold watch in hand, stares at him, the falling girl shouts a name, the old man blows a cloud of pungent smoke through the slowly closing door, the boy in the gardens dodges and weaves chortling through the moonlight toward the basket dangling from the lower balcony, the man in the white suit steps out of the elevator, giving instructions to the small crowd that follows him like ducklings. Touring the building and grounds Davies feigns obliviousness, but a slight smile enlivens his habitually impassive features as he glides among the ghosts; they nod or smile at him and he responds with a simple nod or movement of his hands, or shoulders.

Is Davies a living ghost tour guide or a revenant? And if the second, how many others of those you encounter at the Crescent Hotel, in the dining room, the elevator, the gardens, on the ghost tour, are likewise People of the Past, wandering among us today?

At another point in time, in a possible universe somewhere else, the Gray Man is telling stories in the morgue.

'We once had a ghost tour guide name of David, worked here for years. David was much loved as a storyteller, a favorite feature of the Crescent Hotel, people came across the country to take the ghost tours in this hotel and they all wanted to be on David's tours. He gave so many tours, he was around the haunted areas so much, he got to know all the ghosts personally and in the end he decided he wanted to be with them, on the Other Side. One night he laid down on the floor of the meat locker and held his breath till he died. They found him the next day, and he was smiling.

'But as many of the staff will verify, David is still here, in some form. Sometimes he may be seen flitting about the halls of the Crescent Hotel, recognized by his black cloak and the worried expression he wore perpetually in life. Not in the summer, too many people around, but in the winter, when we have a lot of two-for-one offers. And if you don't see David you might hear him, if you listen really hard, in the sound of the wind, still telling his stories, over and over and over. Unto eternity. Thanks for taking the tour with me. You'll find the traditional tip jar by the door on your way out. Come back again for more Tales of the Crescent Hotel!'

Each human mind, yours for example, contains more potential interactions between neurons than there are subatomic particles in our entire universe - the better to perceive the endless parallel universes, infinite dimensions, multiple vistas, untold stories, unwritten symphonies, unimaginable realities out beyond what we know today. The more we look the more we will see.

Chapter Twenty-Two:
Hide and Go Seek

Many years then rolled away,
during which Granada
was not honored by a royal guest.
The palaces of the nobility
remained silent and shut up;
and the Alhambra,
like a slighted beauty,
sat in mournful desolation
among her neglected gardens.

Washington Irving
Tales of the Alhambra

22

CHAPTER TWENTY-TWO
Hide-And-Go-Seek

For Kathleen

For certain periods of what we all call Time, the triple-towered, limestone fortress at the top of the hill has stood empty and silent, unoccupied but for small creatures, birds, bats and a few ghosts, waiting for the next owner, the next identity. In those periods – near the beginning of the twentieth century, during the Depression, during World War II – with no living people in the rooms, no voices in the halls, not even memories because there are no living beings to remember, within those stout stone walls there is no time. The carpets and woodwork and plumbing deteriorate over decades of our time, the seasons change, one winter and summer much like another, and the lingering spirits do but observe – mostly. But anything that happened during any of those eras fo disuse could have happened in any of the others.

The boy stood staring into the forest, listening, wondering what was hiding in those trees and which way to go to reach the open air again. The girl tugged on his sleeve but he did not notice until she tugged harder, whispering 'Look. *Look!*'

She was pointing at something against the sky above the trees: towers, square and gray, on some great building higher than everything else on the horizon, either close and big or far away and huge. Without talking they started off through the undergrowth in the direction of people, where snakes and panthers and black bears did not go.

As the sun was beginning to set and the sky to change color, they lost sight of the building.

'Climb a tree,' she said.

'You climb a tree,' he said.

'I can't climb trees.'

'What tree?'

She revolved in a clearing, one finger in her mouth, showing the possibilities to her Teddy. She put her ear to Teddy's snout. 'That one there.'

And indeed, it looked possible. The trunk was curiously bent from about the height of the boy's waist before it rose straight up again and from the bend the lower branches were easily reached. But it was not a stout tree and he felt it sway as he climbed and then sway back and he yelped, afraid to go any higher; but when the tree swung back to upright he saw the towers of the gray building again and saw that they were very close.

When he got to the bottom of the tree the girl was crying.

'What's wrong?'

'Hungry,' she said, 'Cold. Thirsty. Lost. Teddy's frightened.'

'It's all right,' he said. He tried to put his arm round her but she shied away like a frightened animal. 'That place is over there.'

'Don't want to walk anymore.'

He kept looking into the forest in the direction of the building knowing that if he looked away he would lose it. 'Can't stay here,' he said.

She burst into loud crying and sat on the ground, hugging Teddy very tight.

'It's right there,' he said. 'Real close.'

She stopped crying to wave away a cloud of biting midges.

He felt a drop of rain on his face.

They crept closer to the massive building in an unexpected clearing on a hilltop, an ancient stone mansion with hundreds of windows, mostly broken. All around, crumbling rock walls gave indication of overgrown flowerbeds. An old fishpond was filled with sludge. A disused road twisted away downhill into the forest. There were no people. The sun was beginning to slip below the trees.

As the boy was peering through windows and around corners for signs of life the girl found a small door, partly open. Steps within led down into pitch darkness. She stared into the dark, more afraid of what might be in there than she was of staying outside, until the thunderbolt came. The boy had been slipping quickly from one hiding place to another, enjoying the game he was playing, until the thunderbolt. They were each first aware of a white flash that illumined the whole side of the edifice towering above them, and then of a great crackling sound and lastly of an earthshaking, earsplitting, heart-stopping crash of thunder, as though the heavens were splitting apart over their heads. And then the sudden downpour, raindrops the size of beetles.

They sat uncomfortably on the stairs, soaked to the skin, watching the slashing rain through the narrow doorway as the light faded. They huddled together against the darkness of the night outside and the unknown emptiness behind them, unspeaking.

After a long time the girl, whose name was Mavis, said, very quietly, 'Teddy wishes we never got off the train.'

Awhile later the boy, Davey, said, 'Too late now.'

Eventually the thunder died away and the rain settled into a steady drizzle. At last the sky lightened and then the sun rose, bringing birdsong and the clean smell of wet leaves. The light slowly revealed the stairs behind them, not very many, a doorframe without a door. They could see part of a polished floor and when they slowly peered closer, descending one step at a time, the floor was revealed as long and empty, laden with dust, leading to a distant set of double doors where a boy stood watching them, silently.

Davey waved. The boy did not wave back. 'Hi!' Mavis shouted and ran along the wooden path toward him. He turned and disappeared through the double doors. They both called out but the strange boy did not answer. They ran along the polished floor, sometimes slipping in the dust, and through the swinging double doors to where a wide carpeted stairway with wooden rails rose up. From somewhere far above they heard a light laugh. Looking up, they squinted in the rays of sun that poured down through the skylight, silhouetting the boy several levels above them, looking down. They started up the stairs, turning every half dozen steps and the boy above turned too, but more slowly, as though to allow them to catch up to him until they were one floor below and he drew back from the rail and was lost to sight.

At the top of the stairs, breathless and suddenly very thirsty, Davey stopped to catch his breath but Mavis tugged his arm and pointed along a dim corridor. The strange boy was there again, standing at the end of the hallway, throwing a ball against a wall and catching it, though if its impact made any sound they could not hear it. He watched them watching him and threw back his curls, laughing, a strange, hollow-sounding laugh as though from far away that echoed along the corridors and down the stairwells, seeming to fill the entire huge building.

They ran toward him, enchanted by his gaiety, but he slipped to one side and disappeared from view. At the end of the hall they turned the corner and found another set of stairs, narrower, leading down again, and there was the boy standing at the bottom, looking up, beckoning them down. They raced down the stairs, stumbling from weakness, their clothes still wet on their bodies, to catch up to their fascinating new friend. He led them, with gestures, into and across a great room with stout columns, gaily painted like a carnival, past a big white fireplace filled with ashes and through wide, dusty, glass-paned double doors into an even larger room, the ceiling too high to be seen, with tall windows on all sides, scattered with broken furniture; and through another set of swinging doors with one small window only into a place of metal tables, great ovens and sinks and a wall of cupboards.

The boy stopped at the end cupboard door, and turned to face them, his ball under one arm. He was in a corner, now there was nowhere for him to run to, so fast as to almost seem to disappear. His clothes were different. Knickerbockers, jacket with a huge collar, all velvet.

'What's your name?' Davey said.

'Is this your house?' Mavis said.

The boy stepped aside from the door and it swung open. He grinned and cocked his head. Mavis ran to look inside. She turned to Davey.

'Food!' she said.

Davey followed her into the closet and saw stacks on stacks of cans, large and round, smaller, flat and oblong, many with the labels long gone, others showing pictures of fruits and vegetables and pigs and turkeys and fish, an Aladdin's cave for two very hungry children.

'Is all this yours? Can we have some?' Davey asked but when he turned for an answer, the boy was gone. On the far side of the kitchen a door opened, then closed, apparently by itself, or the wind.

Mavis was holding a can wrapped in a mouthwatering picture of plump peaches. She thrust it to Davey to open, and they searched the kitchen for implements. In the back of a metal drawer, otherwise empty but for grime and spider webs, he found a small knife. He jabbed the top of the can, making dents and a small hole though which juice spurted, and suddenly threw the knife down in frustration. He started to cry. 'Where's that boy?' he said, and then, shouting, 'Where did you go? Come back!'

Mavis was standing next to him, quietly, offering him her find: an old fashioned, wooden-handled can opener. He had seen them used and after a few tries managed to work it far enough around the can to pry back the jagged lid, drawing a little blood. He sucked his finger. Mavis reached eagerly for the shining gold fruit, but 'Wait,' Davey said, and poured the peaches and juice into a small pan that was only a little rusty. When they had eaten all the peaches and drunk the juice, 'What else?' Mavis said, and went back in the storage closet.

Later, after several helpings of pork and beans, pea soup, sardines, pickles and an extra-large can of mixed fruit salad, by which time Davey was more adept with the can opener, Mavis was sick and Davey felt like he was going to be.

'Let's find the boy,' Mavis said and they went back into the echoing dining room. Broken chairs, overturned tables, scattered trays, racks of glasses and cups and napkins still folded into ornamental shapes were covered in dust that made them cough and sneeze. Behind a black curtain Mavis found a pile of linen.

'Bedsheets,' she said.

'Tablecloths,' Davey said and pulled off the top layers in a cloud. Beneath, the pile was clean and inviting. Mavis jumped onto the pile and wrapped herself and Teddy up in one of the cloths and Davey did the same, laughing and rolling and falling.

'I want to see the boy again,' Mavis said, yawning.

'He'll come back,' Davey said, 'bet you anything.'

Moments later they were asleep.

When they woke they began to explore the building, calling out to their friend but receiving no response. The hallways were lined with sternly closed doors, all painted glossy black but chipped and dusty. Mavis tried a few of the doors but they were all locked. Some corridors were too dark to venture down, but those near the skylights over the stairwell were lit by the rays of sun that poured down, thick with motes.

They listened. They could hear no sound in the building.

'There's no one here,' Davey said.

'Why?' Mavis said, as she often did.

'We could live here,' Davey said,' it can be our house.'

'Where's the bathroom?' Mavis said. They found them at the ends of the halls, but they did not work.

'We have to remember our way to the outside.'

'And to the food.'

'I know where that is.'

'Let's go get some now.'

'I want some peaches.'

'And pickles. And cherries. And Teddy wants to see the boy again.'

They ate, and played a game of banging on the pots and pans with big spoons, and saw a rat. Mavis screamed and it scurried away. They turned on all the faucets. One of them, over a big metal sink, started to gurgle and then exploded with an issue of crud and yuk. They jumped back, afraid to go closer, watching the rust and mud ooze and spurt. Outside it began to grow dark again and they had to fumble their way through the dining room to their makeshift bed. They spoke in whispers and Mavis told Teddy not to be scared. She fell asleep the moment they lay down, but Davey was awake for a long time, listening for sounds, trying to distinguish the wind and cicadas and coyotes from movement or activity inside the building. He almost thought he could hear voices mumbling, somewhere above. He decided he would stay awake all night, in case of danger. He wished the boy would come back. He closed his eyes. When he woke up, light was streaming in the big windows, and Mavis was gone.

Davey looked in all directions around the big dining room, expecting to see her, or catch her hiding, waiting to jump out and surprise him, but there was no sign of her, just very still, very dusty broken furniture and spider-webs everywhere. He went through the swinging doors to the great kitchen and checked the pantries. In the garish lobby he listened carefully but could not hear her, giggling in hiding, or running up and down the stairs. He called out, quietly at first and then much louder, beginning to panic. He looked out through grimy windows, in case she was outside but found no trace. The stairwells were empty and so were all the halls as far as he could see. Up the north stairs and down the south, running now, shouting, angry and frightened at the same time. He didn't want to be alone. Why would she go away? Where?

She was sitting in the lobby with her back against a column, talking into Teddy's ear.

'Where'd you go?' he said.

"I was with the boy,' she said, 'we played and played.'

'Is he here?'

'No. He says only two of us can play at one time. Not all together.'

"What's his name?"

248

'Don't know. Boy. He showed me a special room. It's my room, where I can keep things I find.'

'Where is it?'

'Under the stairs. Up there. I'll show you.' She scrambled to her feet, Teddy upside down under her arm, and ran to the south stairs. As she climbed up the stairs almost too steep for her little legs he saw that her skin was filthy and the dress that had been soaking wet and then covered in dust was now stiff and encrusted. His own clothes were in the same condition. He would have been in big trouble if he got that dirty at the Children's Home.

'Only once, you can only see it once, and then it's my room and you can never ever come in.'

'I don't care,' he said.

She pushed open an unmarked door and let him peep in. It was small, with no windows and a slanted ceiling, empty. 'That's all!' She closed the door. 'You can't look in my room ever, ever again. If you can't find me, that's where I'll be.'

'Is he going to give me a room, too?'

'Don't know. This one is special, my special place.'

'I know. You said that. I don't want your old room.'

'Special, special!' she said, and danced along the hall, leaning Teddy from side to side.

In the kitchen the faucet was now running clear water. Davey let the water run over his hands, watching the mud slide away.

'You should wash up,' he said.

'No,' she said. 'Don't want to.'

'Want to go exploring tomorrow?' They sat among the cans, some open and empty, some half-full but the food inside covered in dust already, some freshly opened and filled with gleaming fish and jellied meat and fruit salad.

'No,' she said. 'I want to stay here and never ever go out.'

'I wish we had some bread,' he said.

Next morning he woke up alone again. He climbed up to her secret room and listened at the door. He could hear her whispering. To Teddy? Or the boy? He didn't care. He was going to go exploring anyway. It was just not so much fun by himself.

He found a neglected orchard, with small green apples on spindly trees. He bit into one but it was hard. He kept trying till his teeth hurt, then threw it away. Later his stomach hurt. He went back to the big house. Mavis was standing on the top step, crying. 'We thought you'd run away', she sobbed, 'me and Teddy were sad.'

'Where would I go?' he said. 'This is our house. This is where we live.'

"You and me and Teddy and the boy.'

'Why doesn't he come around when I'm awake? Doesn't he like me?'

'One at a time. He says he can only be with one of us at a time. He shows me things. In the rooms. He's funny.'

'Does he ever talk?'

'No, not ever. Only sometimes. I tell him everything I'm thinking, he just listens. I make up stories. All the time, stories. About us. About people coming to help us. Sleeping in a bed. Cake. Animals that talk to each other and go exploring and find things they like and bring them home to keep in their special room.'

'I don't care if he doesn't like me. Don't like him.'

'Well, I do, so there!' And she started to cry again, quietly this time, her tears falling onto Teddy's head.

'Want some jam?' he said.

'What kind?'

'Don't know. Berry.'

After they had eaten far too much jam straight out of the can her face was covered in blue stains. He wet a napkin at the faucet and tried to wash her face, but she screamed and ran off. He sighed and washed his own face, equally smeared. He supposed she would go to her Things room but when he turned around she was standing, holding Teddy by one leg and twisting from side to side. 'I wish I had a pretty dress,' she said. 'I would wash my face if I had a nice dress to put on.'

'We could wash that one,' he said.

'How?' she said.

'You have to take it off. We can wash it in the sink. Let it dry.'

'I have to wear something.'

He fetched a tablecloth. 'Wrap up in that,' he said. She started to pull her dress over her head. 'Wait,' he said, and turned his back, afraid of something but not sure what. When she was all wrapped up he took the wet napkin and carefully cleaned off layers of grime from her cheeks and chin until she told him to stop. It took a long time for the dress to dry. She tried to walk about, holding her makeshift robe up with one hand and Teddy in the other but she kept treading on the tablecloth and after tripping and falling a few times she screamed in

250

frustration and then began to cry, loudly, telling Davey that she hated him, the boy didn't make her wash, he didn't care if she was dirty as anything; she was going to be his friend and no one else's and she lay on the floor and screamed some more.

'You sure cry a lot,' Davey said. He had been examining a chair and saw that a missing leg lay in the dust a few feet away. After several tries he figured out how it went together. 'There,' he said, 'fixed it.' She pouted. He set the chair up. 'We got a chair,' he said. 'You want it? It can be your chair. Look.' He sat on the chair and it promptly collapsed. Her tears turned to laughter.

'Do it again,' she said, 'do it again!'

Days and nights went by. They soon learned that if they ate too much they would throw up, and they learned to go to the toilet outside, and they learned not to talk to each other if one of them was feeling short-tempered. Mavis would find objects she liked and take them to her Things room. Sometimes she did not come out all day. Davey would linger on that floor for a while, listening to her lecture Teddy in a sing-song imitation of the teachers from before the train journey, and then wander about the building, wishing he had someone to play with.

Late one afternoon, just before dark, they heard voices outside the building. Davey peered though a broken pane.

'They've come to take us home!' Mavis started to run toward the voices but Davey held her back. 'Shhhh!'

'Who's there?' She whispered, impressed by his seriousness.

'Don't know. Two guys. Don't like them.'

He took her hand and they climbed up the north stairs to where they could hide in the shadows behind the railing.

The front door was shoved open and a face peered into the lobby, unshaven, dirty and wearing an old army cap. After a moment he called back to his companion: All clear. He squeezed through the opening and into the lobby, small, scrawny and unsteady on his feet. The second man was obliged to shove the door further open to allow for his bulk.

'What is it?' he said, his voice slow and deep.

'Quarters,' the smaller man said. 'Look what we got, Jeremiah. Dry, empty... '

'How do you know it's empty?'

'Hey!' he shouted. The echoes came back from the floors above, died away.

Mavis looked at Davey. He shook his head. She held her hand tightly over Teddy's mouth.

'Know what we're gonna do? Know what we're gonna do, Jeremiah? We're gonna build a fire, we're gonna get warm and we're gonna sleep good tonight. Where's that jug?' He took a long swig from a gallon can, rattled his head and burped. 'Let's git some of this here firewood in a pile,' he said. They began to gather broken pieces of furniture into a heap in the middle of the lobby, Jeremiah moving slowly and deliberately as though attempting to maintain his focus, the little man scampering in spurts and chuckling. 'Oh, Jeremiah, we struck it right tonight, just in time afore the sun goes down, huh? Huh, Jeremiah?'

Davey and Mavis crept quietly up the stairs. When they reached the floor with Mavis' Things room she said, 'I'm going to play with my things,' went into the room and closed the door. Davey sat on the bare wood floor for a while, listening to the voices of the men coming up from below, louder and more raucous as each minute went by. He crept back down the stairs to where he could watch them unseen.

The fire was blazing dangerously.

The two men were circling the flames, staring at each other, one with a blazing firebrand and one with a cold steel blade, one silent and one gabbling, one or both apparently about to suffer death.

'So help me, Jeremiah, if'n you come any closer I will cut your throat!' The hand pointing an Arkansas toothpick at Jeremiah's big face was shaking. Twice his size, not shaking at all, Jeremiah was waving a flaming brand and laughing.

Davey suddenly became aware of the strange boy in the blue velvet suit, standing close behind him and to one side, watching the two-man dance of death in the firelight below.

'Swear to God, Jeremiah, you get me so mad sometimes, I didn't mean what I said back there, Jerry, don't get so close with that fire! I mean it, Jerry! *Don't come no closer!* You know me, I may go down but I'll go down fighting – back off, man! That's fucking hot, *get back!* See? I mean it, now quit kidding around, Jerry or one of us is going to get hurt and there ain't no medics in the immediate vicinity, *we need to look out for each other, soldier* - Please, Jerry, I'm begging you, don't do it, it's already been a bad night, don't make it worse, Jerry – no! Alright sucker, come and *get it!*'

The boy suddenly screamed, so loud, close to Davey's ear, a

medley of bloodcurdling screeches and mournful wails, broken only by an uncontrollable giggle that served to heighten the horror and before he had run out of breath Jeremiah and his companion had forgotten their differences and left the building.

The boy ran away, laughing, turning back to Davey as though inviting him to chase, to play hide-and-go-seek. But Davey was afraid of the fire and he ran to fill empty peaches cans with water from the faucet, splashing the burning broken chairs and tables, running to refill the cans, shouting for Mavis, stamping out the last sparks before the floor itself caught fire. The lobby was filled with acrid steam and smoke and Davey's eyes were streaming. When there were no embers left glowing, just a pile of soaked and sodden charred brands, he fell back against a column, slid down and sat with his head in his hands, relieved that the building had not been burned to the ground, sick with the knowledge that their secret house in the woods had been discovered.

Late spring turned to early summer. The air was still and moist. They lay about in their favorite places in the long, hot afternoons, playing in the grounds outside or on the balconies in the early mornings and evenings. Davey had managed to close the front door, though not all the way. His pants were ripped down one side and he grazed his thigh frequently. His hair was long enough to bother him, hers was growing out in all directions. She hated to wash. He could barely distinguish her features under the dirt, and she developed a hacking cough that made her voice so husky he could hardly understand her. Days went by without the strange boy appearing, though Mavis said that he had not left, just did not come around when Davey was there. But she would never be still, she was always off playing around the halls, chasing the boy that Davey never saw, sometimes stopping to hack for minutes on end, the painful abrasive explosions echoing along the hallways and down the stairwells like smoke pouring down from a blaze on an upper floor. He continued to attempt to mend broken furniture, with occasional minimal success.

Every morning and evening he would station himself on the highest balcony, watching the barely perceptible road for men with fire and knives.

One full moon night they were playing on one of the upper

decks when they heard the sound of an automobile chugging somewhere below, coughing and wheezing but unmistakably drawing closer, until it abruptly stopped and then they could hear much laughing and shouting. Mavis and Davey waited by the railing, wondering, but pulled back out of sight when a ragged group of youngsters appeared around the bend of the old road, wandering and tripping and falling into each other, and laughing all the time, although they all fell quiet when they reached the base of the building. The moonlight threw long shadows and everything was blue.

'What are you, chicken?' the young men challenged each other. 'Ain't afraid of *ghosts* are ya?' They lit lanterns and swigged from dark bottles.

'Hey! the girls go first!' Screams and, 'You're supposed to be tough, you go first!'

'No way – I ain't scared of any guy in school but this place gives me the heebie-jeebies...' And they all laughed hysterically, repeating, *Heebie-jeebies!*

'We have to go in – we can't go back and tell the others we were scared to go in, they'd love that...'

'I'll go in. Ghosts are not real.'

'Go ahead!'

'If someone comes with me...'

At last, they agreed to all venture in together. They leaned against one of the front doors till it scraped inward, leaving an opening only wide enough for one person at a time to squeeze through. Heebie-jeebies went first. Once through he implored the next one to hurry up and not leave him in here alone, and outside they all held their mouths and pretended they had left, till he started to sound really panicky and then they all cracked up and leaned on the door some more till they could get inside the building. Once inside they stayed together in a group, whispering, flashlights turning in all directions, lighting now the stairs, the reception desk or the gaudily painted columns, observed from the shadows on the north second floor landing by Mavis and Davey.

'I don't like them,' she whispered, 'make them go away.'

'Easy,' he said. Finger to his lips he led her quietly to where the empty elevator shaft yawned dangerous and deep. He lay down with his head over the edge, took a deep breath and screamed.

The laughing and joshing in the lobby came to a sudden stop. Mavis joined in the screaming and between them and the elevator shaft they produced sounds unearthly enough to freeze the blood of the most valiant quarterback. It was fun watching them all scrambling over each other to get out the narrow exit. Before he realized what she was doing, Mavis dashed out to the balcony where she and teddy could scream some more and that sent the intruders running and stumbling and bumping into each other as they raced down the hill, each without regard for any other, screaming, too: and that set off the coyotes and the hoot owls plus the cicadas and the frogs. The hills were alive that night. Davey and Mavis rolled around on the deck, holding their bellies.

Later, the still-terrified, still intoxicated explorers would pour out their tales of horrible things seen and heard in that spooky old mansion on the hill, including a walking corpse with a dead baby in her arms, strangely shrunken. And even those villagers who were skeptical of the legends of departed spirits lingering within the forbidding walls of the ruin on the hill experienced a cold chill of fear like a feather of ice trailed up the spine.

From that moment there would be no going back for the reputation of the grand old lady of the Ozarks - haunted, forever.

A few mornings later, when the leaves were beginning to drift down from the trees, Davey opened the last can of peaches. He counted the remaining cans, mostly without labels, and wished they had not opened so many, so recklessly, and left so much food for the rats.

There's people down the hill,' Mavis said. 'Maybe they would give us some peaches.'

Davey suggested they go and look for people. But Mavis would not leave the building. She went into her Things room and closed the door.

Davey ventured cautiously down the old broken road that ran downhill into the trees, holding a stone. He was gone for a long time.

It was just beginning to turn dark when Mavis and Teddy heard the sound of the front door being forced. They waited in the shadows on the second floor. A head and shoulders came in through the opening, retreated. The door scraped open and a man came all the way in, reaching back a hand to a woman with long black hair. He led her through the shadows to the center of the lobby, its carnival colors dim but discernible in the golden light of sunset, and watched her as she looked around in wonder.

'So – what d'you think?'

'What *is* this place?'

'I don't know. I come on it hunting. Eureka Springs is down the hill, they probably know. I don't go to Eureka Springs.'

'What's wrong with Eureka Springs?'

'Too many weirdos. So what do you think? It's like a movie or something, this is a castle, right?'

'Chateau, yes, it's like something out of old Europe, right out here in the middle of nowhere and you *found* it?'

'You like it?'

'Its.. interesting... kinda spooky. You think it's haunted? I bet it's haunted.'

'You reckon?'

'Don't you feel it? I'm getting the shivers, just standing here and it's so humid out there, my shirt is soaking...'

'Feeling a draught, baby? Come here, let me warm you up a little...'

'Here?'

'Why not?'

'Here?'

'It's kind of romantic, don't you think?'

'Romantic? It's haunted, it's filthy and there's not even a bed, what kind of girl do you take me for?'

'Who needs a bed? Come here. I have some ideas, and you know what, you can make as much noise as you like, there is not a soul around to hear...'

'Except ghosts... It's creepy here, I don't know, let's go back out to the river...'

'Time we get there it will time to get you back, listen, come here, I got something I wanna do...'

'You always do...'

Since they had stopped arguing and were kissing so nicely, Mavis and Teddy thought it would be a good moment to introduce themselves and ask for help.

The pair scrambled out through the falling door, stumbled to a pick-up truck and clambered in, cursing all the way. The engine fired and the truck roared away as Mavis came out onto the steps holding Teddy. She saw the woman looking back at her through the receding rear window of the cab.

Mavis ran down the steps and made Teddy wave to her. The

truck stopped, though the engine continued to roar. A door opened and the woman stepped down and stood, looking. Mavis and Teddy both waved. The woman waved back.

Towards sundown, after a sudden rain, Davey emerged from the dripping trees. He limped to the front of the building and sank down onto the steps, holding his ribs where he had been kicked. One eye was badly blackened, he had bruises on his bare arms and legs and he was bleeding from a cut on the head. He had cried all he could, now he could only sit, glad to be back at their house but badly frightened by the rest of the world, especially the boys his own age he had attempted to befriend. He wished he had not told them where he lived. They had stood about him in a circle, taunting him, shoving him from one to another, calling him dirty names. Throwing his stone at them had been a mistake. There were many stones lying on the muddy ground and the boys were experts. Only the arrival of the blacksmith had brought their vicious game to an end, and he had given Davey a final cuff to send him on his way back out of town.

Leaves swirled as the light failed and a strengthening wind stirred everything he could see. There were puddles all over the ground. He saw something lying in one of the puddles. He went over to the puddle, peering in the near-dark, and stooped painfully to pick up the rain-sodden bundle of filthy fur. Teddy.

He climbed the stairs slowly, halting on every other step, hauling himself up by the banister. He listened at the door of her Things room. He thought he could hear her voice, very quiet, though it could have been the howling of the wind as it battered the building from outside, the clatter of swinging shutters, or the groaning of bending trees. He was alone, with no friend or ghost for company, completely alone; and for the first time he felt afraid of the vast, empty building.

Where did she go? Why did she leave Teddy? Will she come back? He sat against the door in his soaking clothes and screamed and screamed, and almost choked as something rose up in his throat. He spit light red blood from his broken teeth and darker blood from somewhere deeper inside. And then he saw the boy.

He was standing silently at the end of the hallway, as Davey and Mavis had seen him the morning they first ventured into the building. Davey struggled to his feet and waved to the boy, but the boy turned away. Davey saw his golden curls flash as he turned the corner out of sight, but his side and his head hurt too badly for him to give chase. He shouted and heard his voice echo through the empty halls, the garish lobby and vast and shadowed dining room. *Where is she? Where did she go? Did you hurt our friend*? His cry echoed up through the stairwells and along the passageways and into the rooms and out through broken windows into the storm. *Did you hurt our friend?* He listened for a long time for an answer but none came.

He climbed slowly to the roof of the building, terrified in the wind and sky lit up by lightning and crushing thunderclaps overhead so loud he could not hear himself bawling into the night. There was nothing but tree tops to see in any direction save one – the town below. And he could not go there.

In pain and frightened, with the temperature falling fast, he lay awake in their nook by the stairs, looking out into the darkness, shivering.

As the weak light crept down the stairwell he woke from a nightmare of flailing fists and bad words and Mavis screaming for help, to find he could barely move from stiffness and pain. He called out to Mavis.   She was there somewhere, he had heard her voice in her Things room. He called again, though it hurt to take a deep breath, but there was no answer.

Winter came early that year and hit very hard. The rains came, and then the ice. Davey breathed his last in the cubbyhole beside the stairs on the second floor. He closed his eyes and dreamed that Mavis came back with Breckie and they had toys and food and a new pair of pants and she wasn't coughing at all and he wasn't sweating and they went up onto the top deck to play like they used to and then he dreamed that it was only a dream and he was really going to die and then he saw them, skipping along the hall toward him and bouncing the ball as all the light faded.

Stand in that cubby hole and listen; you may hear a bouncing ball, on the walls or floor of the hallway and, faint and hollow, a shouted protest: *It's not fair. It's not fair.* And whose voice is calling?

It is said that a building where a child died in misery will always be haunted by restless spirits: they come and stay for a time and leave and others take their place; and they return to be observed by different generations of the living, those closely involved with the Crescent Hotel, residents, staff, guests and guides. And so it will always be: whatever the name or function of the monumentally improbable edifice at the highest point of the ancient Ozark mountains, it will provide a sanctuary for those spirits of the departed obliged to wander, perhaps for eternity, or perhaps only until the day the walls come tumbling down; the only way to know how those things work is to be dead.

Since that period of neglect and decay, the years of the second world conflagration, the Crescent Hotel has known continuous popularity as a place of relaxation enjoyed by thousands. Occasional reports come in from guests or employees, of youngsters dressed like extras in a Depression-era movie misbehaving in the halls, hollering and whooping and laughing and running up and down in the middle of the night. They are seen in every part of the building, but all three are never seen at the same time. They are all there but on different floors, looking down over the stair-rails and laughing. Like certain sub-atomic particles they do not exist in one place, they are here, there and everywhere, they are the orphans.

CODA

So – how's death treating you? Getting used to it yet?

How do you deal with the boredom? The same predictable behaviors, the same futile ambitions, self-destructive illusions, noble sacrifices that go for naught, willful disregard, pettifogging pettiness day after day, year after year, into centuries... I can't stand it – and I've hardly started!

It's not going to change. Not ever. That's a given. But there might be more going on than you're aware of. The living can only see one thing at a time, two at most. They do their best, most of them, most of the time. Well, some of them, sometimes. But you, being dead, have a choice: you can stop watching, seek inactivity, remain aloof, and eventually seize up – you will still be around, there's nowhere to go, but after a few hundred years of impassivity you won't feel a thing, not even boredom. Or you can get involved with the living, engage in their lives. Mingle.

That's not much of a choice!

What did you expect? Bliss?

Listen, the flexible factor here is you. Whether you're in heaven or hell is your decision. The secret is: keep your sense of humor; even in the bleakest of times, remember the cosmic joke and do your best to make things better. You can turn your back and go to sleep, or step up and step in. Ghostly detachment; entanglement – you have the choice, always. But the longer you rust, the harder it is to get your motor going again.

So if I stick around and stay awake, would it be okay –

Yes?

Could I... could I put the fear of God into Billy Bull?

Unlikely, Mr. Davies. You'd be advised to concentrate on the bigger picture.

NOT THE END

AFTERWORD

The characters in these stories are either of my own invention, or survive in scraps of inherited ghost stories, or they take the names and biographies of historical personages about whom I know only what there is to read in books. The rest I made up. Was Powell Clayton the way I try to suggest he was? I don't know, but since no one is still alive to put me right, I have presented him and Michael and Theodora and all the other historical personages in this book as I imagine them. If you imagine them differently, I look forward to reading your books.

Keith J. Scales

The Author

KEITH J. SCALES, actor, director, writer and lifelong student of supernatural lore and legend, is currently Tour Manager for the 1886 Crescent and 1905 Basin Park Hotels in Eureka Springs, Arkansas - both of which have well-deserved reputations for being haunted.

Born and raised in London, England, Keith has been an all-round professional theatre practitioner for 50 years. His many original works for the stage include line-for-line English versions of the principal ancient Greek plays. Study Fellowships have taken him to Ireland, Japan, Greece, Prague, London, the west of England, the south of France, Eastern Oregon and Northwest Arkansas.

Keith has now turned to preparing several novels and scores of short stories - written in the small hours after performances, rarely submitted - for publication at last. He chose Indie publishing over the cumbersome agent/editor/publisher route and congratulates Amazon and Createspace for providing good alternatives.

Also by Keith J. Scales:

A forthcoming CD version of *House of a Hundred Rooms,* performed by Scales.

He has at least two further books in mind featuring the 1886 Crescent Hotel, one much more serious, one a complete farce.

The Overlook Chronicles

Coming Soon: Stories long, short and tall of the collisions and collusions between the characters who still inhabit the mythical town of Overlook, somewhere between the frontier and the fantastic, the town that Time left behind, a long way from anywhere you would know.

Volume 1	*The Cloverleaf Development* - novella
Volume 2	*Overlook and the Otherworld* – short stories
Volume 3	*Overlook Anniversaries* – short stories
Volume 4	*Overlook Overdoes It* – short stories
Volume 5	*Overlook Un(re)solved* – 3 longer stories
Volume 6	*Duplicity City* – full-length mystery

"The Cloverleaf Development... kept me thoroughly entertained and intrigued for the two or so hours of reading time it requires... Keith J. Scales has packed more into his 130 pages than many a novelist manages with a 300-page canvas. It is filled with quirky characters, humor and observations about small town life, and it is definitely a "great little read."

Sam Statler

"A short while ago I had the great pleasure of reading *The Cloverleaf Development* . I'd also read one of Keith Scales's stories in an anthology of short stories - and been most impressed. Both of these stories take place in a town called Overlook..."

Clare Dudman
Keeper of the Snails

Made in the USA
Columbia, SC
30 August 2018